Just Making Do

Dia Webb

Published by Dia Webb
Publishing partner: Paragon Publishing, Rothersthorpe
First published 2021

ISBN 978-1-78222-833-2

Cover illustration © Cheryl Thornburgh
cherylannthornburgh@gmail.com

Book design, layout and production management by Into Print
www.intoprint.net
+44 (0)1604 832149

To my family, past and present.

Chapter 1

Margaret was going to be late for work at the bakery. It was raining hard as she hurried from her parents' terraced house where she had left her toddler. It didn't help that her little girl was such a slow eater, picking at her food and stopping to day dream while Margaret became more and more agitated. She believed in giving the child breakfast before handing her over to her mother, feeling it served as a disciplined routine, but at times it was more of a torture for them both. Thankfully, Diana, her seven-year old, had left home earlier, walking the half mile into the town to her Infant School.

The job at the bakery was vital to her since Jack, her husband, had been admitted to the sanatorium over sixty miles away. He had been sent at first to Hawley in their home town of Barnstaple, where very few came out alive, but Margaret's mother had gone to the doctor and made such a fuss that he was then sent to Hawkmoor County Sanatorium on Dartmoor, where some people did eventually recover. He had been there for over eighteen months and it was still uncertain whether he would ever walk out. Tuberculosis was a killer.

Margaret's mother was a kind woman but a force

to be reckoned with. Working-class she may be, but she knew how to stand up for herself and her family. Margaret was fortunate that her parents lived in the next street. The front door of their small, terraced house was almost opposite the back door of hers. The support she had from her parents enabled her to earn enough money to pay the rent and even put a little bit by into her Post Office account.

Margaret and Jack had married too young, started a family too soon and struggled with their health while knowing that money was short and jobs in their part of the world were few. In any case most women stayed at home, leaving their husbands to bring in the money to support the family, although the absence of so many men fighting in the war had softened attitudes to some extent, even in the traditional South West of England. Jack wasn't going to be doing any fighting, apart from fighting for his life. His chances of returning to the family were similar to those of his brother-in-law returning from serving his country, but Jack had a positive outlook and a hard-working wife.

As Margaret crossed the Long Bridge over the River Taw, a sudden gust from the South Westerly wind blowing from the estuary almost hurled her into the road. She gripped the railings to regain her balance and looked down into the swirling waters of the river below. Bending her head and turning it away from the cutting rain which lashed her face and plastered her hair to her head beneath her headscarf, she reached the end of the bridge, crossed the road and ran up the High Street to the bakery. She was six minutes late.

'I'm sorry, Doreen, I couldn't get her to finish her breakfast,' Margaret said, hanging up her dripping mac and scarf and putting on her apron, ready to serve in the shop. Some days she was asked to help in the bakehouse, cooking and decorating the cakes. She loved doing that and showed a considerable flair and willingness to learn. But today wouldn't be one of those days. It was Tuesday and one of the two Market Days for the town. Margaret would be wanted to serve in the shop. She dabbed at her wet face with her hanky and began to put on her white hat.

'No, Maggie!' Doreen said, lifting a tray of Chelsea buns and putting them in the window. 'They want you back in the bakehouse. You'd better be quick. There's a panic on out there. We're very short-staffed today.' She'd just have to manage on her own in the shop, Doreen thought. It would be Tuesday. Of course, it could be worse: Friday was even busier. Margaret's eyes lit up as she hurried through the door to the passage-way leading to the bakehouse at the back of the shop. Beautiful smells wafted towards her – freshly-baked bread, scones and dough cake just out of the ovens. This was her favourite moment; scents and sounds of kitchen activity, banging of trays on tables, pounding of dough, and the bakers calling and chiding one another, teasing and laughing. She loved it all and wanted to be part of it, creating and organising, learning all that they knew and more besides.

She stepped into the bakehouse, her feet echoing on the shiny stone floor. Bert looked up but his usual welcoming smile was missing. Margaret looked round quizzically. Where was everyone? There were only two bakers to be seen, Bert and Frank, his young apprentice. They were running around the bakery taking loaves of bread from the ovens and picking up uncooked rolls to go in, shouting instructions to one another.

'Frank, knead that dough while I finish these custard tarts,' Bert shouted.

'First, Bert, pass me that bowl near you,' Frank pointed, stretching out one arm to receive it while balancing a tray of small loaves he'd just taken from the oven. Master and apprentice had disappeared. It was a dual act, each on equal terms as each man, with an expression of desperate concentration on his face and an occasional frantically jerking glare at the large clock on the wall, did the work of two men. Margaret was thrilled. Her adrenalin raced.

She was wanted to come to the rescue and she was ready. With a quick assessment of where she could be most useful, she made towards the piping bags laid out on the far table in the corner of the room. This was going to be her moment to prove that she could do the work without assistance. Looking around at the rows of naked fairy cakes, just waiting to be dressed up for display in the shop window, she reached for the icing bowl and the palette knife.

'No, no, Maggie,' Bert shouted, 'we don't want you here. Well, we do, but there's something we want you to do that is more important. You'll have to manage on your own for ten minutes, Frank. I'm going out to the yard. Finish my custard tarts and watch out for those cakes in the second oven.' Pulling Margaret by the hand from the bakehouse, they left Frank frozen to the spot with his mouth open. Once in the yard, Bert looked at Margaret and started to explain.

'Now you see, Maggie, we are in a tight spot today. We've Minnie, who usually comes in to help in the shop when we're short of staff, off sick, and Percy from the bakery visiting his father, who's ill in Bideford. George helps out on Tuesdays and Fridays with the baking but he's hurt his back lifting a sack of flour. Now, to cap it all, Ron, who drives the van for our deliveries, has broken his leg falling over at his allotment. It was so careless of him. I don't know what he must have been thinking of. He knows how busy we are.'

'But wasn't it an accident, Bert?' Margaret asked, concerned about her colleague, although she hardly knew him.

'Well, yes. But he should have known better and been more careful. He knows it's our busy time leading up to Easter.'

Bert led Margaret towards the van, parked on its own in the loading yard.

'Now Maggie, this shouldn't take long. We want you to drive the van and do the deliveries for today to Landkey and Swimbridge.'

'Drive the van?' Margaret was confused. 'But I can't drive, Bert.'

'Of course, I understand that. I didn't think you could but you're a bright girl and will pick it up in no time.' He pushed her towards the front of the Morris van and opened the driver's door.

'Now, the van is loaded up with all the deliveries and there's a list of customers and the costing for each item. Some are orders but it's all written down. And here's the satchel with the purse for the money. There's some change in it to start you off. Oh, and here's the map.'

'But I can't drive, Bert.'

'That's why I'm going to give you a little bit of instruction now, Maggie. Right. Now get in and sit behind the wheel.' Bert pushed the terrified Maggie into the driving seat. 'Oh! You can't see over the dashboard, can you?' he frowned. 'Just a moment, I'll fetch you a cushion.'

He disappeared and Maggie could hear him shouting to Doreen for a cushion from the shop, and telling Frank that he should have taken the cakes out of the oven.

'Now, here we are. Sit on this, Maggie, and I've brought you my woollen jumper to go behind your back. There. That's better isn't it? You can see fine now. Right. Let's get started.'

Margaret's hands gripped the steering wheel, her knuckles showing white. It had been a short amount of instruction and she'd had trouble keeping the motor running and had stalled the van several times when pulling away and trying it out around the yard. But Bert had gone back to the bakery and she was on her own. He'd driven the van out onto the road by the river and she'd been left to get on with it. Margaret sat to attention, back like a ramrod, neck stretched so she could look through the windscreen at the road ahead. The thick woollen jumper behind her enabled her feet to reach the pedals. Accelerator, brake (using her right foot), clutch and gear stick. Then there was the handbrake. She kept saying them over in her head, trying to visualise them without looking down. Gears one, two and three, oh, and neutral. You had to stop the stick in neutral and use the clutch pedal twice when changing down. Double-declutch Bert had called it.

'She won't get up a hill without you doing a double-declutch, Maid,' he'd warned. 'First gear is for starting and for hills, up or down. Oh, and be careful starting off on a hill. If you don't hold it on the clutch, you'll keep slipping backwards, so keep the handbrake pulled up and don't let it go until you feel her keen to pull away.' Bert had made the van sound like a young filly trying to get over a jump instead of a motor vehicle.

'She'll get 'ee there, Maid, don't you worry.' He had such confidence in the van and brushed off her apprehension with a shrug.

'You can ride a bicycle can't you, Maggie? Well, there you are then. She's ticking over lovely now so put her in first and get on.'

With a wave of his hand, he'd promptly disappeared back into the yard and made for the bakehouse.

Chapter 2

It was twelve noon on a sunny spring day in mid-March and nothing stirred in the tiny raised garden in front of the kitchen window of the Devon Longhouse. Nothing, that is, except a gentle wind with the chill of winter lingering in it as a stern reminder of what had been a bitterly cold February. Sunnybank, cream-washed, with a thatched roof, like a picture from an old chocolate box, faced south and looked down the stony, winding lane which ran from its front door to the road below. The approach to the house was by a five-barred gate. Between the road and the gate there was a grassy space for vehicles to turn into on the rare occasions that someone might call. Behind the house a two-acre green splat rose steeply to a wood of oak and beech. On its western boundary an ancient hedge ran parallel to the lane, and on the eastern side were fields which made up most of the small holding of twenty-seven acres. To the west the road wandered through countryside which rolled and dipped gently down to the village of Swimbridge, and to the east it climbed, first steadily and then steeply, cutting and curving its way through fields and woods to the village of West Buckland.

It was from this direction, at a quarter past twelve every day except Sunday, that Stan Webber cycled on his homeward journey. He was postman for the villages of West and East Buckland and he covered the round on his bicycle, sometimes pedalling and sometimes pushing it up the steep hills and along potted, muddy tracks to farms and cottages. His working day was a long one and it was only half over.

Stan was also the smallholding tenant of Sunnybank, which was owned by Earl Fortescue, whose Estate was centred on Castle Hill, Filleigh. The family home was presently occupied by pupils and staff of a large school which had been evacuated there in 1941. The Earl and his family had moved out and were living in a large house on Exmoor.

Back at Sunnybank, Lil looked out of the kitchen window at their dog Bruce, an old Welsh Collie, who had been lying motionless for almost two hours on the little strip of lawn which served as the front garden. As if he'd been given his cue, Bruce began to stir, stretching his legs, opening his eyes and getting slowly to his feet. After a huge yawn, a snap at a passing bumble bee and a thorough shake, the dog moved to a well-worn spot at the edge of the garden and sat down. Head raised, and sniffing the spring air, he pointed his nose in the direction of the West Buckland road. Without bothering to look at the clock, Lil decided it was time to put the potatoes on to boil.

Although the lives of Stan and Lil were ordered by the tending of animals, the sowing and harvesting of crops and the turning of the year from spring though to winter, the daily pattern of work for each of them was quite a different one. They had no children, a loss now accepted by them both, and Lil spent much of the day alone, busy with the unending chores necessitated by a draughty old farmhouse with no mains water, gas or electricity supply. Not that Lil would have liked a piped water supply. She could taste the difference between tap water and their own sweet well water. In any case, it had been she who had found the water when they'd first moved into Sunnybank as a young married couple back in 1928. The house had been unoccupied for at least a year and the water from the old well had dried up. Stan thought there must be water somewhere below ground in the splat behind the house. Lil had seen her father divining water with a small hazel branch and just knew she would be able to do it.

Stan had cut and trimmed a good branch shaped

like a letter Y. Lil, holding the two arms of the branch, one in each hand and with the main shoot of the Y pointing outwards, had spent over an hour walking about the field, stopping, changing direction and watching for the strongest movements from the hazel branch, which occasionally took on a will of its own as it swung downwards, pointing to possible sources below the rough pasture.

Leaning on the wooden gate at the eastern side of the splat, Stan watched his wife with curiosity and some doubt. After quietly noting the point of the hazel shoot's most violent reaction, he took his pick and spade and began digging while Lil went indoors to prepare tea. She would be glad when they no longer had to fetch water every day from Orchard Mill. It was while he was digging two days later, only nine feet down, that Stan struck water. It had been a thrilling moment for them both and marked their first big achievement as a partnership.

The sound of Bruce's gentle barking brought Lil out of her day dream and she went to the scullery to fill the kettle. Moving the wooden hand pump to and fro, fiercely at first and then slowing as the water flowed, Lil thought about her morning. Monday. Washday. She never liked lighting the copper, but at least it had been a dry morning and she had already been able to pick in some of the clothes from the line which ran across the top of the vegetable garden. She put the kettle on the hook hanging over the black range in the kitchen and threw in two more logs. She would have to go up to the woods in the afternoon. They were almost out of lightings and there wouldn't be enough to light the range the next morning.

Wiping her hands on the sides of her apron, Lil walked outside and stood on the front step. Bruce was on his feet now, his tail wagging. Shielding her eyes against the brightness of the spring sunshine, she looked up towards the West Buckland road to see Stan in the distance, freewheeling down it. With an age-defying leap from his vantage point to the foot of the front door steps, the old sheepdog raced off down the lane like a puppy, skidding to a halt inside the five-barred gate at the bottom. Seconds later, Stan turned off the road and, crossing the bridge over the stream which formed the southern boundary of their land, he drew up at the gate.

Back in the kitchen, the clock on the dresser showed twenty-five past twelve. Lil stirred the stew and salted the potatoes. Apart from the Christmas and Easter Festivals, the pattern of her work varied little from one week to the next. On Sunday there was Chapel in the morning. Stan drove her to Swimbridge in their Austin Seven and while she enjoyed the hymn singing and the worshipping together with other village folk, he occasionally called on relatives or friends nearby, catching up on their news and passing on happenings from the villages of West and East Buckland. Having a good 'tell' was his life's blood and no incident was too small or trivial to go unrecorded. But Stan didn't enjoy being away from home for long and was always happy to return to the peace of his beloved Sunnybank.

They ate a cold 'dinner', as they called it, on Sundays of meat from Saturday's roast, with pickles and boiled potatoes. In the summer they would have some of their own grown lettuce and tomatoes with it. In the afternoon they sometimes received visits from sisters or brothers and their wives and children, or, on rare occasions would visit them. Lil, who had grown up in a large family, loved 'comp'ny' as she called it, and living at Sunnybank with no neighbouring house in sight, she was lonely. Of course, tradesmen called and that brought news and further contact with the village. Some even came from Barnstaple, six miles away.

The rest of the week was marked by washing, baking and cleaning, but in March Lil started the spring cleaning; not an easy undertaking in their old cottage with Stan bringing in mud on his boots every day. They rarely went out during the week. There was little time for socialising or going to the shops in Swimbridge or Barnstaple. In any case Stan hated going to Barnstaple and rarely ventured beyond Swimbridge.

But dinner was ready. Stan, having wheeled his bike half way up the lane and pushed it in alongside their car in their homemade garage, walked up the narrowing, rocky path to the farmhouse, followed closely by Bruce. After a quick wash and a change of clothes out of his uniform and into his dungarees, he seated himself at the top end of the long kitchen table, ready for his dinner.

'Well, Maid,' he said, looking up at Lil as she ladled stew into his plate, 'what do 'ee think about us 'avin' some evacuees?'

Chapter 3

Margaret had driven the van up Newport Hill and stopped on a straight piece of road on the way to Landkey. She had only stalled the engine a couple of times and applied the handbrake immediately, pushing her foot onto the clutch, and after a bit of fumbling, started off again. She already felt exhausted and hadn't reached any customers yet. Fortunately, she had only seen one car which overtook her, and after that an AA man riding a motor bike and sidecar which came towards her. He saluted her as he passed, although Margaret couldn't understand why.

She decided to take a good look at the map. The route through Landkey Village and Swimbridge was vaguely familiar to her as she had taken the bus from Barnstaple to South Molton last December to see a friend. But now she had to turn off somewhere on the right to Landkey Town. There were two customers on the way who had placed orders and then she had to stop in the centre by the church for customers to come to the van.

Margaret started the engine and took a turning on the right marked Landkey Town. Soon after, she found two cottages next door to one another, stopped and delivered the orders of loaves and carrot cakes, the same for both customers. They were sisters and liked a chat. Margaret had to politely tear herself away and drive on to the bottom of the hill where she stopped by the church.

Almost immediately, a queue of customers formed and eagerly bought what appeared to be the local favourites of iced buns and coconut cakes. On she drove to Landkey Village, coming back onto the South Molton road after the detour to Landkey Town. There were a few stops before parking at the bottom of the hill near the butcher's, which was where Bert had told her to park. Again, there was no shortage of people coming to the back of the van to choose from what Bert had packed there. Some people were disappointed but those who had placed an order were secured of their delivery. After carefully updating the list of sales she had made, Margaret checked the map and set off up the hill from Landkey, in the direction of Swimbridge. With a few stops before the bottom of the village, she parked near the shop at what was already a gathering point of eager customers. After about quarter of an hour, she had finished the business in Swimbridge and was ready to set off again.

Margaret was exhausted, but apart from a few embarrassing stalls and grating noises as a result of her inexperienced driving when trying to find first gear, which resulted in a few guffaws from the local youth, she was beginning to enjoy herself.

Now it was time to turn left and get off the main road and drive up Station Hill. Margaret set off and feeling more confident, soon put the van into second gear. The narrow road out of the village was steeper than she thought, and the van started to struggle. She would have to get it down again into first gear. Double-declutch. Oh no! She fought with the gear stick and jumped on the clutch several times. The van started to slip backwards, and she got the handbrake on, pulling it up tight. The engine stopped. She sat shaking, wondering if the van was going to slip backwards down the hill. Suddenly, a young man appeared from a gateway on the opposite side of the road.

'Are you all right there?' he shouted in a friendly way as he walked across the road and stood alongside the van. She wound down the window.

'I only learnt to drive this morning,' Margaret replied, 'and I'm not much good at it yet.'

'I don't like driving cars and vans meself,' the young man said. 'I'm more used to tractors and steam rollers, something with a bit of go in 'em. Where have you come from?'

Margaret looked more closely at the stranger

and was surprised that he should be driving at all.

'The bakery in Barnstaple,' she answered.

'Where are you going?' he asked, looking behind her at some of the remaining produce in the back of the van. He was fresh-faced and boyish with fair hair, and looked as if he should still have been at school. Margaret picked up her list which she had placed on the front seat next to her.

'I have to turn right at the top and go as far as Sunnybank, making one stop on the way.'

'Oh,' he said cheerfully. 'You'll have a good welcome there. I hope you're hungry.'

Margaret wondered what he meant.

'I'm related to the lady there. Nephew. But everyone around here is related to everyone else in a roundabout sort of way. I'm Wilfred and I live at Landkey. We have our bread from Darch's but I expect yours is all right,' he said slightly begrudgingly.

'Now let me help you get going again,' he added. He came behind the van and shouted, 'Start her up and keep the handbrake on tight and gradually let up the clutch as you use your accelerator. I'll stand at the back so I can put my weight behind the van to help you, but be careful now. I don't want to be run over.'

He had a very loud, deep voice and Margaret thought that the whole of Swimbridge must have heard him shouting instructions to her.

'That's it. Right foot down and left foot up very slowly. Well done!'

Fumes and smoke issued from the back of the vehicle and poor Wilfred could hardly be seen.

'Now gradually release the handbrake,' he bellowed. 'Good! Good!'

A great roaring noise followed as the gear engaged and the van began to pull slowly away, gaining momentum and gradually climbing Station Hill. Margaret could just see Wilfred in the driving mirror, clouded in smoke but waving happily. She almost cried with relief as she reached the top of the hill and turned right, keeping in a noisy first gear. It had been a frightening experience, but she and the van were still in one piece. She continued on her way along the narrow road to West Buckland. She soon stopped at a large, country house on the left which had a bell hanging above the centre of its roof. Margaret had turned into the drive between two stone pillars when suddenly a maid servant, dressed in black with a white apron and cap, came running out to see her. Margaret was directed around the back of the building to a courtyard with stabling on three sides where two grooms were hard at work.

Having handed over the order, she was signalled to turn around and depart from the premises, which she did without a word having been spoken. She drove back onto the road and made for her final stop. Sunnybank. Margaret realised that it was gone two o'clock and she had had nothing to eat or drink since leaving the bakery that morning. She suddenly felt very tired. If she hadn't had to make one last delivery, she'd have pulled in somewhere and drunk from the flask of tea that Bert had given her, and she would have eaten one of the cakes left over from the morning's sales. She thought that she'd better get on as she was probably already behind her time to arrive at her final customer's home.

After about two miles, she drove around a sharp bend in the road and saw the sign for Sunnybank on the left. She turned into the grassy area leading to the gate. She decided to open the gate and drive up the steep path as far as she could. She got out of the van and opened the gate, drove through the gateway, stopped the van and shut the gate behind her. The path went up as far as a rough building on the left which looked like a sort of garage, although somewhat rickety and homemade. She chugged on up in first gear as far as the building and stopped the van.

Margaret went to the back of the van and collected the order, together with some of the remaining rolls and cakes that had not been sold, which she put into the large basket. She had a keen sense for business, and it would be good if the day resulted in an increase of sales compared with those of the previous Tuesday. She walked up the narrowing, rocky path, went up the steps and knocked on the front door.

Chapter 4

Loud **barking came** from inside the house and a man's voice cut through it with a shout. 'Bruce! Lay down!' A woman's voice followed with a gentle reprimand.

'Stan, you know I don't like that dug in yer. Where's 'e been hidin'? Under the bench I s'ppose. Come on Bruce. Out!' the woman ordered.

The door opened and the dog rushed past Margaret, almost knocking her off the top of the steps.

'Oh, sorry dear. 'E won't hurt you. 'E loves everyone. Come in! Come in!'

Margaret followed the woman into a huge kitchen with a black range, two old armchairs either side of it and a large, cream-painted dresser on the wall to the left of the door. A long, wooden table took up much of the room, with chairs facing the window and one larger chair backing onto the door. A wooden bench seat fixed to the wall ran around the table on the two other sides. The man was seated up the far end, drinking a cup of tea and eating a scone smothered in clotted cream and what looked like strawberry jam. He looked up.

'Us don't know you, Maid, do us, Lil?' he asked with a pause between bites on his very large scone.

Margaret's mouth started to water at the sight of the plate of scones laid out before him. There wouldn't be any cake sales here she thought to herself.

'No. I'm afraid Ron has broken his leg, so I've had to take his place. Sorry I'm late but I didn't know the round and I didn't know the way and – well I couldn't drive until this morning and I'm not much good now,' she finished lamely.

'You poor thing!' Lil came forward and took the basket from Margaret and put it by the dresser.

'You must be tired out. Fancy getting' you to do all that. Wasn't 'ee scared?'

'Well, yes I tried to tell Bert that I couldn't – ' Margaret emitted a long sigh.

Lil directed the exhausted Margaret to sit on the bench facing the room.

'Now, you just sit there, you poor girl, and I'll bring in the dinner that Ron would have eaten if 'e'd come. Us always gives him dinner, don't us, Stan? And don't worry about being late either.' She disappeared to the scullery and returned carrying a huge plate of steaming stew, enough to feed two people. Margaret was confused. What was it that Wilfred had said? 'I hope you're hungry.'

'That's very kind of you, Mrs. Webber.' Margaret

was wondering if all the tradespeople received the same treatment.

'Lil. Please call me Lil, and this is Stan. And what's your name, dear?'

'I'm Margaret. Margaret Partridge.' Lil smiled and nodded at the plate she'd put down on the table.

'Good. Now get that inside 'ee and you'll feel a lot better. There's rice pudding for afters.'

'What about a drink for 'er, Lil?' said Stan, reaching for another scone and ladling cream and jam on it.

Margaret started on the stew, which was delicious, and Lil returned with a tray on which there was a very large, brown tea-pot, a jug of milk and a cup and saucer.

'Thank you so much,' Margaret said. 'I didn't expect to have this welcome. It is lovely and a real treat.'

Lil sat down at the table and poured tea for herself and Margaret.

'Oh no, dear. Everyone's welcome here. 'Tis a treat for us to see folks. We had our dinner a few hours ago but Stan 'as been working in the vegetable garden and popped in for a little snack.' She chatted away while Margaret ate the food put in front of her.

'I've got your order in the basket there,' Margaret

said. 'And there are some extra little cakes and two pasties that have not been sold. You can have them at half price if you like.'

Margaret had no authority to sell the food at a reduced rate but thought it was better than taking it back to the shop.

'Well, us won't say no, will us, Stan? That'll be just the thing for you to take on your post round for your lunch tomorrow.'

Stan stood up, walked across the room and looked into the basket.

'Bootiful,' he said. 'And see 'ee next week, Maggie.' With a somewhat toothless grin, he walked towards the door.

'Must get on while the weather keeps up. More teddies to put in and then I'm off to do the milkin'.'

'And I really must get back to the bakery, Lil. That was a lovely dinner, but I know Bert will want to finish up at the shop.'

Lil handed Margaret the money for the bread order and the extra for the cakes and pasties.

'Please thank Bert for puttin' in some fresh yeast for me. I makes me own bread in between times. I'll walk down to the corner of the lane with 'ee, Margaret. I 'spect you left the van near our garage didn't 'ee?' Lil asked.

'Yes, Lil. I should have left it down by the gate really.'

Lil smiled and shook her head. 'No, no dear. Always drive up as far as you can and save your veet.'

They walked out of the front door with Lil carrying the basket. Margaret stood on the top step for a while and looked down to the bottom of the lane and across the road to the fields and woods beyond. It was breathtakingly beautiful and quiet, except for the sound of the birds and the faint rustle of the wind in the trees behind the house.

Suddenly, Margaret realised that she hadn't been to the toilet for hours and now felt a real urgency to go before the drive back, which would take about half an hour. She looked up at Lil who understood the situation immediately.

' 'Tis over there,' Lil pointed in the direction of the vegetable garden. 'Go across the yard and through that gate. Walk across the top of the vegetable garden and the toilet is at the far end. 'Tis a painted, wooden 'ut with roses growin' round the door. Mind you there's none flowerin' yet but they'm nice when they come out.'

Margaret was somewhat confused but set off, walking in the direction of the distant hut while spotting Stan working at the bottom of the garden tilling potatoes. She reached the hut and went inside, fastening the door with a hook on the inside.

It was dark, even in daylight and she wondered how they managed in the depths of winter and at night. There was no way of flushing the toilet, so she came out and shut the door. It was just a bucket with a wooden seat over it.

So, this is the country, Margaret thought.

'Thank you, Lil,' she said. 'It would have been an uncomfortable drive back to Barnstaple.'

They walked down to the van and Margaret put the basket and the money bag in the back and got into the front seat.

'Now you can come out and see us any time,' Lil said, her hand on the van door.

'I'd love that,' Margaret answered, starting up the van and doing some gear grinding.

Suddenly she stopped the engine.

'What's the matter, dear?' Lil asked.

'Well, there's nowhere to turn around and Bert didn't teach me how to go backwards. I don't know what to do.' A feeling of panic started to come over her.

'I can't drive so 'tis no use askin' me,' Lil said. 'But you sit tight, and I'll fetch Stan. 'E'll sort it out for 'ee.'

She started to run back up the lane calling out to her husband.

'Stan! Stan! Come down yer a minute. Poor Margaret can't drive backwards down the lane.'

Stan's head appeared over the hedge above the garage.

'That's all right, Maggie. Don't do a thing. I'll show 'ee,' he shouted.

Margaret got out of the front seat. She thought it would be safer for Stan to drive the van all the way to the bottom of the lane and take it onto the road, facing in the direction of Barnstaple. Two minutes later, he appeared and sat in the driver's seat. He started the van and showed her where the reverse gear was. Margaret thought it was quite a battle to get into reverse gear. She waved to Lil and sat in the passenger seat next to Stan. He backed the van down the lane, and she got out and opened the gate. Stan reversed through and she followed him, shutting the gate behind her. She was aware that some animals were grazing in the bottom field, although she couldn't see any at that moment. Stan had parked the van on the road ready for her to drive off.

'I can't thank you enough,' she said. 'Earlier today, another member of your family helped me when I was stuck on the hill coming up from Swimbridge. He said his name was Wilfred.'

'Wilfred!' Stan laughed. 'What was 'e up to out of school? That boy was born with an oil cloth in 'is 'and. 'Tis a wonder 'e didn't take the van apart. 'E's a character, be Wilfred!'

Stan got out of the van and Margaret got in behind the wheel.

'Now drive safe, Maid. You done well today.'

She started the engine, waved and drove off. Yes, she thought to herself. All things considered, she had done well.

Chapter 5

James Webb finished his shift at Barnstaple Junction Station at 4pm. He had started early and set off with a railway colleague at 8.30 am, walking along the tracks in the direction of Instow. They had to check the points on the line from Barnstaple. The weather was dry but cool and they needed the extra layers under their railway uniforms. Apart from standing aside to see the occasional passing train going by in the up or down direction, all was quiet. There was just the sound of the birds which the workers interrupted by the clang of their metal tools used to hit the rails, checking for cracks, and the crunch of their boots as they walked on the stones between the wooden sleepers.

There were few houses between Barnstaple and the little seaside village of Instow, and the wildflowers and unruly, stunted trees alongside the track parted now and then to give glorious views of the Taw estuary. The men spoke little to one another except when they sat down at one of these viewpoints to eat their lunch and drink from their flasks of tea. It was a good day; a peaceful one. Even the wind had dropped, and the stillness was calming.

'It's only a half day for me, Jim,' said his colleague.

'Oh yes, John. I'd forgotten that. See you tomorrow then.'

John started to walk away along the track back towards Barnstaple. Jim waved him goodbye and took a deep breath, closing his eyes and filling his lungs with the clean, fresh air. He loved the stillness and the peace. He had survived four battles in the '14 –'18 war and had been wounded twice before eventually being discharged. He had been part of the British Expeditionary Force and had seen more than enough turmoil, loss and sacrifice. After the war, he and his wife and two young children had moved to North Devon and he took up a job on the railway, a link with the area from where he had come. They had lived in Southampton, but some members of both families had worked at the locomotive and carriage building works at Eastleigh. The opportunity had come to move to the South West and they took it, together with the renting of a cottage owned by Southern Railway. There were three railway stations in Barnstaple but Jim worked mostly out of Barnstaple Junction.

After working along the line towards Instow, Jim checked his watch and turned to make his way back towards the station. When he got close to it, he stopped to look to his right at the allotments which were within easy walking distance from where he lived. There were a few older men and one woman working, weeding and turning over the soil. Some plots still had some leeks and winter cabbage hanging on, enough for a few more meals, Jim thought. He worked his allotment there but without a great deal of enthusiasm.

Back at the station, he checked out and walked the six or seven minutes to his house. There was no-one at home, and he changed out of his uniform and put on some old trousers and a shirt and pullover, washed his hands at the sink in the scullery and sat down in the kitchen in his own small armchair next to his beloved wireless. He turned it on and played with the knobs, eventually finding a station; this time it was Hilversum, which would play him some classical music. Ah yes. Beethoven's Pastoral Symphony. Perfect. He closed his eyes and after a few minutes he started to fall asleep. His gentle reverie was broken by loud calls and laughter. His wife was back with the grandchildren.

'Grampy! Grampy! What's that you're listening to?' Diana shouted. She always had to know what he was listening to and would often stay sitting listening quietly with him. She sat down on the floor at his feet.

'Everything all right, Florrie?' Jim asked without showing undue concern as to whether it was or not.

'Yes. We've been to the park and I'm going to get them some tea. Margaret's not back yet and when she is, she'll be tired out. I hope that shop's paying her extra for all the time she puts in there. I'll put the kettle on. Now Mary, love, sit down here and play with your toys. Here's the box. Oh! You like to empty it out all over the floor. Well, that's fine then.'

Beethoven's Pastoral continued to cut through the sounds of the preparations for tea, preceded by the reminder from Granma that Mary should use the potty and Diana should go to the toilet upstairs. Jim stayed in his chair, turned off the wireless and Florrie brought his tea to him to have on his lap. The others sat round the table. It was a simple tea of bread and butter, spread thinly, a small slice of cheese each and after that some home-made cake that Margaret had brought over in the morning. Jim had some sliced Spam with a few cold potatoes left over from dinner, and a good slice of cake.

'Drink up your milk now, Mary. Mummy will be here in a minute.' The little one was starting to get grizzly. She was tired.

'What are you going to listen to next, Grampy?' Diana asked.

'I'll see what I can find on the wireless in a minute,' he answered, turning it on and twiddling with the knobs, resulting in a series of cracks and whistles and snippets of sounds, not many of them musical. Suddenly there was a piercingly loud whistle as he hit upon a station where the reception was not going to result in anything remotely musical. Diana covered her ears and Mary started wailing.

Florrie groaned. 'Oh, Jim! For goodness sake, turn that thing off until the girls have gone home.'

At that moment the door opened and Margaret walked in.

'Mummy! Mummy!' Mary cried, stretching out her arms.

'Sorry I'm so late, Mum. No. I won't stop for a cup of tea thanks. I'd better take them straight away. It's been a very unusual day. I'll tell you all about it if you come over in an hour or so,' she said, picking up Mary.

'Diana, bring that bag of things and put those toys in the box for Granma. Say "Thank you" girls. Mum, thank you for giving them tea. See you later. Bye, Dad.'

Jim looked up from his newspaper and waved. Florrie followed Margaret to the front door. 'They've been very good,' she said and smiled as she closed the door behind them.

'Well Margaret,' her mother said, sitting down at her daughter's table two hours later. 'What's been happening today? You look tired out.'

'I had to drive the delivery van, Mum. We were very short-staffed today and there was no-one to drive the van.'

'What? When did you learn to drive?' her mother asked, puzzled.

'This morning, Mum. And I really can drive now, or sort of,' Margaret answered proudly. 'I've been to Landkey and Swimbridge, and I've met some lovely people, and the last customers gave me dinner and were so kind. I hope Bert lets me drive the van again.'

'Well,' said her mother, 'let's hope he pays you more for doing that, dear.'

'Oh, I forgot to see if there's been any post today,' Margaret said. 'I came in the back way with the children earlier, so I haven't been to the front door. I'll just go and see.'

Every day Margaret looked for a letter from her husband. There never was one as the regime at the sanatorium would never allow Jack to sit up and write a letter. Part of the treatment for tuberculosis was to ensure the patients stilled their breathing and moved as little as possible. They spent long hours on their backs, but Margaret knew that Jack was hoping to progress to being allowed one pillow for part of the day.

She went out into the narrow passage leading to the front door. There, on the mat was a small white envelope. It was addressed to her in a scrawling, feeble hand. She gasped and picked it up, ripping it open as she ran back into the kitchen.

'Look, Mum. At last, news from Jack. They must have let him get out of bed to write this.' She removed a single sheet of paper from the envelope and read the message aloud.

Dear Marj,

at last I am allowed out of bed for just enough time to write a letter. It feels wonderful. I have had another x-ray. Sister is coming now so I must close. Give the children a hug from me. Your loving husband,
Jack.

There you are, Mum. He must be getting better, don't you think?'

Florrie made an effort to sound enthusiastic. 'I hope you are right. It shows progress anyway. Now you get some rest. Have an early night. You've had a very full day.'

They hugged one another and Florrie made her way back to her own house. If only she could feel confident about her son-in-law's progress. She'd seen too many die from the disease in her time. She decided to be optimistic, especially when in the company of her daughter. She opened the front door and entered her house, only to hear Jim's voice calling from the kitchen.

'Florrie! Is that you? Can you make me some cocoa? I want to go on to bed.'

'Coming, dear,' Florrie sighed. Her husband was a hard worker and had come out of the war never the man he had been when he went into it, but it would be nice if he could boil a kettle, she thought.

Chapter 6

The ward was quiet following the usual routine of bedpans, washing, breakfast and doctors' rounds. The morning started very early and now most of the patients were having a sleep. Some of them were lying flat but a few had been promoted to having one pillow. Jack lifted himself to an upright position and swung his legs over the side of the bed. After being allowed up for about ten minutes on Monday, surely, he could get to the toilet himself for once.

Suddenly a booming female voice rang out from the end of the ward.

'Mr. Partridge! What do you think you are doing? Get back into bed this minute.'

Sister Bailey came speeding through the ward, passing the rows of parallel beds on either side, the only warning of her approach being the faint crackling sound of her starched white uniform. Even the patients who were sleeping stopped snoring as if in obedient homage to the terror of Ward 4. She stopped at the bottom of Jack's bed.

'Well?' she said with a challenging glare.

'I just thought that because I was allowed up on Monday to write a letter, Sister, I could get up to go to the toilet. I thought – ' His voice petered out lamely under Sister Bailey's unblinking, fixed expression. Without taking her eyes off her patient, she replied.

'You are not paid to think Mr. Partridge. I am paid to think, and I think that your best chances of recovery are to do as you are told, get back into bed and rest.'

'Yes, Sister. Sorry, Sister,' he answered, swinging his legs back into bed and getting into the horizontal position. Still looking straight at him, Sister Bailey put her voice up a semitone.

'Nurse Oldfield! Get this patient a bottle immediately. Why didn't you see what he was up to and stop him getting out of bed?'

Nurse Oldfield appeared, straightening her apron and adjusting her cap.

'Sorry, Sister. I was in the sluice. I thought they were all resting.' Sister Bailey looked away from Jack.

'Yes, well you have to have your eyes everywhere in this job. Don't just stand there. Get the patient a bottle.'

'Yes, Sister. Right away, Sister.' Nurse Oldfield shot off down the ward.

'And don't run, Nurse,' Sister Bailey shouted, turning back to Jack.

She looked at him earnestly for a moment. 'You

seem to be showing signs of improvement Mr. Partridge. We may promote you to having one pillow and, if you do as you're told, to two pillows later.' Continuing to scrutinize him, a faint semblance of a smile passed across her face momentarily. With a swish of her starched uniform, she turned suddenly and walked briskly out of the ward.

Patients who had been woken by the commotion but were feigning sleep in order to stay out of Sister's bad books, opened their eyes. Nurse Oldfield returned with the bottle and pulled the curtains round Jack.

'Sorry about that, Nurse,' Jack frowned.

'Oh, don't worry, dear. I'm used to it. You have to be in two places at once in this job and I always seem to be getting it in the neck for being in the wrong place.'

She left him and walked up and down the ward, checking that her patients were resting. Nurse Oldfield returned to Jack, pulled the curtains back and went off with the bottle. The patient in the opposite bed looked across at Jack. He had two pillows.

'Blimey! That Sister Bailey woman would be a formidable adversary against Hitler,' he said. 'When she comes on the ward I find myself lying to attention.'

His name was Harry and he'd been in the ward

for longer than Jack.

'I pretend to be asleep when she's on the ward,' Colin said. He was the patient in the next bed on Jack's left. 'It's safer and it keeps me out of trouble.'

They all agreed that was the best way to cope with the Buzz Bomb of Ward 4, as they had named her. The day progressed as most others, without further incident, but there was some disturbance later that night. A patient at the far end of the ward, near the Nurse's Station, had been coughing and was eventually wheeled out and put in a room on his own. While they were waiting for breakfast the next morning, the group of men in Jack's part of the ward talked of how they had woken up several times in the night when lights were going on and off and nurses were quietly calling to one another.

'Poor devil,' Colin said. 'He had a bad night. Anybody know him?'

'He's called Johnny. He came in about six months after me,' Jack said. 'He's an Exeter chap, like me. I was born not far from where he lives. Paris Street. Mind you, it's been badly bombed all around there. I think Johnny's pretty rough. Don't know if he'll make it,' he added gloomily.

'We've seen a few go in our time here, haven't we, Jack?' Harry remarked sadly.

'Yes. Too many,' Jack replied. 'But I've learnt that you have to think positive, not dwell on things.

I reckon I might be allowed a rest time out on the terrace soon. That's what I'm looking forward to.'

'Don't get too cocky, Jack.' Will's voice came from further down the ward.

'You're in Buzz Bomb's bad books now.'

Jack turned his head to reply but saw the far door swing open and the breakfast trolley being pushed through. Nurse Morgan, young and pretty, was one of the attractions on the ward. She had long fair hair and it was arranged into a bun at the back of her cap.

'Morning, gentlemen.' Her smile was enhanced by the bright sparkle in her deep blue eyes. 'Porridge first. It is so good for you. No. Please don't groan, Mr. Roberts. I'll put some extra sugar on yours.'

Nurse Morgan had a kind word for everyone.

'You're looking chipper today, Harry. Won the pools or something?'

'No, Nurse, but the sight of you is enough to cheer anyone up, even an old bloke like me.'

'Old bloke?' Nurse Morgan stopped at his bed and poured milk on his porridge. 'There's life in the old dog yet. I can tell that by the way you're looking at me, you cheeky man.'

'You've made me feel ten years younger, Nurse.' Harry's face lit up. She patted his arm and pushed the trolley to the opposite side of the room.

'Ah Jack! I hear you've been trying to escape.'

Jack thought that it must be all over the hospital that he'd attempted to get out of bed the day before. The fact that Sister Bailey was on duty was what made it news to the rest of the staff. He looked up at Nurse Morgan.

'Yes, Nurse. But I thought about it and decided to stay. How could I leave you here with this lot of shirkers?'

She screwed up her nose and blew a kiss at him, moving on down the ward with the trolley to the other patients.

After breakfast and bedpans, the doctors came on their rounds with the on-duty Sister for the ward. Saturday today. That meant Sister Bailey. The young doctors were scared of her but were usually accompanied by one of the older experienced specialists behind whom they could hide. The ward door opened and in came Mr. McNally with Sister Bailey at his side and the junior doctors trailing behind. The group gradually worked its way down the ward and stopped at Jack's bedside. The consultant looked at Jack's chart and peered at the anxious patient over the top of it.

'And how are we today, Mr. Partridge? Eating well are we, and sleeping well?'

Jack thought it was strange to be addressed in the plural. There was no-one else in his bed with him, was there; more's the pity.

'Yes, quite well, thank you, Doctor.'

'I have the results of your recent x-ray which shows some improvement,' Mr. McNally said, stretching out his arm and snapping his fingers without looking behind him. After some fumbling amongst the folders he was carrying, one of the junior doctors put the x-ray into the consultant's outstretched hand. Mr. McNally studied it briefly, holding it up to the light and then passing it quickly behind him.

'Yes. Yes. We have some progress here.' He turned to Sister Bailey and they talked quietly for a few minutes.

'Good, good. Sister, please be sure to keep the windows open. The patients can always have extra blankets if they are cold.'

The entourage moved on down the ward. After the doctor's round was finished, Sister Bailey returned to the ward and briefly explained some of the issues discussed with various patients. She stopped at Jack's bed and looked down at him.

'Well Mr. Partridge, you have earned one pillow and -' she paused dramatically, 'half an hour out on the terrace this afternoon.'

Jack's eyes lit up.

'Thank you, Sister,' he said.

'That doesn't give you licence to charge up and

down the ward, or even to move one inch from that bed unless I say so. Is that understood?' she said, her eyes fixed to his.

'No, Sister, I mean yes, Sister,' Jack could almost have leapt from the bed and hugged her but tried to calm his voice. 'Thank you, Sister.'

With a nod, she walked away. If the sun comes out, Jack thought, it would definitely be warmer outside than in the ward. Fresh air could be taken to extremes and the very name of 'Hawkmoor' told everyone that its situation was high up on Dartmoor. If he was still here in the summer, it would be more bearable, he thought. The bed on Jack's right was still unoccupied, but on the left side of him, Colin was making a thumbs up sign with some of the chaps in the ward.

'I'm going to see the outside of this place at last,' Jack shouted.

'Me too,' Colin chipped in. The feeling of progress and hope had lifted everyone's spirits.

Suddenly the ward door opened and Nurse Oldfield came on duty, walking down the ward, straightening bedcovers and plumping pillows.

'Any news of Johnny, Nurse?' Jack asked. Nurse Oldfield stopped by his bed and lowered her head.

'I'm sorry to tell you that he died about an hour ago.' She was biting her lip and couldn't bring herself to look up at anyone. The ward fell silent.

'He was only a young chap,' Harry said. 'Life's not fair is it, Nurse?'

She looked up at him with tears in her eyes. 'No, it's not fair, Harry. You're right.'

Chapter 7

'I don't know what the problem is,' Stan said, as he pushed his pudding plate away. Rhubarb pie and custard with their own clotted cream was one of his favourites so Lil thought she had caught him in a good mood.

'Well the letter only came this mornin'. The envelope be all dirty and creased and it must have gone astray, 'cos it was sent last week and today's Friday and she's comin' 's afternoon at three o'clock.'

Stan looked up from contemplating his empty pudding dish, wondering if he could cope with another helping.

'Who's comin' 's afternoon?' he asked casually.

'Stan, did you talk to Mrs. Bowden and 'er sister Miss Chugg over at East Buckland about they two evacuees? Why have they got to give 'em up?'

'Yes. Mrs Bowden's got to go to Crediton to look after 'er mother 'cos 'er fell and broke 'er arm. Mrs. Bowden 'ave wrote to the Billetin' Office and told 'em us could 'ave the lad.'

'And what about 'er sister? Can't 'er 'ave 'im?'

'No, 'cos the lad's little brother is billeted with 'er and 'e can't stay there 'cos Miss Chugg's got problems with 'er 'ouse. I forgot to tell 'ee. The thatch caught fire over a week ago and then it rained in the night. There'll be a lot of work to do on the place, so Miss Chugg is going with 'er sister to 'elp out in Crediton.'

Lil frowned. 'When Mr. Bowden passed on a few years back, wasn't Miss Chugg goin' to move in with 'er sister?'

'That's right, Lil, but then the two ladies took on the two evacuee brothers, one boy in each of the two little 'ouses.'

Lil nodded. 'Yes, I know they cottages are not very big. So, does that mean that both boys 'ave to be billeted, Stan?'

'Mrs. Bowden told me that 'er would write and ask the Billetin' Officer to try to keep 'em together. They was almost next door to each other in East Buckland. Anyway, what do that letter say?'

Lil sighed. 'You read it. I got to make up the baids for the little lads.' She left the room and went upstairs. Stan took the letter out of the crumpled envelope and read it. It was from a local government official named Mr. Andrew Morgan.

Dear Mr. and Mrs. Webber,

Mrs. Bowden of 2, Beech Lane, East Buckland, has written to inform me that she and her sister, Miss Chugg, of Corner Cottage, Beech Lane, East

Buckland, are no longer able to keep the evacuees formerly billeted with each of them, due to unforeseen circumstances. I understand from Mrs. Bowden that you would be willing to house the two boys concerned, which would be especially helpful in enabling them to stay together.

The boys are Jimmy Cooper, aged nine, and his younger brother Danny, aged seven. Their home is in Poplar, East London, which has suffered considerable bombing in the Blitz. We will let you have details of their family in due course, together with information regarding the money granted to you to help with the cost of care.

Mrs. Ellington-Smythe, one of our volunteers from the Evacuation Panel, would like to call on you with the boys on Friday next at 3pm. Mrs. Bowden highly recommended you, and in offering these children a home, you will be playing a vital part in helping the War Effort.

Many thanks,
Yours faithfully,
Andrew Morgan.

Stan lit his pipe and drew on it. The boys would be pupils at Filleigh Primary School so there would be no change to that arrangement, although they could go to Swimbridge to school. Best to keep them where they are used to going and where they are known. They could help out with the animals. P'raps they'd like that. Not many farm animals in London, that's for sure. He was just thinking about how the boys would like feeding the little goslings when they hatch out when his musings were interrupted by the sound of a distant vehicle. He turned from his seat to look out of the window towards the bottom of the lane. It was the baker's van. He saw Margaret getting out and opening the gate. She drove through, got out again and shut the gate behind her and drove on up to the garage.

'Lil,' he called, getting up and going to the foot of the stairs. 'Look out of the window and see who's comin' up the path. 'Tis Maggie.'

Lil came hurrying down the stairs. 'Margaret,' she said, determined to call the arrival by her full name. 'I thought she was only comin' on Tuesdays. Hello, dear. What a nice surprise to see 'ee. Us'll 'ave seen 'ee twice this week now. Come in and sit down. What's 'appened to Maurice?'

'Hello, Lil, hello, Stan. No, it's me again. It looks like I'll be coming every Tuesday and Friday for a while. As you know, Maurice is the new relief driver taking Ron's place until his leg mends, but Maurice can't do Tuesdays and Fridays 'cos he's got a stall in Barnstaple market and won't give that up for anything. That's only fair. He grows a lot of his own produce but Bert isn't pleased and says he's being "UNREASONABLE".' Margaret mimicked the offended tone that Bert had used.

'Good to see 'ee, Maid,' said Stan. Lil took the basket and directed Margaret to the table where a place had been laid for Maurice.

'Well, you won't be takin' anybody else's place for a while, Margaret, will 'ee?

Us'll see 'ee regular.' Lil smiled. 'Dinner is all ready and then I'll tell 'ee the news about this afternoon.'

'I'll go and get on then, you two.' Stan knocked out his pipe and put it in a pot on the mantelpiece. 'Come on then, Bruce.' Bruce slunk out from under the table and the two of them went out.

'Oh, that crafty dug gets in 'ere. 'E knows 'e's not supposed to be indoors but Stan encourages it. Trouble is, Margaret, I come way down in the peckin' order round yer, with every vour-legged creature and two-legged ones way above me. But there's something I want to tell 'ee about. Best thing is, you read this letter that was 'eld up in the post. It only came this mornin'. I'll go an' make a pot of tea.'

Margaret finished her pudding and then read through the letter that Lil had handed to her.

'It all seems rather sudden, Lil. They're coming this afternoon with – ' she paused and read in a rather posh voice, *Mrs. Ellington-Smythe.*

Lil nodded and she and Margaret cleared the table.

'Come on Lil, I'll wash up. I've finished my round and you've given me a lovely dinner. Let me help you get ready for them and then I'll go. They'll be here soon.'

They cleared up, wiped the table and set out some tea things and a plate of cakes that Margaret took from the basket.

'Let me pay for those as well as my bread,' Lil said.

'No Lil. Just pay for the bread. The cakes are my treat and they are cheaper anyway if they've not been sold by the end of the day.' Lil settled up with her order and looked at Margaret.

'Is there something wrong, Lil?' Margaret asked, picking up her basket and preparing to leave.

'Well, I was going to ask 'ee if you'd stay a bit and be 'ere when they come. I'm so nervous and I'm bound to say the wrong thing.'

'I could stay if you're really sure I won't be in the way. I've finished the round a lot earlier than last time. I know the route now and can drive the van better.'

Lil sighed. 'Oh good. Stan will come back in soon and 'e won't think of the sort of questions us women would.' She looked up from setting down the tea tray. 'Talk of the devil!'

Stan walked into the kitchen but this time he stopped Bruce slinking in and hiding under the table. 'Out you go, dug,' he said.

'They'm 'ere, Lil. Not 'alf past two yet.' He looked out of the window to see that a car had been left at the bottom of the lane and a woman was walking up to the house, accompanied by two boys.

'I'll put the kettle on,' said Lil, all of a fluster.

Margaret sat in the corner by the fire, trying to be out of sight.

It took some time for the three newcomers to reach the steps to the house. The boys kept stopping to look at the animals; some sheep who had wandered from the far field into the field by the lane. The lambs were a big attraction, but suddenly they scampered off at the arrival of four geese and a gander who came towards the visitors, their necks stretched out and making an awful, penetrating screech. Stan went outside to greet the party as they came up the steps to the front door, carrying their little cases and leaving them at the bottom of the stairs in the hall.

'Oh! Hello, Mrs. Smith. I'm Stan Webber. Come in, come in, boys.'

'I'm Mrs. Ellington-Smythe,' said Mrs. Ellington-Smythe, with a slightly admonishing look at Stan. 'And these are Jimmy and Danny. Take off your caps, boys and say "Hello" to Mr. and Mrs. Webber.'

Jimmy said 'Hello' and Danny looked down at the floor and then at the bright, red glow from the range. Lil introduced herself and Margaret to the new arrivals and invited everyone to sit at the table. She had found a bag of odds and ends of toys she kept for when her nephews and nieces visited.

'You can sit on the floor over there if you want,' she said, giving the bag to Jimmy.

'Or you could go outside on the step and meet Bruce,' Stan said, looking closely at Danny, who appeared anxious and uncomfortable.

The boys took the toy bag and went outside and sat on the top step. Bruce came up to them, tail wagging, and was immediately fussed over and cuddled.

Back in the kitchen Mrs. Ellington-Smythe went through some of the formalities of billeting and produced forms which Stan and Lil read and signed, but not until they had got Margaret to read them through first and received a nod of approval from her. When the formalities had been completed, the boys were called inside and everyone sat around the table and had tea, the cakes proving a big success with the young ones. Lil made an effort to talk to Jimmy. She wanted to put him at his ease.

'We don't know London, Jimmy,' she said, smiling at him.

'It's a big place, Missus,' he replied, through a mouthful of cake. 'And we was bombed.' He swallowed, and looked serious for a moment.

Danny said nothing, just looking on but in another world.

'Jimmy!' put in Mrs. Ellington-Smythe, 'We WERE bombed!' She looked at him, waiting for him to repeat what she had said.

'Was you, Missus? I didn't fink you was bombed 'ere in the country.'

Mrs. Ellington-Smythe thought she would have another try at working on Jimmy's grammar. 'WE weren't bombed but—'

'You just said you was.' Jimmy wiped his mouth with the back of his hand while looking straight at the lady. Margaret thought she should jump into the conversation to avoid any more confusion on both sides.

'Did you see the geese, boys? They scare me a bit, but I think you have to shout back at them when they cackle and hiss at you. I've tried that and they turn and waddle away.'

Jimmy smiled and looked at his brother. 'We'll do that won't we, Danny?' He put his hand on his younger brother's shoulder, as Danny looked up at him with a little worried smile. Jimmy looked around the table at everyone and said, 'I talks for 'im cos 'e don't talk no more. Not since the bomb fell in the street at the back of our 'ouse. We 'ad a rabbit 'utch at the end of our garden wiv two lovely young rabbits. They was both killed in the blast. 'E ain't talked since.'

Silence fell around the table. Sunnybank was another world, Lil thought. She looked at Margaret, who was trying to wipe away a tear.

'Us'll do our best for the boys, won't us, Stan?'

Mrs. Ellington-Smythe got up to leave. She was biting her lip.

'I know you will, Mrs. Webber, and I will send you further information in the post very soon. Thank you.'

She smiled and stretched out her hand. The ungrammatical mixture of the English language in both Devonshire and Cockney accents now suddenly seemed of little importance.

Stan stood up and nodded.

'And you can call us "Uncle" and "Auntie,"' he said. 'Now boys, what about comin' and 'elpin' me with milkin' the cows?'

They shot off down the steps and along the path towards the milking shed.

The three ladies looked at each other and smiled.

Chapter 8

It was Saturday and Margaret sat at the kitchen table and picked up her pen. Mary was having a late morning sleep and Diana was in the front room tinkling on the old piano that Grannie had passed on to them when she died in January. The piano had been at Aunt Maggie's house in Reading and had been brought down to Devon recently in a friend's lorry. The instrument was badly in need of tuning. Diana had not given them any peace since the piano had been carried into the little front room, whose window looked out directly onto the pavement. Their terraced house was small, but at least the noise being made in their 'best room' didn't sound too loud as it travelled to the rest of the house, as long as the doors were kept firmly closed. The girl had asked if she could have piano lessons. She had asked the same question every day for the last week. Margaret had hedged her answers with various excuses other than the real reason.

'You're still very young Diana,' and, 'You'd have to practise every day, you know. I don't think you'd keep it up.' How could they afford it when Jack was away at Hawkmoor and she was the only earner? There was the rent to pay each week and food and clothes to buy. Dad had offered to help by paying for a term's lessons to see if the little girl would take it seriously and practise. It was good of him. Perhaps it was worth a try. Margaret opened the note pad and started writing. She had looked in the local paper and found three advertisements put in by different piano teachers in Barnstaple. She would write a letter to each one of them and find out about their qualifications and their fees. After twenty minutes, she put down her pen and read through one of the letters. Diana was still playing what sounded like a little tune she had made up and its faltering melody was quite restful as its sound filtered gently through the wall into the kitchen.

Dear Miss McEvansoneya,

I read your advertisement in the local paper and am writing to ask if you would be willing to take on my daughter, Diana Partridge, who is seven years old, as a new pupil. She is a diligent child, and since we have been given a piano, it has been difficult to get her away from it.
Would you kindly inform me of your fees and let me know if you have a vacancy?
I look forward to receiving your reply.

Yours sincerely,

Margaret Partridge. (Mrs.)

Margaret folded the letter and put it in the envelope. She wouldn't mention it to her daughter until she had received replies from the three teachers. She sealed the three letters and stamped them, listening for any sound from the cot upstairs. Mary was still asleep and the sound coming from the front room continued. Surely the girl was bored by now? No, she was playing more than one note at a time. Chords. The musical investigation was continuing happily so Margaret decided to write a short letter to Jack. She had received an encouraging one from him yesterday. He had been allowed out to sit on the terrace and would be able to enjoy fresh air regularly, as long as his health continued to improve. It was a sign of real progress but she knew she mustn't become too confident. One of his early jobs was working in a dry cleaner's and the steamy, muggy atmosphere in the back of the premises where the clothes were cleaned and pressed had probably led to his illness. Margaret thought she would tell Jack a little about the good people she had met at Sunnybank, but of course she would also tell him about how she had arrived at their home. He would be amazed. She finished the letter with an ambitious sentence to give him something to think about.

So, I can drive now, Jack. And when you come home and can get back to work, we will save up for a little car and I will teach you how to drive.

She signed off the letter and addressed the envelope and sealed and stamped it. She put it with the others. There were sounds of stirrings from upstairs so she called Diana from the front room.

'Run up to the post box at the top of the road, Diana, and put these in the box. And remember what Granma says.'

Diana took the letters.

'Wait till you hear them drop,' she answered. Her mother smiled.

'Good,' she said. 'Go on then and we'll have our dinner when you come back.'

Chapter 9

When Margaret arrived at the bakery early Tuesday morning the following week, Bert had already loaded the van.

'I can't get any more in there, Maggie,' he said, sighing and wiping his brow after all his efforts. 'You'll most likely sell it all with next Friday being Good Friday. We'll be closed then and on Easter Sunday, and the Monday of course, so folks will be buying more this week. I'll be here until early evening 'cos you won't be back 'til late. I've packed you a flask of tea and a pasty and some hot cross buns but if you finish up at Mrs. Webber's you'll be fed again. She'll know to expect you later today.' He closed the back of the van door and grinned.

'Twice a week to Sunnybank and you'll soon have to go on a diet.'

Margaret agreed and thanked him for the picnic. She would make sure to eat it well before she reached Lil and Stan's. With the load she had on board, she wouldn't get to them until much later than usual anyway. She sat in behind the wheel, waved to Bert and set off. She enjoyed the drive from Barnstaple, leaving the houses behind and seeing the hedges and fields either side of her. An earlier shower had ceased and the sun shone on the fresh green leaves on the trees, and on the last of the primroses in the hedgerows, now in colourful contrast with newly emerging bluebells. With a deep sigh of satisfaction, Margaret forced herself to think of the day ahead. The basket would feel heavier when she had to walk up some of the long paths with the orders. There were a good number of customers who had ordered Simnel cakes and hot cross buns, although many of the country folk liked to make their own, which presented difficulties acquiring some of the vital ingredients. Margaret loved to cook and knew that the substitution of almond essence for ground almonds and dried eggs for fresh eggs resulted in a poor substitute for the real thing. Still, with rationing it was a case of 'make the best of it,' and it was good to see people making an effort to enjoy the Easter Festival in spite of Herr Hitler.

When Margaret had completed the Landkey part of the round, she drove on towards Swimbridge and stopped at a grass verge near a gate and started to eat her picnic. After eating the pasty and one of the buns, she decided against tackling the second one and put it back in the bag. The tea went down well and she could almost have fallen asleep but didn't dare close her eyes in case she did.

Driving on, she finished the Swimbridge round and headed for Sunnybank, after delivering to the large house with the bell on the roof. She knew better now than to drive to the front of the house, so motored around the back to the courtyard where the stables were. She was received with a 'Good Afternoon' and sent off with a 'Thank You,' which was progress, she thought. They always seemed to be in a hurry there. Perhaps Lil and Stan could tell her something about the owners and the staff.

Arriving at Sunnybank late in the afternoon, Margaret parked in the usual place and walked up to the front door with her basket. In no time she had been greeted, fed and watered and was enjoying a cup of tea and a chat with Lil. Because it was later than usual, Stan was out tending to the animals, helped and hindered by Jimmy and Danny.

'We've 'ad a letter and all sorts of information from Mrs. Ellington-Smythe, Margaret.' Lil handed the letter across the table. 'Us'll get money allowed for the boys' bed and board, and a bit of 'elp to clothe 'em. I reckon they'll grow fast, especially Jimmy. What that boy can eat! But us don't mind. They'm good lads and 'ave 'ad it tough in London.'

Margaret read the letter. Yes, they had had it tough.

'Oh,' Margaret looked up. 'So, they didn't come with the first wave of evacuees because Jimmy had measles at the time. Then the little chap caught it, and by the time they had regained their health, they suffered the effects of the Blitz. No wonder little Danny is as he is. Has he said anything yet, Lil?'

'Not a word, but I can see a little smile on 'is face now and then. You see, Margaret, us couldn't 'ave any evacuees when they came down 'ere a few years back, 'cos us had Grannnie and Granfer Cook 'ere lookin' after. My mother couldn't walk much and Dad suffered with 'is 'eart. They couldn't 'ave managed back 'ome on their own, so us moved 'em in yer with us. It was a lot of work but they'd been good to us and us wanted to pay 'em back as best us could.'

'Well, I don't think the boys could be anywhere better,' Margaret said, folding the letter and handing it back. She went to pick up her basket and Lil settled up for the order.

'I won't see you on Friday, Lil because it's Good Friday. Are you going out over the weekend?'

'Yes. I'm going to visit my sister in Landkey on Saturday. Stan will drop me off there in the car but 'e never stays; just says, "Hello," and waves, and off 'e goes, back to where 'e likes to be most. There's no changing' 'im.'

She paused and said, 'Why don't you come? You could get a bus from Barnstaple and walk the little way to my sister's 'ouse. She's expecting me about 'alf past two, and I don't stay much after vour.'

'That would be lovely, but I may have to bring

one of the children with me. Mum would have the little one. I did tell you last time I was here about my family. Jack wrote to say that he has been allowed to sit out on the terrace, so he is showing signs of progress. But without the help from my parents, especially my mother, I couldn't do this job and bring in money to keep body and soul together. I don't like to put upon her too much. She's a willing horse, and is always running around helping someone or other. In any case, would it be all right for me to turn up without an invitation? Your sister doesn't know me and I don't want to intrude.'

'No, you wouldn't. Edith likes to meet new volk. I'll write down 'er address and draw a little map to show 'ee the way there from the bus stop near the shop. 'Tis only a short walk.'

Lil scribbled down the details on a scrap of paper and handed it over to Margaret.

'I hope I can come, but it will depend on Mum.'

Margaret moved to the door and set off down the steps as Stan and the boys were coming along the top lane from the cow shed. They were some way off and Margaret had to get on back to Bert, so he could finish up and get home.

'Thank you, Lil. Lovely dinner as always. I don't know how I will be able to pay you back.'

They smiled at one another and Lil shook her head. 'You don't 'ave to, dear. I don't do it for that.'

Margaret waved to Stan and the boys as they turned to go up to the front door. They waved back and Jimmy shouted, 'Bye Mrs. P. Mind them geese now!'

Chapter 10

The scullery door opened, and Florrie came bustling in, dressed and ready to go out.

'Have you finished your dinner yet? You don't want to miss the bus, Margaret. Oh, good. You're all ready. It's a nice day so we are going to the park, Mary. You can bring your ball but give it to me and I'll put it in my bag.' Margaret settled Mary in her push chair and she and Diana put on their coats.

'Thanks, Mum, we won't be long gone. We'll be back before tea.'

'Don't worry, Margaret. Dad is listening to his wireless so I'm glad to get away for a bit. The music is fine but the racket he makes finding it is terrible.'

'I thought he was going to the allotment today?'

'He went this morning but not for very long. You know he isn't too keen on it, but he says he's put in some seeds and that some of the potatoes are coming through. Right. Off we go, Mary.'

'Sings, sings,' Mary shouted.

'Yes, you can go on the swings and Granma will push you.' They went out the front door, followed by Margaret and Diana. They all walked over the bridge together, Margaret and Diana turning left at the end of it to the bus station and the other two turning right to the park.

The bus to South Molton was at the bus stop and they got on and sat waiting for it to go. Margaret looked at the piece of paper on which Lil had scribbled directions. The bus conductor took their fares and gave them the return tickets as the bus set off.

'I don't know the lady we are going to meet, Diana, but she is the sister of my new friend, Lil – Mrs. Webber to you.'

'Is that the lady with the naughty geese, Mummy?'

'That's right, but they have other animals. I haven't seen them all, but I know there are cows and two pigs and chickens, and —'

'Is there a horse? There's got to be a horse or it's not a real farm, is it?'

'I wouldn't call it a farm because it's not big enough for a farm, but if we are invited there some time, we can find out about all the animals.'

They chatted away until the bus approached the bottom of the hill near the shop at Landkey.

'Right, Diana. This is where we have to get off.'

They stood on the pavement and Margaret pointed to a narrow road leading off the main road and close to where they were standing. She took her daughter's hand.

'We walk down here and look for an unmade road on the left.'

It was very quiet and the houses dropped away after a few minutes. They came upon a narrow muddy lane which was gutted with tyre tracks.

'I think we turn down here, Diana, but other than that one bungalow on the corner, I don't see another house, do you?'

They walked on with some difficulty on the uneven surface of the lane. Just as Margaret was thinking that they must have taken the wrong turning, the lane opened out to give onto an open piece of ground full of every sort of vehicle one could imagine, but only one of them in its whole state. That one was a car parked facing them as they approached. On the left of this graveyard of what had been cars, vans, lorries and bikes, was a huge shed, its double doors open, with sounds of metallic clanging and banging coming from inside. There was a wide path leading to the shed and another leading straight on to the little cottage ahead of them. They followed that path in silence, after looking at one another questioningly. At first, they couldn't work out where the door to enter the cottage was. The building seemed to be the wrong way around and they were looking at it side-on. Where was the front door? Where was the back door, or the side door? As they stood thinking about it, a door at the side, concealed by a tall shrub, against which a motor bike was leaning, opened suddenly and a tall woman with dark hair came out.

'You must be Margaret, and is this your daughter?'

The woman had only a slight facial resemblance to Lil, but her confident manner was entirely different from the gentle stillness of her sister.

'Yes, this is Diana, our elder daughter. Lil said you wouldn't mind us calling on you and meeting her here this afternoon.'

'No, of course not. I'm Edith. Do come in. Lilian is inside. We're just about to have a cup of tea, but I expect you'd like some lemonade, Diana.'

They entered a small scullery with a table with three chairs tucked in under it. There was a sink and work top and a cooker with a kettle boiling on it.

'Go on through and I'll come in with the tea tray in a moment.' Edith opened another door, almost squashing them against the wall to do so. Margaret and Diana went up a step into a sitting room. There had been a fire burning in the grate but today being warm and sunny, the fire had been allowed to go out. The room was almost filled by an armchair and a sofa, with a drop-leaf table against the opposite window on which was growing a large aspidistra. Margaret wondered how many people lived here and how they all fitted in. There was no sign of Lil, but her voice came from a further room beyond the far door.

'Is that you, Margaret?' She appeared at the door and welcomed them with a warm smile.

'You made it then and with this lovely little girl. Are you Diana, dear?'

'Yes, I am. I think you are Mrs. Webber, but you don't look much like your sister.'

'Diana, that's not polite to make personal remarks,' said her mother, correcting her, and shaking her head apologetically at Lil.

'Everyone says that so don't worry,' said Lil, smiling. 'Come through to the parlour.'

They followed Lil through the far door, coming immediately to a narrow staircase on the left and a door to outside on the right. Straight ahead of them was another door and they followed Lil through it to the parlour.

'Sit down,' Lil said, indicating another sofa which had an armchair on its either side, the arms of which were touching those of the sofa. Lil sat in the armchair furthest from the door and Margaret and Diana sat on the sofa. The room was very small and rather cold, with pictures on every wall of animals of various sorts. It was quite claustrophobic, Margaret thought, but inwardly chided herself for thinking it. Edith entered the room with a large tray with tea and cakes and a glass of lemonade on it. She set it down on a low table which touched everyone's knees as they sat looking at each other. Edith handed the lemonade to Diana and poured the tea.

'Help yourselves to the cakes. I made them this morning,' she said,

'My sister is a wonderful cook. 'Er made they cakes and that lemonade.' Lil said. 'And 'er 's secretary of the Landkey Mothers' Union. 'Er keeps 'em all in order there, don't ' ee, Edith?'

'The trouble is,' Edith shook her head, 'Some people volunteer to do things and don't do them. It makes organising much more difficult when you can't rely on people.'

'I can understand that,' agreed Margaret. 'I expect you end up doing a lot of the work yourself, Edith.'

Edith raised her eyebrows as she looked up at the new visitor.

'I can see that we are going to get along well,' she said, looking at Margaret intensely. 'You know what they say, "if you want a job done well, do it yourself." Have another cake, Diana.'

Diana wasn't fond of coconut cakes but found the lady rather frightening and didn't dare to refuse. 'Thank you' she said, choosing the smallest one on the plate.

'I'm sorry to hear about your husband, Margaret,' Edith said, her face softening a little, which suddenly made her look quite attractive. 'I know you told

Lilian all about his illness. It is a terrible disease, but I believe he is improving.'

Margaret smiled. 'Yes. He is making good progress now and we pray that he keeps it up.'

Edith paused and said quietly, 'We will remember him in our prayers.'

Lil said, 'Edith and George are "Church" and I'm "Chapel" but us still speaks to one another.' The three women laughed, and Edith said, 'Now Diana, you've sat here very quietly, but would you like to see my garden? We can all go out the front door and up onto the lawn.' She stood up and the others followed her out of the room.

Outside the front door, which was really the side door, they went up some steps onto the lawn. The contrast from the approach to the cottage was remarkable. There was not a weed to be seen in the immaculate lawn, nor in the little borders that surrounded it, where spring flowers were in full bloom. There was a bench at the far end with a privet hedge behind it to shelter anyone seeking refuge from the wind. Edith led the way and invited them to sit down.

'How beautiful!' Margaret's eyes widened in admiration. 'Who looks after this?' she asked. 'It's so- so-different.'

'Different from what you had to walk through to get to the back door?' Edith asked, laughing at Margaret's difficulty in finishing the sentence politely.

'When we bought this place, the most important thing for George was to have plenty of space for him to run his business, agricultural and motor repairs. He's good at it and our son is following in his footsteps. So, the house and any space for a good garden was limited but I am determined to hang onto this,' she said. 'And there is a little plot at the side of the workshop for a few vegetables. That and this little garden is all I am allowed, and I have to fight to keep that.'

Diana had escaped and was looking around the garden and heading back around the corner towards where they came in. Suddenly, a very tall fair-haired young man almost bumped into her.

'Oops,' he said, stopping suddenly. 'I thought I heard voices coming from Mother's garden. Is she back there sitting on her favourite seat, 'cos I want a cup of tea.' He walked past the little girl and up onto the lawn.

Margaret sat up, surprised, but recognising the young man as her saviour from when she couldn't drive the van up Station Hill in Swimbridge.

'Hello Wilfred,' Lil said, smiling at him. His overalls and his hands were covered in grease, but his ruddy smile was welcoming.

'Visitors, Mother?' he asked. 'Have they left any

tea and cakes for me?'

'Wilfred!' his mother chided him. 'Where are your manners?'

'I've left them in the workshop, Mother, and I'm gasping for some refreshment.' he replied.

'This be my friend, Margaret, and her daughter, Diana,' Lil told her nephew.

'Yes, I almost bumped into the young one but we know each other from a few weeks back, don't we?' he said looking at Margaret.

His manner was very confident, Margaret thought. It was difficult to tell how old he was. He was still at school and now he'd be on his Easter holiday, but a few weeks back, surely, he should have been at school then.

'Oh, so you're the van driver Wilfred was telling us about, Margaret. Wilfred was glad to help you. He was off school that week with a bad cough,' Edith explained. As if on cue, Wilfred put his greasy hand to his mouth and coughed into it.

'Where's that tea, then?' he asked loudly.

'We'll go back to the kitchen and I'll get it for you,' Edith said, and the three women stood up and walked around the outside of the house to where Margaret and Diana had entered it. Diana stayed exploring the pretty garden and the little pond where tadpoles had hatched and were wriggling in its clear water. The wild bluebells growing in the hedge were reflected in it. It was much nicer being outside, she thought. Wilfred followed the adults and remained outside the kitchen door, leaning against the wall, whistling quietly and looking up into the blue sky. There was a worn, wooden garden seat nearby and Lil and Margaret sat down on it while Edith went inside and prepared a tray of tea and cakes for the young worker.

'Where's your father, Wilfred?' his aunt asked.

'He's driven the tractor that we repaired to South Molton, Auntie. He'll get a lift back or come home on the bus. Anyway, I must get on. Good to see you both,' he said as he took the tray of tea and cakes that his mother was handing out to him. Margaret and Lil stood up.

'That won't keep him going for long,' Edith remarked. 'Are you two off? I know you have to get back, Margaret. Lilian told me you could only stay for a little while.'

'I think we should be going, Edith. I don't want to be away too long. My mother is so helpful during the week, you see. I'll collect Diana on the way out.'

'I must go too, Edith. Stan says 'e'll wait in the car by the shop for me, and you can catch the bus back to Barnstaple from the bus stop on the other side of the road, Margaret.'

'It has been such a treat to come here,' Margaret answered. 'I don't get out much, other than to go to work, so it's been a real change. Thank you very much.'

'Be sure to come again.' Edith replied. 'Ah, here's your daughter.'

'Goodbye, Auntie Edith,' Diana said, without prompting.

'That's nice,' Edith said. 'You can come again too,' she said, 'and here's another coconut cake to take with you.' She put it in a bag and waved as they set off.

'Thank you,' Diana said, gritting her teeth.

'See 'ee next week, and love to George,' Lil shouted as they left, wending their way through the myriads of vehicle parts.

'And to Stan,' Edith shouted back, 'Haven't seen him for months, tell him.'

They started walking towards the Landkey shop, to the decreasing, percussive sounds of Wilfred's efforts on the repairs in the workshop.

''E's not too fond of school, Wilfred,' Lil said.

'No. I rather guessed that,' Margaret replied. 'But he's clever in his own way, isn't he?'

'Oh yes. 'E can mend anything, and make things. 'E's what they call "knowing,"' Lil said.

'Yes.' Margaret answered thoughtfully. 'I think I understand what you mean.'

Chapter 11

Margaret and the girls sat at the breakfast table. After they had finished eating, Margaret put two little parcels on the table, each one wrapped in green coloured paper and tied with a yellow ribbon.

'Happy Easter, girls,' Margaret said as she handed a parcel to each of them. 'Mummy will help you unwrap that, Mary.' Mary was already ripping open the parcel, pulling off the bow and sending strips of green paper in all directions.

'Ooh! It's a lollipop,' said Diana.

''Olliop,' shouted Mary in agreement, having unwrapped the object but not really knowing what she was looking at.

'It's a carrot lollipop,' Margaret explained, 'and you can lick it. What do you say?'

'Thank you, Mummy,' answered Diana. Mary had already made a start on her lollipop but took a breath to say, 'Ta.'

'Rabbits like carrots don't they, girls?'

'Yes, but they're not going to get this one!' Diana laughed.

It was obvious that no-one would be able to separate Mary's lollipop from her, human or rabbit.

'After we've cleared the breakfast things, we're going over Granma's. She and Grampy have a surprise for you.'

'Happy Easter, Mum and Dad,' shouted Margaret as they entered the kitchen of her parents' home.

'The same to you,' Florrie replied. 'Come and sit up at the table and you can see your Easter surprise. Jim, turn that off for a few minutes.'

Without a word, Jim turned off one of his favourite orchestral pieces, Dvorak's New World Symphony, and looked up and smiled at his grandchildren.

' 'Olliop,' shouted Mary.

'You haven't finished the one you're licking yet,' Diana said.

'No, love, it isn't a lollipop. It's an Easter treat from Grampy and me. Here you are.' Florrie handed the young one a pretty cloth bag.

'Ta,' Mary said, putting down her lollipop on the table and looking closely at the bag which had a pattern of baby rabbits and chickens printed on it. She was so intent on examining the bag that she had to be reminded to look inside it. The little girl opened the bag and took out a cuddly, hand-knitted rabbit in shades of browns and greys with pink ears and blue eyes and a big white bobbly tail.

'Ooh, Ooh,' she kept saying. 'Ooh!'

'I think she likes it,' said Jim.

'Mum, it's so sweet. Where did you get it? Thank you.'

'Well, I know you're good at knitting but you're always busy knitting their cardigans and jumpers so I asked Mrs. Teague to make it for me and she wouldn't take anything for doing it. "You're always doing something for other people," she said.'

'She's right, Mum. You are.' Jim looked across at Mary, who was clutching the rabbit under one arm and licking the lollipop at the same time.

'What are going to call it, then?' he asked.

'We'll have to talk about that, Dad,' said Margaret.

'There's something for you now, Diana,' her grandmother smiled, passing the little girl an envelope.

Diana took it, while feeling very disappointed but trying not to show it. A plain, white envelope didn't look very interesting. She couldn't think what it could be about. The adults all leaned forward in expectation while Diana opened the envelope. A little card fell out onto the table. Diana picked it up and looked at the printed writing on it.

'Read it out then, Diana,' her mother ordered.

In a faltering voice, the little girl read the words on the card.

'Happy Easter. Your present is ten piano lessons starting next week. Make sure you practise! Love

from Granma and Grampy.'

Diana looked up, her eyes big and her mouth open in surprise.

'Really? Really?' she screamed. There followed a short silence then she shouted, 'Thank you. Thank you, Granma and Grampy.' She got up and dashed over to kiss each of them. 'I will practise. I will,' she shouted, her eyes shining.

'Mum and Dad. It is a lot for you and I really appreciate it. Thank you. You know that I had some replies to the letters I wrote to the local piano teachers. You remember I showed you their adverts in the local paper? There was one in particular I liked the sound of, and I went to see her last week. I think she'll suit Diana very well. She wants to meet you, Diana on Tuesday before you start your lessons so that you know where she lives.'

'Don't you have to go to work on Tuesday, Margaret?' Florrie asked.

'Yes, but only in the morning and it will be in the shop because Bert is going to drive the route himself that day. Diana and I are going to meet Miss McEvansoneya at 2.30 and then we will go to Nicklin's Music shop and buy the music books that Diana will need for her lessons.'

Diana was looking anxious about something.

'Miss Mac-ever-so-only-a. Is that how I say her name?'

They all laughed.

'No.' Margaret said.' Your new teacher said you may call her "Miss Mac." All her pupils call her that.'

Diana breathed a sigh of relief. ' "Miss Mac." That's a lot easier,' she smiled.

'Well, if you've all finished,' Jim said, about to switch on his wireless.

'Just one more thing.' Florrie took an envelope from her apron pocket and pulled a letter from it. 'I'd been saving this to tell you about it on Easter Day. We got it in the post on Thursday, but I wanted to keep it as a surprise. It's a short letter from Alan. Your Dad knew about it, but we could hardly believe it.'

'From my brother?' Margaret looked puzzled. 'Where is he?'

'We don't know that. Somewhere with the Eighth Army but he can't say where. You know that. I'll read it to you.

Dear Mum and Dad, I hope you are all well in lovely North Devon. I am still having a busy time with all my mates, but we may be getting leave soon. I will let you know more when the top brass tells us our services won't be needed for a little while. How is Jack getting on? How much longer will he be in that sanatorium? Looking forward to seeing you all before not too long. Sorry I can't tell you exactly when. Your loving son, Alan.

P.S. I hope you haven't got rid of the Monopoly Game.
Isn't that a lovely Easter present, Margaret?'

'It certainly is. That's wonderful news.'

They all smiled, and Jim switched on the wireless.

Chapter 12

Stan finished the morning milking and let out the cows. He carried the bucket of milk to the house. There wasn't time to clean out the stalls or he'd be late for picking up the post from the Post Office at West Buckland. He had a quick wash at the sink and went upstairs to put on his uniform. Lil had left him a brown paper parcel with his lunch in it by the front door, which he usually had at 10 o'clock. Somebody on the round always offered him a mug of tea.

'A bit more milk today, Stan,' Lil remarked, waving him out of the front door.

'"Tis much better,' Stan answered as he set off down the path to take his bicycle from the garage. 'See 'ee later.' Bruce sat by the garage looking miserable as Stan freewheeled down to the gate at the bottom.

It was a steady climb up to West Buckland and Stan managed most of it before getting off and pushing his bike up the steepest part. He collected the day's post which had been brought out earlier by van and deposited at the village post office, and set off to deliver the letters to the houses in the village. This was the easy part of the round and he got through it quickly but stopped to hear news of Mrs. Bowden and Miss Chugg from their neighbour, Mrs. Carpenter. She reminded him that they were both caring for their elderly mother in Crediton, who was keeping them on their toes with various jobs that she thought badly needed doing.

'I 'ad a letter from Miss Chugg last week. Their mother's leading 'em a terrible dance. 'Er's got 'em clearin' out all the cupboards and paintin' the kitchen when they only went up there last year to do the same. Slave driver! That's what she be. Slave driver! Anyway, I've wrote to tell 'em they repairs to the damage done to the thatch is goin' well. The workers from the Filleigh Estate 'ave been at it for two days and I've kept 'em goin' with mugs of tea. That's mainly so as I can keep a close eye on 'em.'

Stan thought that knowing the sort of eye that Mrs. Carpenter kept on her work-weary husband, the workers had better get on with it.

'You'm the right person for the job, Mrs. C.,' Stan said. 'The two ladies be lucky to 'ave 'ee keeping a watch on things.'

He was just about to move on when she stopped him.

'How are they two boys doin' at your place, Stan?'

'They'm settlin' in well, thank you. They like the animals.'

'Nice enough boys, Stan, but a bit wild. 'When

they was livin' nearby, that Jimmy was tearin' all over the countryside, up trees, and in the river over at Shallowford, swimmin' in 'is pants an' comin' back 'ome in a filthy state.'

'Well, Mrs. C., they never could do that in London, could 'em?'

'Maybe not, but it made a lot of work for the two sisters. They was good to take 'em on.'

'I 'spect they boys 'll settle -' Stan tried to cut in.

'And then that Jimmy, 'e dragged the poor tiddler of a brother after 'im and 'e got 'im – '

'Yes, I know, but 'e loves 'is brother an' won't see harm come to 'im,' Stan said. 'Us can be sure of that.'

Stan got on his bike and waved goodbye. Her heart was in the right place, Stan thought. That was the main thing. Not that he envied poor Mr. Carpenter, he decided.

Once Stan had delivered to the village, his round became more demanding with walks up lanes, often to only one dwelling, or through gates and across fields to farms. At ten o'clock and about two miles from the village, he ate his lunch while sitting on a log near the entrance to Little Bridge Farm. Fred Baxter, who farmed a fine herd of milking cows there and loved every one of them like pets, came out of the nearby barn.

'Ah, Stan. Come in the kitchen and we'll have a cup of tea. Barbara will be pleased to see you.'

They went inside and sat down at the table. The kettle was boiling away on the Aga and Mrs. Baxter entered the kitchen, carrying a basket of eggs from the chicken coop.

'Hello, Stan. We heard you and Lil have taken in those boys. How's it going?'

'Early days yet but us'll do our best for 'em,' Stan replied.

'I'm sure you will. They are lucky to be with you and Lil.'

She poured boiling water into the teapot and took some freshly baked biscuits out of the oven.

'You can try one of these biscuits. They're not what I'd like them to be what with the rationing but at least we're lucky enough to have eggs on the farm here, instead of that powdered stuff that folks in the towns have to put up with.'

'Thank you, Mrs. B.,' Stan said, taking a biscuit and biting into it. 'They'm very good. First prize.' He nodded appreciatively.

Mrs. Baxter smiled at him and looked at her husband.

'There you are, Fred. Somebody likes my cooking.'

She shook her head.

'He's always like this around this time of year.

The weather is going to turn cold, they say and so Tom Connibear is coming over to kill one of our pigs next week. Fred can't do it and it's time for it to go because it's reached its weight but -'

'We could hang on a bit longer, Barbara,' Fred interrupted. 'We don't need the meat just yet and Gladys is good company for Nellie.' Fred pushed the biscuits away and sat looking crestfallen.

'Honestly, Stan. It's hopeless! Anyone would think we're running a zoo instead of a farm.'

'That pig follows me about and understands everything I say,' Fred replied. 'It's more intelligent than some people I know, naming no names, but a few of them live not far from here.'

'You see, Stan? He's like that with every animal on the farm,' Mrs. Baxter said wearily.

Stan stood up. ''Tis true. Us gets fond of our animals 'cos us spends so much time with 'em.'

'That's for sure,' Mrs. Baxter answered, with a rueful smile. 'I could name some of those animals in the divorce case on a charge of causing marital neglect.'

'Thanks for the tea,' Stan said and left the pair sitting in contemplation.

There was not a lot of post for East Buckland that day and Stan cycled on to West Buckland School, a fee-paying school for boys, and known by the locals as the 'big school.' The grounds were looking very pristine and two of the gardeners were working on the large lawn and borders at the front of the school. Stan stopped to talk with one of them. His name was Percy and he had been employed at the school for many years and had his nose close to all the happenings there. Any inside information could be delivered by him, but no-one knew quite who his sources were or how he seemed to know more than most of the teaching staff.

'What's the news today then, Percy?' Stan asked, smiling at the old chap. Percy straightened up from working on the rose border and rested on his hoe.

'Terrible, Stan. Not news I wanted to hear. Two of our "boys" have been killed. One was a pilot and his spitfire got shot down and the other lad went down with his ship in the Atlantic. The Head announced it today at Assembly. The two of them were here in the thirties. I can remember them. Friends they were and a mischievous pair. I used to tell 'em off for kicking their football into the vegetable garden.'

He took out his handkerchief and wiped his eyes. Stan stood silent. What can anyone say? He shook his head.

'So sorry. So sorry.'

Percy looked up at Stan. 'Somebody's sons. Our boys. Our poor boys.'

Stan took the post to the office. The secretary was sitting at her typewriter but didn't look up. Stan left the post on the table near her and walked out. He rode his bicycle slowly back to Sunnybank without the usual feeling of wellbeing.

Chapter 13

Diana thought that Saturday would never come. She and her mother had gone to meet Miss McEvansoneya on Tuesday, and the first piano lesson had been arranged for the following Saturday morning. Diana was to walk over the bridge to Miss Mac's home at Barbican Road, a little further on from Trinity Church. Miss Mac gave the impression of being quite strict but there was something gentle about her which Diana liked. The lady was tall and slim with auburn hair arranged back in a bun. She wore glasses and had a delicate complexion, and was dressed in neat but subdued-coloured clothes, which did not allow her to stand out in any way.

Diana arrived at the front door and reached up and rang the bell. Someone inside stopped playing the piano and Miss Mac opened the door.

'Hello, Diana. You found me then. Come in and sit down. I am just going to finish with Jennifer's lesson and then I'll be ready for you.' She showed Diana into her music room which was where they had talked on Tuesday.

'Sit on the sofa and you can listen to Jennifer finish playing the last page of her Schubert piece.'

Schubert. Grampy often listened to music by Schubert, but as Jennifer started playing, this didn't sound like the music Grampy had been listening to. Of course, this was piano music and Grampy often played music where a whole orchestra was coming out of his wireless. That must be it, she thought. It sounded lovely all the same.

'Yes, Jennifer,' Miss Mac was saying. 'It is much better but try to bring out the melody in the right hand. That means you will have to tone down the left hand so that the melody can find its way through. I'll see you next week and don't forget to catch up with your theory. We'll look at that first, next time.'

Jennifer got up and made a face to Diana as she turned away from the piano, obviously not liking the idea of doing theory, whatever that was. She picked up her music and put it in a lovely case with a shiny handle, like a bar, and put on her coat. 'Thank you, Miss Mac', she said, as she went out.

'Goodbye Jennifer. Now come and sit at the piano, Diana.' Miss Mac smiled.

'Oh good. You have brought the books I recommended.'

'Yes. Mummy went and bought them at Nicklin's the same afternoon but I can't play anything from them yet.'

'Of course, you can't, dear. That's why you're

here; to learn how to play and how to read music. Now first of all, sit and look at the keyboard and be sure that your tummy is in the centre of the piano. That's right. Shuffle that way a little. Good. Put your right hand over your knee, and keeping the same shape, lift it and lightly touch the keys with your fingers. Perfect! Now do the same with your left hand. That's the shape I want your fingers to be in when you are playing. Now we are going to find middle C. It's just to the left of those two black keys in the middle of your tummy. There are lots of C keys on the piano but only one called 'middle C.' Can you move your hands away a moment and find any more Cs? Yes, that's right, you can play them. We only have seven letters in the musical alphabet: ABCDEFG. We repeat them over and over again as we go up to the high notes and say them backwards as we go down to the low notes.'

Miss Mac found an 'A' and said ABCD and stopped. 'You say it for me and play all the white keys from there.' She paused and encouraged Diana to take over playing the notes and saying their names as she progressed up to the top of the piano. 'Let's say them backwards now but we have to start on this very top one and say 'C.'

They went all the way to the very bottom note saying the letter names together.

'Now Diana, you will only need to play on the

keys in the middle of the piano for quite some time, but at least you know that all the other keys have the same names.'

The teacher opened the book and the lesson went by quickly, during which Diana was taught two little pieces using the reading language of music to work out what each note on the page was called and where to find it on the piano.

'To help you learn the note names, I want you to look at this stave. It's a sort of ladder,' said Miss Mac. 'But the notes live in the rungs **and** the spaces between the rungs. We call them line notes and space notes. There are twenty-one altogether. I will give you some little rhymes to help you learn them, and I want you to know them by next lesson.' Miss Mac got up from her seat at the side of Diana as the doorbell rang.

'Ah,' she said. 'That will be John. Put your music away now. I'll see you at the same time next week. You concentrated very well.' Diana put her books in the bag her mother had given her and left the room, remembering at the last moment to say, 'Thank you.'

She walked home, all the way, saying to herself, 'FACE face,' and 'EGBDF Every Good Boy Deserves Favour.' She wasn't quite sure what 'Favour' meant but would ask her mother when she got home. She decided she would concentrate on learning the 'treble clef notes' as Miss Mac had called them, and then move onto the 'bass clef' ones in a few days' time.

Diana opened the front door and went straight to the piano. She took the book with the little tunes she had to learn out of the bag and sat at the piano.

'Diana! Is that you back from your lesson?' her mother called out. 'Dinner's ready.'

'I'm coming in a minute, Mummy, but I have to practise first.'

Chapter 14

Lil **went upstairs** carrying a large patterned china jug of hot water for the boys to wash themselves. She poured the water into a matching bowl.

'Time to get up, boys. You don't want to be late for school 'cos the bus won't wait for 'ee.'

Jimmy stirred and got out of bed but there was no movement from Danny.

'Hurry up now, boys, and come down for breakfast.'

Five minutes later, Jimmy appeared at the kitchen door. He sat down at the table and Lil came in with two plates of fried egg and fried bread. 'Where's Danny, then?' she asked.

'That's just it, Auntie. I can't wake him up, can I?'

'I'll go up and see 'im. You start on that breakfast now, Jimmy.'

She put the second plate down on the table and hurried upstairs.

'Come on now, dear. You'm goin' to be late for school.'

Lil pulled the bedclothes back but the sleeping boy still did not stir. She felt his face. It was hot and damp. What could be the matter, she wondered.

She shook him gently and he opened his eyes and started to sit up, coughing and sneezing suddenly.

'Oh, you poor boy. You've got a chill. I know you'm hot but you must stay in baid and keep warm. Auntie'll bring 'ee a cold drink and something to suck. No school for you today.'

Lil wiped his forehead and settled him back down in the bed.

'I'll be back d'rectly with something for you to drink.' Lil ran downstairs and looked at Jimmy accusingly. 'Ave you two been in that river over at Shallowford?

''Tis only May and that water be very cold. That poor lad upstairs 'as a chill.'

Jimmy looked guilty. 'Well yes, Aunt, but the sun was shinin', and we didn't go in the deep bit.'

'But you two was in they wet clothes for too long Jimmy. You'm usually very good at looking after Danny. 'E can't go to school today and not for a few days either.'

'Sorry Auntie. I didn't fink – '

'Well you must, Jimmy. He's not so tough as you be. Now, take your lunch bag and get down the lane or you'll miss the bus.'

Somewhat deflated, Jimmy picked up his lunch and ran off down the lane just as the bus to Filleigh pulled in. It was fortunate that the boys hadn't had to change their schools when they moved to Sunnybank. The children from West and East Buckland all went to the Primary School at Filleigh. The two brothers had settled very well and made friends, or at least, Jimmy had made friends. Danny tagged along wherever his brother went, which sometimes led to a few hair-raising incidents. The little boy still hadn't spoken but settled diligently to his work in the classroom and was watched carefully and kindly by his teachers.

After school Jimmy took the bus back to what was becoming 'home.' Lil stopped him going upstairs to see his brother. 'He's asleep,' she whispered. ' 'Tis the best thing for 'im so us won't go wakin' 'im up. Change into your boots and take these cakes for you an' Uncle. 'E's in the far field checkin' the snares.'

'Thanks, Auntie,' Jimmy replied, wondering what the 'snares' were. He changed into his wellington boots, and taking the little picnic, ran off in the direction of the shippon and the field beyond it. The land sloped down from the gate and the field flattened out to a broad pasture with the stream running on its far right. All was still and green and fresh, and three cows were grazing contentedly at the water's edge. There was no sign of Uncle Stan so Jimmy walked on to a further gate and went through it, fastening it securely behind him. Stan was working on something near the upper hedge of the field. Jimmy walked towards him and could hear him muttering to himself.

'Fancy me 'avin' to till teddies in my best field. Damn shame!'

Stan looked up as Jimmy approached him. 'I bain't pleased, young Jimmy,' he muttered, continuing to work on a circle of wire which he was fastening in some way in the hedge.

'What's up then, Uncle?' Jimmy asked, wondering what all the wire was for.

' 'Tis the Min. of Ag., Jimmy, that's what be up,' Stan replied looking very aggrieved. 'They wants me to till two acres of teddies in my best field 'ere. I know 'tis only two acres but this is bootiful pasture land for they cows. Trouble is, the Min. of Ag. comes and checks that 'tis done proper, or else.'

'Uncle, 'ere's some cakes.' Jimmy opened the bag, and Stan took out a large cake and started eating it. Jimmy took his and they sat, side by side on a mound of grass.

'So, where does Mr. Minofag live, Uncle? 'E don't sound too friendly.'

'That be the government, Jimmy. The Ministry of Agriculture to give it its proper name. There be an even longer name, if I remembers it.' Stan swallowed the last of his cake and looked up at the sky for inspiration. 'The Ministry of Agriculture,

Fisheries and Food. There!' He nodded with satisfaction at having remembered the offending Body.

'Blimey!' Jimmy looked at Stan in sympathy but without much understanding.

'I know us 'as to do it for the War Effort, to feed folks, but – ' Stan paused from fiddling with the wire, ' 'Tis still my best field.'

'Sorry, Uncle.' Jimmy folded the empty paper bag and put it in his pocket.

'When d' you have to plant the teddies? And what's 'teddies' anyway?'

' 'Tis our word for potatoes. I 'ope my tractor won't play up. 'Tis not in good shape. 'Twas second 'and when I bought it. But first things first, Jimmy. You can 'elp me with these snares.'

'And what's snares, Uncle?'

'Oh Jimmy, you be all questions.'

Stan turned his back on the work he was doing at the hedge and pointed down at the field as it dropped away to a green flat pasture.

'Tell me lad, what do 'ee see?'

'Just the field, ain't it?' Jimmy answered.

'Right! And look at the grass there, boy.' Stan pointed at the grass, looking lush and growing well. 'Look 'ard now, Jimmy.'

'It's movin' like the wind's blowin' through it.'

'You'm getting' warm, lad. But there bain't no

wind today so how come the grass is movin'?'

'Ooh!' Jimmy let out a shriek. 'There's a rabbit. And another one.'

Stan picked up a large stone and aimed it at the pasture below. High into the air it went, dropping with a thud and scattering rabbits in all directions.

'There's hundreds of 'em, Uncle,' Jimmy shouted.

'That's just it, Jimmy. Now us knows 'ow true that sayin' is.'

'What saying, Uncle?' Jimmy asked looking up at him quizzically.

' '"To breed like rabbits." While us 'ave bin chattin' 'ere, some of em 'ave popped another twenty or so. It can't go on, boy. Us 'ave got to get they numbers down or the blighters'll eat everything in sight.'

'Do mean you got to kill 'em?' Jimmy looked anxious. 'That's sad if you 'ave to kill 'em.'

'That's as maybe, but 'tis war time and us 'ave got to work for the War Effort. Do our bit, work the land as best as us can and that means sortin' out they rabbits. 'Tis them or us.' Stan looked at Jimmy. There was no arguing with that. Jimmy looked at the lower part of the field, seeing the grass waving with the movement of hundreds of rabbits, who had now become the enemy.

'I understand, Uncle. Can I help you?'

Stan smiled. 'Yes, Jimmy. I'm goin' to show 'ee 'ow to set snares in this hedge. As the rabbits run through, the wire tightens and –'

'Ooh. Yes. But we won't tell Danny about this, will we, and we won't let him come to this field. I can make up somefink to keep 'im away.'

'Good lad. But these yer snares won't get many of 'em. On Saturday, I'll 'ave a bit of a party 'ere. A shootin' party. There's folks I know who sell rabbits to butchers in Barnstaple, to they shops in Butchers' Row. Rabbits make good eatin', see. You can come an' watch as long as you stand well back, Jimmy. Us don't want you getting' shot, do us?'

'Well, Uncle, I'm not sure 'cos there's Danny to look after. And even if he stayed in the house, the noise of the guns going off would -' His voice dropped down and he looked agitated.

Stan interrupted him. 'Auntie's off to see 'er sister Edith on the Saturday afternoon, and if Danny be better, 'e can go with 'er.'

Jimmy nodded. 'Are your friends really coming wiv their guns on Saturday afternoon, Uncle?'

'Oh yes. Jimmy, they'm comin'. Three o'clock sharp, an' us'll see what can be done about this lot. You can be the bag boy. And there'll be plenty to bag up if us 'as anything to do with it.'

'Auntie,' Jimmy said, handing over the last of the potatoes he'd peeled for Sunday dinner. 'Why didn't you go to Chapel today?'

'Good boy, Jimmy. And you too, Danny. That's lovely the way you peeled that teddy.' She put the potatoes on to boil. 'Well, Jimmy, I wanted to see that young Danny 'ere didn't go dashin' all over the place. Another quiet day and 'e should be fit for school tomorrow. Now 'elp me clear the table, boys, 'cos dinner won't be long.' They took the peelings into the scullery and put them in a bin for the pigs and Lil went back to wipe the table.

'Oh, Stan! What be doin' of with that gun on the table? 'E sneaked in when us turned our backs, boys.'

'I be cleanin' it, Maid. What do 'ee think?'

''Tis nearly dinner time. 'Ow long is that goin' to take?' Lil and the boys looked at the large gun and Danny looked up at his brother.

'He ain't goin' to use it, Dan. It goes over the door, just for decoration, see.'

'A couple of minutes, then the table be all yours,' Stan said generously.

''Ow did things go after I dropped 'ee off at George and Edith's?' Stan thought he would distract her for a while.

'Oh, Margaret was there with young Mary, and she and Danny got on fine.' Lil stirred the stew. ' 'E was so good with the little maid and she liked 'im too. Then Wilfred took Danny into the workshop.

You liked that, didn't you, love?' Danny smiled up at her.

'We 'ad to fetch 'im out of there when us had to leave, an' 'e was all oily, so what he and Wilfred got up to with all that messy machinery, I don't know!' She turned away from the range to see that Stan was packing up his cleaning rags and putting the gun in its place above the door.

'At last!' Lil sighed and wiped the table. The boys laid the cutlery out and Lil set out the dinner plates. They all sat down and Lil started to serve out the food.

'I see you found the stuff I put in the shed then, Lil,' Stan remarked, with more of a statement than a question.

'Yes, thank you, Stan,' she replied curtly, giving him a reprimanding look. They ate their meal in silence until all the plates were scraped clean.

'Does anyone want some more?' Lil held the serving spoon over the large saucepan.

'Yes, please, Auntie,' Jimmy said and Danny nodded.

'Not bad for chicken stew, be it, boys?'

Stan looked at Jimmy and winked.

Chapter 15

Margaret opened her mother's front door and called out.

'Hello, Mum. It's only us.' She and Mary walked into the kitchen, but all was quiet. There was no sign of either of her parents, and they were always at home on a Saturday morning.

'Hello.' Mary ran through the kitchen to the scullery, followed by her mother.

'Hello Ganma, where are you?' The little girl was finding her voice at last and wasn't shy about using it.

A voice came from the back yard.

'I'm out here, at the mangle.' Florrie sounded tired and feeble.

'Mum, whatever are you doing? It's not washday.' Florrie was trundling wet sheets through the clothes mangle, and there was another pile of them on the ground in the clothes basket.

'What's happened? Let me help you.' Margaret pointed Mary in the direction of the little yard away from the sopping wet clothes. 'Mary, here's Granma's peg bag. Get them ready for when we put this washing on the clothes line. Good girl to help.'

'Oh Margaret, your poor Dad has had a terrible

night with another attack of his malaria. He sweated so much that I had to keep changing the sheets. He's still in bed now and will stay there and rest until the worst of it is over.'

Margaret lifted the sheet away from the mangle.

'Are these rinsed, Mum?' Her mother nodded.

'Yes, they're all rinsed but I'm running out of energy.' Florrie leaned against the side of the shed, took her handkerchief from her pocket and wiped her forehead.

'Right. Now you go in and make yourself a cup of tea and have a sit down, and I'll put these things on the clothes line. I'll keep Mary busy. She can pass me the pegs.'

'Thank you, dear. That's such a help.' Florrie went into the house and put on the kettle. After about five minutes Margaret and Mary joined her in the kitchen.

'I've brought you some cakes that Bert said I could have, Mum. I don't know how fresh they are.'

'They'll fill a hole, dear. That's the main thing.' She sat Mary on her lap.

'Look at these lovely fair curls, Margaret. She's just like Shirley Temple, isn't she?' Florrie ruffled the little girl's hair.

'She's more like her Daddy, Mum. He is fair-haired and had the same sort of hair when he was young, I think. Now tell me about Dad.'

Florrie set Mary down on the hearth rug and gave her the box of toys.

'Well, you know that your Dad came back from the war in poor shape. He joined up as a young professional soldier back in 1904 and was in the British Expeditionary Forces. We think it was when he was on a campaign in Africa that he picked up malaria. The trouble is you can never rid yourself of the blessed thing. He'll be fine for a large part of the year, then suddenly – ' her voice trailed off and she sighed.

'At least he came home alive from the war, Mum. Many didn't.'

'Yes, Margaret, that's true.'

'And he survived four battles.'

Her mother nodded slowly. 'But don't forget he was injured twice. We've still got the cap badge with the dent in it made by a bullet. It skimmed the top of his head.'

Margaret smiled ruefully.

'It's no wonder he likes to relax listening to his music on the wireless. He never talks about the war does he, Mum?'

'No, never. But when Alan joined up for this war, and went off, well, he was all over the place. Started shaking and couldn't settle himself. "Another war?" he said. "How many more are we going to lose, on both sides?"'

Margaret sat on the floor to play with Mary.

'Any news of Alan coming home on leave? It's all gone quiet since the time he had in the desert. Perhaps things will start to turn for the better now.' Margaret thought it was time to be optimistic and to try to lift her mother's spirits. It was rare to see her like this.

'No news. And I think that is what has worried your Dad deep down.'

'Well, I have some good news in a letter from Jack. He's been allowed to go out on daily walks to start to build up his strength. I thought I'd try to visit him next weekend. I could get the train from the Junction Station and I'd have to change at Exeter for Bovey Tracy. It would give him such a boost to see us. I'll take Mary, but Diana has her piano lesson in the morning so perhaps she could come to you when the lesson is over?'

Florrie sat up and smiled. 'Of course, she can. That's wonderful news Margaret. You've cheered me up. Jack must be doing much better to be going on walks.'

Florrie got up and went into the scullery.

'I'm going to take Jim a drink and see how he is. Then we'll get a bit of dinner, so stay here.'

'I'll help you, Mum. Diana will know to come over here when she gets back from her lesson and finds we're not at home. After dinner, I'll bring in the bedclothes and iron them if you can keep Mary occupied, although she may need a sleep as she didn't sleep this morning and was quite wakeful last night.'

'Teeth, I expect. Her cheeks look a bit pink.' Florrie went upstairs with a drink for the invalid.

The front door opened and in came Diana.

'Hello. Anybody there?' she called out as she walked into the kitchen.

'Di-yi-ya,' Mary answered in a deep voice.

'We've been helping Granma because Grampy isn't very well. He's upstairs in bed,' Margaret explained.

'Oh, I wanted to tell him about my piano lesson.' Diana took out her books and turned to a page she'd been working on. 'It's this piece here. You see, you have to move your right hand from where it usually lives to another part of the keyboard, and at the same time you have to play more than one note at a time with your left hand. Then, after that, you – '

'Hello, dear.' Florrie came into the room carrying a washing jug, towel and flannel. 'He's starting to feel slightly better, but will stay in bed for a day or so. Let's get you all something to eat.'

'Diana, you can show me that music when we go back home but can you play with Mary while I help Granma?'

After a while, they all sat down to boiled potatoes, sliced Spam, tomatoes, and a tiny piece of cheese each. Florrie cleared away the plates.

'I've got a surprise now,' she said, and went into the larder and returned carrying a large dish on which wobbled a pink blancmange in the shape of a rabbit.

'Oohs' and 'Aahs' came from around the table and Mary clapped her hands.

'Don't ask me how I turned it out of its mould, Margaret. It's a miracle.'

'It has all its parts in the right places, Mum, so well done.'

'You know I'm no cook dear, but it looks good,' Florrie said, placing it in the centre of the table.

'Margaret, can you serve it out? I don't know which part to cut into first.'

'Ears, ears!' shouted Diana.

Mary picked up her spoon and banged it on the rabbit's tail.

'Well, I think I know what you girls want, but please can we have some manners?' Margaret served the blancmange into the four dishes and into one for her dad.

'A plate of this would be good for him, Mum. Not too difficult to get down and it's very cold.'

'Yes, I'll take it up to him. The rabbit has been sitting on the marble slab in the larder, so it has set well. The last time I tried to do it, the poor creature collapsed in a heap.'

Florrie picked up a spoon and the plate of blancmange and went upstairs to Jim.

'We'll wait for Granma to come down and all eat it together,' Margaret said. 'No Mary. We're waiting for Granma.'

Florrie returned to the table and they all started on the blancmange.

'I love these blue and white plates, Mum. Willow pattern, aren't they?' Margaret had finished her pudding and picked up the plate, holding it above her head to look underneath it for the design and make of the crockery. Mary thought that they were all supposed to look at the underneath of their plates, and suddenly picked up hers. There was still a great deal of the rabbit's hind quarters left in the dish which promptly fell on her head. The other members of the little group looked on aghast, yet speechless.

'Oh blimey!' Mary said with pink blancmange falling down over her eyes and nose. Florrie started laughing helplessly. She could hardly get her breath and began coughing. The family all knew that once Granma started laughing, it was difficult to stop her. Wiping her eyes and refusing a glass of water from her daughter, she blurted out, 'Where did she learn that?'

Margaret began to bang her mother on the back but Mary, sensing she was the comedic centre of entertainment, shouted out, 'Oh blimey!' once again, upon which Diana started laughing.

'Don't encourage her, Diana. Just ignore her,' Margaret insisted. But it was too late, the damage was done. Florrie tried to gain control of herself but continued with occasional outbursts, engaging in a duet of giggles with Diana. Meanwhile, Margaret went to find a flannel to clean up Mary, who was thoroughly enjoying all the attention.

After everyone had calmed down, Diana said, 'Can we have rabbit blancmange again soon, Granma?'

'Preferably without the comedy act, Mum. A certain person may try to do a repeat performance.'

Just as Florrie managed to get herself under control, there was the sound of the front doorbell ringing. Getting up from the table, she went into the passage and opened the door.

'Oh, Mrs. Shaddick, what can I do for you? Are you all right? You look upset. Come in. Come into the front room.'

Florrie showed the lady into the parlour and the two women sat down on the sofa.

'It's my husband, Mrs. Webb. I thought he was getting better, but he was taken bad in the night and we had to fetch the doctor. He died this morning.

It's been a terrible shock. I've come to ask you – '

Florrie put her arm round her neighbour.

'Of course, dear. Of course, I'll come. You want me to lay him out, don't you?'

Mrs. Shaddick looked up at Florrie with a tear-stained face.

'I know you always help people round here with that and I can pay you what you want, but I didn't know what else to do or where to go.'

Florrie caught hold of Mrs. Shaddick's hands.

'Now, dear. There's to be no talk of paying me anything. I never do it for that. I always wanted to be a nurse, but when I was a girl my eyesight was very poor until I had an operation, and then it was too late. I married, and that was that. So, you see dear, I love to help people in some way, and if this is the way, then that's fine. I'll come along later. I have to see the family off and clear up. Oh, and I have to check on Jim upstairs, 'cos he had a bad night with his malaria but he's a bit better now.'

Mrs. Shaddock got up to leave and Florrie followed her to the front door.

'I'm very sorry about your loss,' Florrie said.

'Thank you, Mrs. Webb. Come when you can.' Florrie closed the door and gathered herself before returning to the kitchen. Margaret looked up and read her mother's mind.

'We must be getting home now, girls. Say "Thank

you," to Granma. Have you got your music bag, Diana? Good.'

They went out to the front door and Margaret turned to her mother.

'Mum, do you have to?' she asked pleadingly.

Her mother looked at her and said gently, 'No, I don't have to, but I want to.'

Chapter 16

'Friday today, Danny. Last day at school before the weekend.' Jimmy whispered over the backs of the children in front of him to the line where his brother was sitting.

The morning assembly had ended with a rendition of 'All Things Bright and Beautiful' and the Headmistress, Miss Rose had stepped forward to the piano to talk quietly with Miss Harding, who was nodding in agreement with whatever Miss Rose was saying. The Headmistress then left the room and Miss Harding turned towards the children.

'Jimmy, stop talking, please. Anyone who doesn't behave will not be allowed to stay and see the big surprise we have for you this morning.'

The whole school, all fifty-seven of them from age five to eleven, looked up at her with anticipation.

'Pass your hymn books along your rows, so that Monica and Colin can collect them and hand them to Mrs. Oliver in the front here. Now, remain seated, but we want you to move back and make a big space in the front of the room. You don't need to talk about it. You will see that we have moved the desks out, so there should be plenty of space if you shuffle back.'

Mrs. Oliver and the new, young teacher, Miss Gibbons, shooed the children back and settled them down. Miss Harding was very strict, and the children sat quiet and watchful. What could the surprise be?

'This term,' Miss Harding continued, 'we have all been concentrating on birds in our Nature lessons. We've learnt about all sorts of birds and we've grouped them into their "habitats". What does that mean? Yes, Amy.'

'Where different birds live, Miss.'

'Good! Can anyone think of a type of habitat?' Amy looked pleased with herself and put up her hand again.

'Yes, George,' Miss Harding said.

'Woodland habitat.'

'That's right. Oh, you're all waking up now. Yes Jimmy.'

'Farming habitat, Miss.'

'Well done, Jimmy. We mustn't forget that because it's all around us isn't it?'

Danny turned around to look at Jimmy with big eyes.

'Ah, but we can't continue because I think our visitor has arrived with a very special guest of his own. You must be as quiet as mice because his guest gets very nervous if there's the slightest noise.'

The door opened and Miss Rose entered followed

by a tall man carrying a bird on his gloved hand. They went to the front of the room. The children sat up and gasped. Miss Rose put her finger to her lips.

'This gentleman is Mr. Hamish Macmillan, and this is his bird, Flash. We won't greet them with any applause as Flash doesn't like any sudden noise. I will let Mr. Macmillan tell you all about his amazing bird.'

Mr. Macmillan stepped forward.

'Hello, children. I have come to tell you about me and Flash. I am a falconer and this bird is a falcon. It is a bird of prey. Does anyone know any other birds of prey?'

'No calling out, children,' Miss Rose cut in. 'Hands up if you want to talk to Mr. Macmillan.'

Several hands went up. Mr. Macmillan looked pleased.

'Yes.' he said, looking at a young boy in the front.

'Buzzard, sir.'

'Good, any other birds of prey?'

'Kestrel.'

'Sparrowhawk.'

The children were excited and pleased to show off their knowledge.

'Well, Miss Rose,' said Mr. Macmillan, turning to the Headmistress, 'what knowledgeable children you have here.'

Miss Rose smiled and looked very proud.

'The thing is, children, there are groups of birds of prey,' Mr. Macmillan continued.

He looked at the children who were sitting, all eyes and ears, looking at this strange bird, who appeared to be wearing a little hat.

'There are hawks and eagles, owls and falcons, and they all have hooked bills, sharp talons, wonderful eyesight and excellent hearing. They need those things to dive onto their prey.'

One of the girls near the back put up her hand.

'Please sir, what do they eat?'

'Small mammals, insects, reptiles, other birds. Flash here is very fond of pigeons.'

A little girl in the front said, 'Why has he got that hat on?'

Mr. Macmillan touched the bird's head lightly and replied, 'That's called a "hood" and I put it on him to keep him calm.'

He held his bird up for everyone to see. 'When I fly him, I will take off his hood and I will swing a sort of rope, called a lure, which he will land on. On the end of the lure is what looks like a live bird, a pigeon, but it is a fake one. Flash here will fly high in the sky and dive on it, gripping it with his claws. As a reward, I will give him some meat, a dead chick.'

'Ugh!' Some of the children didn't like the sound of that.

'Don't forget that the buzzards you see around here dive on mice and other creatures for their food,' Mr. Macmillan continued. 'Buzzards are hawks, but Flash is a falcon, as I said, and in particular, a very special sort of falcon. He is a peregrine falcon and has the fastest dive, or "stoop" as it is called, of any other bird in the world. A peregrine falcon can spot prey, that is food, from very high in the sky using his marvellous eyesight, and dive onto it at a speed of nearly 200 miles an hour.'

There was a united intake of breath from the enraptured young audience.

'But why don't I show you what he can do? I am going to take Flash onto your playground. I will go on out and set him on his perch and you can see for yourselves.'

Mr. Macmillan left the room, still with Flash on his glove. Miss Rose came forward.

'Stand up, children, and face the door. Without a word, you will follow Mrs. Oliver and will sit on the grass bank surrounding the playground. There is to be no talking. Flash will not be happy if you make a noise and may not want to show you his tricks.'

The children filed outside and marshalled by the staff, all sat on the grass bank from where they had a perfect view of Mr. Macmillan and Flash, who were in the centre of the playground.

Mr. Macmillan walked to the perch and the bird stepped off it onto his glove. Mr. Macmillan removed the bird's hood, and both stayed still and calm for a moment. Then the falconer suddenly raised his gloved hand and Flash took off, quickly gaining height, up into the clear blue, almost cloudless, sky. Using the rope in his other hand with the lure on the end of it, the falconer twirled it round and round, over his head, like a lasso. He continued to do that, whistling and calling to the bird, which could hardly be seen, when suddenly, Flash dived from what appeared to be nowhere, and landed on the lure, its talons outstretched, forcing the fake pigeon onto the ground. The bird's handler walked over to it and Flash flew up and landed again on the glove, immediately taking the reward of raw meat and tearing it with its hooked beak. Everyone started to applaud, and someone called out, 'Do it again.'

'Yes, please let's see that again,' one of the older children called out.

Mr. Macmillan and Flash repeated their performance a few times and then the falconer turned to the children and started to say,

'Would anyone like to -'

Suddenly, Danny got up and walked calmly towards the pair and offered his arm to Mr. Macmillan.

'Oh, I see that we have a volunteer. What's your name?'

There was silence as Danny looked directly ahead of him.

'Well, young man, you will have to wear a glove and I have a smaller one in my pocket for you.' Danny took it and put it on. Miss Rose and the other teachers all leaned forward anxiously, and the children looked at each other in disbelief.

'We are not going to fly Flash and will put on his hood because he doesn't know you.'

But Danny held out his arm and stood still and calm, yet confident. Immediately, Flash stepped onto the boy's outstretched arm and settled happily on the glove. The two looked at each other, bird and boy. There was complete silence in the playground for a few seconds then Mr. Macmillan stepped forward and took Flash onto his glove and put the hood back on him. Mr. Macmillan walked towards his van, parked nearby and, opening the back door, put the peregrine on a perch inside. Danny was still standing in the centre of the playground. The assembled group looked up at the falconer, waiting for his reaction.

'A round of applause for this young man. I think he is a natural handler, so calm. Well done!'

Everyone clapped and cheered as Danny walked back to his place on the grass. Miss Rose stood up, slightly flustered, and said, 'Now it is playtime, so you may stay out here until the bell goes. Your milk will be brought out to you and Miss Gibbons will supervise the playgrounds. Young ones, on the bottom playground please, as usual. When you come back in, Mr. Macmillan will take his leave of you. But first he will join me, Miss Harding and Mrs. Oliver for a cup of tea.' Miss Rose directed Mr. Macmillan back into the school building, accompanied by the other two teachers.

'Do you take sugar, Mr. Macmillan?' Miss Harding asked, passing him a cup of tea and offering a biscuit. She noticed how closely he observed people and wondered if it had anything to do with his passion for training birds of prey.

'No, thank you, and I would like a biscuit. Did you make these?' he asked, taking one and biting into it. Miss Harding nodded.

'How wonderful! That's what I've missed all the years I've been living here in North Devon. You've probably guessed from my accent that I'm from Scotland and I have been back to my home every summer to fly the birds and see my family. Scottish winters are a bit harsh for me but I will have to get used to them. I'm going home permanently in a few days' time.'

'Oh! That will be a loss to our community here,

Mr. Macmillan,' Miss Rose remarked.

She looked at him more closely, wondering how old he was.

As if reading her thoughts, he said, 'You're probably wondering why I am not serving my country. I had measles as a boy and suffered considerable hearing loss. I have had trouble coming to terms with it and my work with falconry has given me a purpose.'

Mrs. Oliver offered him another biscuit.

'These are similar to shortbread, aren't they? Thank you. We are losing lots of peregrine falcons. Their eggs are being taken from the cliffs and destroyed and the birds themselves are being shot down out of the skies.'

'How terrible!' Miss Harding frowned. 'Whoever would want to do that?'

'There have been egg collectors for many years but now, while we are at war, any messages sent by pigeons from England across the channel are sometimes intercepted by peregrines who don't help the war effort by eating the prey carrying the messages.'

'What if there are messages coming into England from the enemy?' Mrs Oliver always liked to look at things from every angle.

'Well,' Mr. Macmillan looked serious for a moment. 'The trouble is that these peregrines may be brilliant flyers but they can't tell the difference between an English pigeon and a German one. It's just a meal to them.'

They all laughed.

Miss Rose leaned forward and said, 'The little lad who volunteered this morning-'

'Yes. What an extraordinary boy; so still and focussed.'

'He and his brother are evacuees, and he hasn't spoken a word since the family suffered in the blitz in the East End. We are very concerned about him,' Miss Rose said.

Mr. Macmillan thought for a while before replying.

'He will come out of it in time. He is good with animals, I think, and they converse with him and he with them, without any actual words. Don't rush him.'

The end of break bell was ringing and Miss Rose stood up.

'I do hope you will come back and see us some time, Mr. Macmillan,' the Headmistress said, taking his cup and saucer.

'I hope I can, but my father isn't as fit as he was and the estate in the Highlands takes a lot of running. That's why I'm going back. Also, we've got to make it pay, and after the war there will have to be some changes made.'

The staff went back into the large classroom followed by their visitor. Miss Rose stood in front of the children. They were sitting on the floor wondering what was coming next.

'Mr. Macmillan has come to say "Goodbye" children, but has a message for you first.'

The falconer stepped forward and looked at the young faces looking back at him.

'You are the future,' he said. 'You will be the ones to look after the countryside when this horrible war is over, and it will be over. You will go back to your homes, those of you who have bravely come here as evacuees. You will remember today and be glad to have been in this beautiful part of the country, this beautiful school with its green fields and lush trees all around, its streams, hills and valleys. But you will be the guardians of every bit of countryside wherever it is, north or south, east or west, near or far. So, we must protect it, our wildlife, our birds and the eggs they lay. We must not take and collect the eggs from their nests. Their babies must be nurtured and allowed to grow into adults, just like we want you to grow into adults and take care of your young ones, when you are older. Will you try to do that?'

'Yes,' they all replied in unison.

'Thank you, Mr. Macmillan,' Miss Rose said. 'You and Flash have given us a superb demonstration.

We will heed your advice and will try our best to love and care for the wonderful world around us, won't we, children?'

'Yes, Miss Rose,' they answered.

'And now, let's all give Mr. Macmillan a big round of applause for giving us a marvellous morning.'

Everyone clapped enthusiastically as Mr. Macmillan smiled, waved and left the room, together with Miss Rose. Miss Harding came forward and directed the children back to their own classrooms. They were set work based on what they had experienced that morning, writing about it, drawing or painting what they had seen. Danny's teacher, Miss Gibbons, looked over his shoulder and was astounded at what she saw. She went next door to her colleague, Mrs. Oliver, who came in and looked at Danny's work. She gasped quietly and she stared wide-eyed at Miss Gibbons. The boy had drawn a detailed picture of Flash using crayons, showing feathers, claws, beak and eyes in a realistic manner. They were looking at a wild bird, and it could almost have flown off the page.

'Well done, Danny,' said Miss Gibbons, trying to control her emotions but with a wobble in her voice. 'I think that would be lovely to send home to your mother and father, once you have shown it to the rest of the school. And Mr. and Mrs. Webber would like to see it too.'

Mrs. Oliver wiped her eyes. 'I think I've got something in my eye,' she said, putting her hand on Danny's shoulder. 'I'd better go and get it out.' She left the room quickly without looking at her colleague.

Jimmy and Danny raced up the lane and on up the path to the front door.

'We're home,' Jimmy shouted, as they ran into the kitchen.

'Hello, boys.' Margaret was seated at the table, her basket on the floor. 'There

are a couple of cakes here for you. Auntie Lil has gone to feed the pigs but won't be long.'

'We had a smashin' day didn't we, Dan? Oh, 'ere's Auntie.'

Lil stepped into the kitchen and smiled at the boys.

'Jimmy was just saying they've had a good day,' Margaret said, setting the cakes on two plates for them and pouring each of them a glass of milk.

'A man came to the school with a falcon and flew it and Danny went up and held it and it's the fastest bird in the whole wide world, see, and 'e lives with 'this 'ere bird not far from Filleigh. Oh, an' this 'ere bird ain't just any ole bird, it's a peregrine falcon, see. And I've wrote about it an' Danny's done a picture of it, an' we'll show it to you, if you like.'

He stopped, out of breath and the boys took their work from their bags and laid it out on the table.

'That's wonderful, Danny, and what beautiful writing, Jimmy,' Margaret said, amazed at the maturity of Danny's picture, but trying not to show it.

'You'm very good boys and should be real proud,' Lil added. 'Wait 'til Uncle sees that.'

Jimmy and Danny were busy tucking into their cakes.

'I think us should send that to your Mum in London. What do 'ee think, Margaret?'

'Good idea. She will love that. Shall I help them write a short letter, Lil, to go with it? I've got a few minutes before I must be on my way.'

'That's very kind of 'ee, Margaret. You'm better than me at that sort of thing. I'll get 'ee some note paper and a stamp, and find the address. Go in the scullery, Jimmy an' Danny, and wash they messy 'ands then I'll give 'ee a sheet of paper each. After that, you can go an' help Uncle milk the cows.'

The boys grinned and ran to wash their hands. Two minutes later they were seated at the table and writing their letters.

Chapter 17

The back door opened and Florrie entered the scullery, carrying a hand knitted Fair Isle cardigan.

'Diana left this over with us yesterday, Margaret,' she said, handing it to her daughter. 'I can't think why she was wearing it. The weather turned so warm in the afternoon.'

'It's her favourite, Mum, but it is much too warm for this time of year. I'll pack it away for the winter and she won't know.' Margaret opened a cupboard in the kitchen and stuffed the garment in there quickly.

'How did you get on yesterday at Hawkmoor? How is he, dear?'

'I couldn't believe the change in him. He looks so much better, tanned from all the time he has been spending outdoors and, well, like a new man. He's going for a walk every day now.'

'That must be building up his strength, Margaret. Did you speak to any of the doctors or nurses there? When do you think he will be ready to come home?'

'There weren't many doctors on duty, being Saturday, but I talked to a young doctor who had been on one of the rounds with the consultant recently, and he said that the "checks and balances," as he called them, were good. I couldn't get him to say any more than that. There was a very friendly, pretty nurse there. Nurse Morgan she was called. She whispered that Jack may be home "sooner than later," but not to tell anyone that she had said that.'

'That's the best news we've heard for some time. Where's Mary, dear? I can hear where Diana is. That sounds like a little piece she's playing, not all those awful scales and things.' Florrie screwed up her nose.

'Well those scales have to be done and are helping her dexterity, Miss Mac says. She's very pleased with her. Mary is over the road playing with that little four-year-old, Shirley.'

'Oh, yes. The one with the lovely long light brown hair. I'm surprised her mother lets the girl grow her hair so long.' Florrie frowned. 'I'd hate to put a nit comb through it.'

'There's been another outbreak of that in the Infant School and some of the boys have had their heads shaved,' Margaret said. 'I'm keeping a close watch on the girls' hair.'

'How is Dad now? Up and about again, of course.'

'Yes, but it's has taken it out of him, this last malaria attack. He's back at work now, but looks so tired by the end of the day. Not been over the allotment and he's a bit "dark" if you know what I mean.'

Margaret knew that 'dark' meant he wasn't communicating at all.

'Still playing his wireless non-stop, I suppose.'

'Why do you think I've come over here, Margaret? It wasn't just to find out about Jack!'

'He'll come out of it, Mum. In any case, Dad's not the most sociable person you ever met, is he? By the way, I took the children to Church this morning, to St. Paul's up at Sticklepath. The girls went into the Sunday School. I don't go very often. The vicar asked me if I would like to join the Mothers' Union. I thanked him and said that I'd think about it. The people are quite friendly there and it's not easy to make friends when I'm working so much. The trouble is that most of their meetings are in the afternoon.'

'That's nice you went, but hard work walking up Sticklepath Hill with Mary in the push chair.'

'And tricky coming down, too. It's really steep in places.'

Florrie put her hand in her apron pocket to fetch her handkerchief. She pulled it out and something dropped on the floor. She leant down and picked up a rather official-looking envelope.

'I knew there was something else I wanted to tell

you,' she said, taking a letter from the envelope and handing it over to Margaret. Her daughter read it and shook her head.

'An evacuee? You are going to have an evacuee, Mum? I thought that most of the evacuation was over with. It seems there are still some coming in dribs and drabs. And this boy is fifteen. How easy is that going to be for you and Dad?'

Florrie shrugged. 'You see in the letter that this poor lad has family problems and needs to come down to us to relieve the situation at home. We don't know all the details yet, but we do know that his father is away, fighting in the Army and his mother was working in a factory until recently. I think she had some sort of accident using one of the machines and was injured. She's had to stop work and is being looked after at her sister's little house. They can't take in young Bill – that's his name – because they already have a houseful.'

'Where do they live, Mum? Oh, wait a minute. It says here – Bermondsey. That's somewhere in London. Some of the factory work people are doing is bad for their health and sometimes dangerous, too. I wonder how seriously she was injured?'

The gentle sound of the piano coming from the front room stopped and the kitchen door opened.

'Hello, Granma. How's Grampy? Can I come over and see him?' Diana went over to the armchair where her Granma was sitting and kissed her.

'Come tomorrow, Diana. He's getting better but needs a rest. I like the little piece you were playing.'

'It's a waltz, Granma. It's in three time. People can dance to a waltz. The trouble is, sometimes I have to stop when I come to a difficult bit and Miss Mac says I mustn't do that or I will put an extra beat in the bar. You know it would go One Two Three, stop and have a little think, One Two Three, stop and have another little think, and so on. That is wrong so I have to have a little think while I am playing the bar and not at the end of it. Do you know what I mean, Granma?' Granma was not quite sure that she did, but went, 'Mmmmm,' and nodded.

'I used to be able to play a waltz,' Florrie said, standing up and going out of the door into the passage. 'Let me see if I can still remember it.' She entered the front room and sat down on the piano stool, rubbed her hands together and took a deep breath. The others had followed her into the room and sat on the sofa, Margaret knowingly and Diana doubtfully. Florrie started hesitantly but as she relaxed, her memory of that gentle dance spoke of her girlhood, probably sitting at that same piano, many years ago. The melody in the right hand was accompanied by octaves in the left hand on the first beat of every bar and chords on the second and third beats. How did she manage that, Diana thought, if she hadn't played for years? The piece finished with chords in both hands. Florrie sat still and smiled.

'Well, something like that,' she said ruefully.

Margaret and Diana clapped.

'I didn't know you could play, Granma.'

'That's the only piece I can play, dear, and if I had to read the music, I wouldn't know an "A" from a "Z".'

'We don't have "Zs",' Diana said, 'but I think you were very good. Can you play, Mummy?'

Margaret shook her head and replied, 'Almost nothing, Diana. No pieces, just a few disjointed chords. You see, I didn't practise. I always wanted to be out in the street, playing with my friend, Myrna.'

'I like playing out in the street, but I actually like practising. It's lovely when you've got something the way you want it to sound like,' Diana explained, away in her own world.

Margaret looked at her mother.

'That's us told, Mum,' she murmured quietly.

Chapter 18

Stan put down his spoon and pushed his pudding plate away. Lil poured him a large mug of tea and passed it to him.

'Trouble is, Maid, I tilled they teddies a bit late. That field took some ploughing, and my Fordson Tractor is getting' on in years. It gave up before I'd ploughed the full two acres.'

Lil sat down to her cup of tea.

'Can't 'ee get George or Wilfred to sort it out?'

'The job's done now and the teddies be in the ground. Tell Wilfred about it next time you'm over there, will 'ee? They'm good at rescuin' old wrecks.'

'Pity they can't do the same for you then, Stan,' Lil said, laughing. Her husband ignored the remark and lit his pipe. He leaned across the table in a conspiratorial manner.

'Do 'ee know what I 'eard from Arthur Kingdon 's mornin'?'

'Is 'e the postman for Filleigh and out round there, Stan?'

'That's right, 'e be. Nothin' gets past 'e. If a blade o' grass moves anywhere on 'is round, 'e knows it. Well, 'e told me – ' Stan paused and drew on his pipe.

'Well, what did 'n tell 'ee? I haven't got all day to sit yer.' Lil could tell that it was going to be one of Stan's long, flowery yarns.

'That falconer chap who lives way up the valley from Shallowford, 'e flies 'is birds there for part of the year and goes up to Scotland for t'other part. Takes 'em on perches in the back of 'is van. Sleeps in the van with 'em on the way.'

'You'm talkin' about Mr. Macmillan. I don't know 'im but 'e went into the school a week or two back and flew one of 'is birds over the playground. Young Danny loved it and drew that bootiful picture an' sent it to 'is mother.'

'Arthur told me 'e's goin' back to Scotland, permanent-like. 'Is father be very wealthy and owns a big estate but 'e's not too well. 'E's not up to runnin' it and so 'is son has to go back and take on the job.'

'Oh, what a pity! 'E's a nice chap, as I've 'eard tell, but keeps 'iself to 'iself.'

'Funny thing was, that Arthur was just tellin' me all this, when 'e comes drivin' up to where we was talkin' at the gateway that opens onto the lane from 'is cottage.'

'What, Mr. Macmillan, you mean?'

'Yes. That place must be nearly a mile away from where us was standin'. All friendly like, 'e winds down the window and says "Hello." Us gets talkin' and I tells 'im that Jimmy an' Danny was at 'is bird flyin' show at Filleigh School. So 'e goes, "Oh, the little lad who doesn't speak," and I told 'im about the wonderful picture that the boy drew and 'ow 'e sent it to 'is Mum in London. Then you'll never guess what 'e said, Lil.'

'So what did'n say?'

'Only invited Danny and Jimmy to visit 'is cottage next Saturday afternoon. I'd 'ave to take 'em but 'e said that would be all right. After 'e'd drove off, Arthur said that the boys be honoured. There's never been any visitors to that cottage that 'e knows of. A real hideaway, Arthur called it. In fact, that's what the cottage be called. "Hideaway". Arthur says 'e don't even take the post up there. Leaves it in the box on the gate. Mr. Macmillan don't like 'is birds disturbed with people goin' there, Arthur told me.'

Lil looked worried.

'Jimmy an' Danny will 'ave to be on their best behaviour, Stan. And so will you.'

Lil started to clear the table and Stan stood up.

'Tell the boys to come up to the shippon when they get back from school. I'm goin' to teach 'em to milk the cows.' He decided to do an hour's work on the vegetable garden first.

Jimmy and Danny were not too sure about learning to milk the cows. They'd seen Uncle doing it but Jimmy didn't think he fancied trying it himself. When Danny heard Auntie telling them that they could have a go at it, he dropped his head and frowned.

'Look how good you was, Dan, with that wild bird,' Jimmy reminded him. 'A cow is tame, ain't it, Auntie?'

'Well, I wouldn't say that, Jimmy. They have to get used to you. And remember, they'm very big next to young Danny 'ere.'

'I s'ppose so,' Jimmy answered. 'They're bigger than me too, Aunt.'

Stan called out to the boys as they approached the wooden building.

'Come in quietly, boys. You know that, though, 'cos you've been in 'ere with me before. Do 'ee remember what these yer ladies be called?' he asked, indicating the cows standing quiet and tethered at their stalls. 'The one near the door is Buttercup, then there's Daisy and the one with the crumpled horn, 'er 's Madam.'

'Not a flower name like the other two, then, Uncle?'

'That's right Jim, and 'er 's called "Madam" 'cos her can be a bit of a Madam, too! So, mind out when you'm walking behind 'er.'

Stan stood alongside Buttercup and beckoned Jimmy to stand next to him.

'Danny, I want you to get up by 'er 'aid and 'old onto the rope that's round 'er neck. If you smooths 'er neck and keeps 'er 'appy that'll 'elp us, won't it, Jim?'

Jimmy looked uncertain but said nothing. Stan put the three-legged milking stool on the ground alongside Buttercup, turned his cap back to front and sat down on the stool. It was very low on the ground and Stan's knees were bent up to allow his head to be resting against the cow's side.

'Pass that bucket of water, Jim, and give me the cloth in it, please.' Stan took the wet cloth from Jimmy and wiped the cow's udder.

'Us 'as to do this afore us starts milkin' 'er. It's all got be clean, see? Next us lubricates each teat.' He put the cloth back in the bucket.

'Put that bucket away where 'er can't kick it over, Jim, and pass me the milking pail.' Stan pulled the stool closer to Buttercup, pushing his head into a place at her side that seemed to be made just for the purpose.

'Us always milks a cow on 'er right side, see, boys?'

Buttercup tried to turn her head towards Stan as if in agreement, but the rope stopped her, and Danny leant in close to her head and rubbed her nose.

'Good boy, Dan,' Stan said. 'Now, Jim, I be gwain' to wrap my fingers of each 'and around the two front teats, just under the udder, see? Then I squeezes down from where me thumbs be to where me little fingers be. I does that in turn; right 'and, left 'and, right 'and, left 'and.'

There was a squirting sound as the milk flowed and hit the side of the pail that was between Stan's legs. Jimmy smiled and looked at Stan in wonder.

'Us 'as to take care, Jim, the milk don't go back up the udder.' He got up off the stool, making sure not to upset the pail. 'Now you try, young Jim. Act like you know what you'm doin' and Buttercup won't get worried.' Stan put his old coat on the stool to bring Jimmy up higher.

'That's it. Work they front teats. 'Er's got more milk there yet.'

Jimmy's lips were pressed together so tightly that they had disappeared from view and his frown of concentration almost made Stan laugh out loud. Stan coughed to stifle his amusement. Jimmy's hands shook uncertainly as he touched the two front teats. Suddenly Buttercup let out a gentle 'moo', as if to say, 'Who is this person? It's obvious that he doesn't know what he's doing.'

'Oh crikey!' Jimmy said and gripped the teats more firmly, saying 'Right hand, left hand, right hand, left hand.' Nothing happened. No milk flowed. Danny patted Buttercup on the side of her neck and suddenly milk started squirting from each teat in turn. Jimmy was so surprised that the angle of his right hand changed with the shock of his success, and a stream of milk whizzed across the milking parlour and hit Stan full in the face.

'That's it, Jim! You'll make a farmer yet.'

Jimmy carried on milking Buttercup and Stan took over and milked the other two cows, as it was getting near tea-time, and the milk had to be separated, some for the house, some for the churn for collection the next day, and some for the calves and pigs.

It was when Stan was milking Madam that something strange happened. He had told Danny not to go to hold the cow by her halter, but the boy had already taken up his position at the front of Madam's stall and was rubbing her nose and holding her crumpled horn. Danny was swaying his head gently from side to side and the cow stood perfectly still. Stan milked her in half the time it usually took him to do it.

''Er likes you, Dan. 'Er's let 'er milk down without any trouble at all. P'raps you'm a bit small just yet to milk the cows but you can calm 'em down, that's for sure, boy. Well done the both of 'ee. Now you go on back and tell Auntie that Uncle said 'e's pleased with 'ee.'

Jimmy and Danny looked at each other and smiled, glowing with the praise from someone that they guessed didn't give it out much.

Chapter 19

Diana was throwing the ball up against the wall of the house belonging to Mr. and Mrs. Williams in Clifton Terrace. It was the best bit of wall around because there was only one window in it and the people who lived there didn't seem to mind that it was sometimes used for ball games. Mr. Williams was quite deaf, and in any case, the couple lived on the other side of the house and only came into the parlour at the front on a Sunday. Diana was not allowed to play in the street on a Sunday. She was practising her catching but two boys kept cycling their bikes up behind her every time she stepped back into the road to make a catch.

'Missed it again, didn't you?' one of them shouted as he whizzed past her. She ignored him and kept throwing the ball at the wall. She was just getting the hang of it and anticipating the rebound off the wall when a young man came up behind her. She hadn't seen him, and he had walked up the street as if he were looking for something.

'Mind what you're doin' on that bike, mate,' he called out to the other boy who passed quickly and closely behind Diana as she caught the ball.

'See. There you are, love. You made a good

catch there. Buzz off you kids,' he shouted. They sped away in the direction of Clifton Street, which continued on from Clifton Terrace, both roads being intersected by Signal Terrace resulting in the formation of a cross.

'I'm looking for a Mrs. Webb,' the young man said, smiling cheerfully. 'I know this is the street but part of the address on the letter sent to us is torn, and so I don't know what number she lives at.'

'Oh, she's my Granma,' Diana replied, putting her ball in her skirt pocket and indicating the door behind her.

'She and Grampy live at number two Clifton Terrace.'

'Clifton Terrace!' The young man sighed. 'I should have read the address better. I went to Clifton Street.'

'A lot of people get them muddled up, even the postman sometimes,' Diana answered, looking at him more closely and realising that, in fact, he was more of a boy than a young man.

'Wait here,' she said and opened the front door of her grandparents' house and went inside, closing it behind her.

'Granma. There's someone at the front door for you,' she called out.

Florrie came bustling out of the kitchen, taking off her apron and throwing it on a chair.

'It's that evacuee, turned up, I expect,' she said as she squeezed past Diana and opened the front door.

'Are you Bill?' she asked, smiling at the newcomer.

'That's me,' he answered with a friendly grin. 'Bill Donovan.'

'Come in, dear. I'm Florrie Webb and my husband is Jim. This is my granddaughter, Diana.'

'Yes. We've already met. She's good at catching a ball.'

Diana smiled at him. He was round-faced, with bright, blue eyes and fair hair.

'Now let me have that suitcase, Bill.' Florrie quickly snatched it off him and they all went inside.

'And you can call me "Gran." Jim's over the allotment but he'll be back soon. Sit down there, dear, and I'll make you a drink. Did you come down on the train, all the way from London? You must be worn out. Did someone see you off at your end? Have you had anything to eat? Now don't be nervous, I can see that you'll soon fit in here. It's very hard for you to leave your home but you needn't be wary of us. We'll get on fine, as long as you can put up with Jim and his wireless going day and night.'

Bill laughed. He warmed to the motherly lady immediately.

'Is it ok if I go to the toilet and have a quick

wash, Gran?' he asked. 'There's more soot on me than before I started out. I put my head out of the window at one point and got a blast of smoke from the engine.'

'Oh, you don't want to do that, dear,' Florrie said. 'See the view from inside the train. It's safer and it's cleaner. Diana will show you upstairs. The toilet is next to your bedroom at the back of the house.'

Bill followed Diana upstairs, carrying his suitcase and coat while Florrie scuttled about in the scullery, preparing some food. Diana came back into the kitchen.

'He's nice, isn't he, Granma? He told those boys off, you know the ones who keep pestering me whizzing by on their bikes when I'm playing with the ball against the wall?'

'Yes, we'll all fit in fine together,' Florrie said, slicing a loaf of bread and heating the frying pan.

'Now what are you doing for your tea, Diana? Your Mummy finished early at work today, didn't she, and went shopping in town?'

'Yes, she took Mary in the push chair. I didn't want to go. I did some practice and then played in the street. What's the time, Granma?'

'Time you went home, love. Go and lay the table for Mummy for when they get back. You can come over here later if you like.'

'Righto, Granma. I won't be long. I'll be back in

a flash.' Florrie smiled. The child almost lived with her grandparents anyway.

Bill came downstairs and knocked on the kitchen door before opening it.

'It all looks so comfy up in the bedroom you've set up for me, Gran. Are you sure I don't have to share it with anyone?'

'No, Bill, of course not. There's only Jim and me, and Alan, when he's home. He should have been home on leave around now, but we think that leave has been cancelled. Now sit down and enjoy this, dear. We managed to get a rasher of bacon and Margaret brought home some eggs from her friend in the country. She and her hubby have a small farm with chickens and geese and cows and a couple of pigs.'

'What a treat, Gran. Thank you. I don't remember the last time I saw an egg. We have that powdered egg, or we did when Mum was able to cook.'

'You can tell me about yourself later, Bill, but you eat that in peace. I'm just going up the lane to see if Jim's about. He's got nattering to somebody, I expect, probably one of his railway mates from the station. I'll bet he hasn't done much gardening.'

Bill finished his meal and poured himself a cup of tea from the brown china teapot. It reminded him of the one they had at home. Suddenly, he felt very sad and alone. So many of the houses around

Bermondsey had suffered bombing and lives had been lost, although things had gone quiet recently. Hitler's bombers were busy somewhere else. But still, the damage wasn't just to the buildings. Dad hadn't been home for so long and, although he wrote as often as he could, the letters didn't really say anything, just that he was fine and there wasn't much fighting, and never anything about his mates, whether they were still alive or not. The Sergeant was a bit of a tartar, but the Captain was a good bloke and always had time to have a laugh. And was he, Bill, doing ok at school and helping mum out? What about Auntie Gwen and the family? Give them his love, and big hugs to mum and his dear son. Bill could as good as read the letters without getting them out of the envelopes. Where was his dad? And would he come back after the war was over? Would he be the same, jokey dad he was when he went away? And would he be all right?

Bill poured himself another cup of tea and thought about his mum, Eileen. She'd worked six days a week in the engineering factory not far from their home, but the hours were long and she became more and more exhausted. It was on one of her shifts that she suffered the accident which put her out of the job. A lapse of concentration resulted in her left arm being trapped in some machinery. The woman working alongside her reacted quickly and stopped the machine or things could have been worse. Even so, his mother spent a week in hospital and Bill had nursed her on her return home. It became clear that his mother needed care and rest and so her sister, Gwen, who had a young child and was at home for most of the day, said that she was up for the job. He smiled when he thought what Auntie Gwen had said to her sister.

'You may be older than me, Eileen, but just for once, I know best. You're coming to me and there's to be no argument about it!'

Auntie Gwen's home was small, so arrangements were made for the evacuation which brought Bill out of London to the house he had been welcomed into in Barnstaple. He looked round the room. It wasn't grand, but cosy with old furniture, two small armchairs, a square table with four dining chairs arranged around it, lino on the floor and a colourful rug in front of the fireplace. The armchair which backed onto the window facing the little garden at the rear of the house had a small table on its left-hand side with a large wireless perched on it, which seemed to be out of all proportion to the dainty ornaments dotted around the rest of the room. That wireless must be the one that Gran was referring to when she said that Jim had it on day and night. Bill was just wondering what time it got turned off at night when the back door opened. Bill stood up and started to clear away the dishes.

'Sorry, Gran. I should have washed these up before you came back. Hello, Mr. Webb.'

'Hello, my boy. Florrie's told me about you. How was your journey? Straight through from Waterloo?'

'Yes, sir, and I got a seat. How is your allotment coming along? Mum and Dad always wanted a garden where they could grow vegetables, but we only have a yard. The house is empty at the moment, while Mum is with her sister.'

Jim washed his hands at the scullery sink and went and sat down in his armchair in the kitchen.

'Don't you worry about those dishes, Bill,' Florrie said. 'There aren't many and I'll do them later. Go and talk to Jim. It's come over a bit dark suddenly. We're going to get some rain.' Florrie took the plates from Bill's hands and went back into the scullery. Bill sat down again at the table and looked at Jim.

'Do you like gardening, Mr. Webb?'

'Not really, Bill. I saw enough trenches in the last war to dig many in this one, even if it is for food production.'

'I could help you, if you like. I'd love to learn to grow things and I bet you could teach me a lot about vegetables and things.'

'We could learn together, Bill. But don't call me Mr. Webb.'

'Can I call you Gramps, then? I don't have any grandparents, see. Dad's parents died years ago, and Mum's died in the blitz in 1941. She's never got over it really.'

'"Gramps" is fine. My grandchildren call me "Grampy" so you're not far off.'

Suddenly, there was a loud crack of thunder, followed by the sound of the front door opening. Margaret, Mary and Diana came into the kitchen.

'Ooh, Grampy, you know what you say about thunder?' Diana said as they all came and sat around the table.

'Someone's moving the furniture up in heaven,' Bill cut in, standing up and moving from his chair.

'Hello. I think you must be Bill. I'm Margaret Partridge and this is Mary. She's very tired and it's late so we won't stay long but Diana said that we must come over and say "Hello".'

Florrie came bustling into the kitchen.

'Sit down, Bill. They won't bite.'

There was another clap of thunder and Mary started to look worried. She climbed up onto her mother's lap.

'Don't worry, Mary. The clouds are too heavy and will soon drop a lot of rain. Grampy needs it for the vegetable garden don't you, Dad?'

Jim didn't look very enthusiastic.

'I'm going to help with the allotment, Mrs. Partridge.'

'Really, Bill? Just make sure that Dad does his share,' she said knowingly. 'And please call me Margaret or Maggie.'

'Margaret, I've been meaning to ask you if you've had a letter from Jack?' Florrie asked.

'No, Mum. I haven't heard anything since I visited him two weeks ago tomorrow. I can't understand it. Perhaps there's something wrong with the post.'

Florrie nodded. 'We haven't heard a thing from Alan for ages and Mrs. Jenkins next door said they haven't had any post for some time and one of the girls had a birthday and didn't get any cards, so there's something wrong.'

'Maybe the postman's ill,' Diana suggested.

'Ooh, Jim. Hark at that rain. It's pouring.'

They all listened and could hear the rain hitting the roof in a deluge. Suddenly, there was another sound.

'Mum, I'm sure I heard someone open the front door.'

'You're imagining it, Margaret. Who could that be at this time?'

The kitchen door burst opened, and a familiar voice shouted out, 'It's me, of course – Jack.'

Chapter 20

Jack had been home a week and felt almost as if he had never been away. He'd seen the doctor for a check-up and was given a good report.

'You're a lucky man,' the doctor had told him. 'Not everyone walks out of Hawkmoor.'

Jack had asked when he could start work and was told to wait another week and then to find something outdoors but not heavy, manual work.

'Take care of your lungs, or what's left of them,' the doctor had said. He wasn't the most cheerful of men, Jack thought, but perhaps he should heed the advice. The local paper was a good place to start searching for a job. He sat down in the armchair in the kitchen and opened a copy of the North Devon Journal. Leafing through it, he found the page with the list of job advertisements. Looking for something in Barnstaple, he came upon a possibility.

Man wanted at Hopgoods Garage as Petrol Pump Attendant, also able to offer help in the workshop when required. Part-time work initially. Remuneration on application to The Manager, Hopgoods, Taw Vale, Barnstaple.

Jack put the newspaper down on the table and shouted upstairs to Margaret.

'Marj. Come down and look at this. I may have found a job.'

His wife opened the door holding a bundle of sheets in her arms.

'Jack, I want to try to get these washed and dried now that the weather has picked up again. The schools break up for the summer next week and I'll be busier than ever.'

'There's a job here which could be just the thing for me and then you could do less time at the bakery. Here. Read about it. The doctor said I should look for light outdoor work; nothing too physically demanding,'

Margaret put down the bundle of washing on a chair and picked up the paper.

'It sounds just your sort of thing, Jack. You love anything about cars and motor bikes.'

'Yes, I miss my old motor bike that I raced around on before we were married.'

'Today's Thursday,' Margaret said, thinking aloud, 'the day the paper gets delivered.'

She went to the bureau and took out an envelope and a note pad.

'Strike while the iron is hot,' Margaret said, passing them to Jack and searching for the fountain pen.

After ten minutes or so, Margaret had dictated a letter to her husband, which he had written and sealed in the envelope. He was just about to put a stamp on it when he looked up at his wife. 'I'm not going to post it. I'm going to walk there and hand it in at their office. I know where Hopgoods is, that is if it's still opposite Rock Park. Things change when you've been away from home like I have.'

Margaret smiled. 'It's where it was and there's still that lovely climbing rose next to the front door behind the petrol pump.'

Jack was already cleaning his shoes to a mirror-like shine. He put on his coat and checked himself in the looking glass above the fireplace. He was very fussy about his appearance.

'Not a hair out of place, dear. Good luck.' Margaret kissed him.

Jack smiled and went out the back door. Margaret was glad that she wasn't needed at work today. It would give her a chance to catch up at home, especially as Mary had been taken into town with her Granma. Florrie had to fit in her housework in her own home around the cleaning work she did in town and her help with looking after Mary and Diana. Now there was an evacuee to factor into the daily routine. It was a good thing that Margaret's mother had a high work ethic. She couldn't bear laziness in others and had no problem about reprimanding those who didn't come up to her expectations. Margaret had to admit that she was a chip off the old block. She thought that her grandmother had been the same. The attitude probably ran through the female line, like a seam of coal runs through a rock. Margaret completed what she had hoped to do that morning and had prepared a dinner for when Jack and Mary got home. Diana was at school and wouldn't be back until about four o'clock. Suddenly, the back door was flung open and Jack burst in.

'Got it,' he said. 'How about that? I've got the job!'

'Really?' Margaret's eyes gleamed. 'Come in the kitchen and tell me all about it.'

Jack took off his shoes, put on his slippers and sat at the kitchen table.

'I went to the office and handed in the letter, and was told to wait for a few minutes. Then the Manager came out, who owns the business, and asked me to go into a back room to talk to him. I told him that I had been away at Hawkmoor and hadn't been home long but that I was keen to get working as soon as possible. He said he was impressed that I had not waited to post the letter and had come to apply in person. "That's the sort of enthusiasm I want," he said. I said that although I would be working on the pumps, I was keen to learn as much as I could about the maintenance side of motoring. We had a chat for a while and suddenly, he said, "Jack, you've got the job. When can you start?"'

Margaret clapped her hands in excitement. 'Oh well done, Jack! It's not a full-time job, is it? It won't be too much for you, will it?'

'It's not full-time yet, but the motor trade is building up and who knows what will happen when everything gets back to normal after the war ends?'

Margaret looked thoughtful.

'I don't have to tell you it hasn't been easy while you've been away. Thanks to Mum's help, I've kept a job going, paid the rent and even saved a little bit in the Post Office. I'm determined that we don't pay rent for the rest of our lives, Jack. It's money down the drain. There may be a chance to own this little house one day, and so I want to have enough saved to put down a deposit for a mortgage to buy it.'

Jack raised his eyebrows and nodded.

'That's one of the reasons I wanted to marry you, Marj. You're a worker and can look ahead. Your ideas are enough to scare me, though.'

'Why shouldn't we buy our own place, Jack? We may be called "working class" in today's times, but after the war things will change. And we're going to be part of that change. You just see.'

Chapter 21

Lil looked out from the kitchen window at the rain steadily falling and showing no sign of letting up. The first week of the school holidays is a sure sign of wet weather, she thought. They'd finished their dinner and the boys were sitting at the kitchen table, looking lost. Lil found some paper and two pencils in the cupboard.

'''Tis time you wrote another letter to your mother, you two. She sent you a little parcel so 'tis only polite to write and thank 'er. Danny, you could do a nice drawin'.'

Jimmy and Danny turned and knelt on the wooden bench and looked out the window. Jimmy sighed.

'Can't we just go out and help Uncle? We could put our boots on.'

'''Tis like a mud bath out there. You'm not g'wain out 'til it dries up or I'll never get 'ee clean again.'

'Ooh, look, Auntie. It's Mrs. P. driving the van up the lane.'

'I'll put the kettle on. 'Er'll be soaked.' Lil went out to the scullery and the sound of pots and plates signalled a late dinner to greet Margaret's arrival.

Having removed her raincoat and shaken it at

the front steps, Margaret stepped into the kitchen.

'Oh, dear! What a way to start the school holidays!' She put her basket down as Lil came from the scullery with a plate of food to greet her friend.

'Terrible, Margaret. The boys want to go up with Stan to the shippon but I just told 'em 'tis much too muddy.'

'It's pouring down, boys. You'd be soaked in no time. I've brought you something for wet weather.' Margaret opened her shoulder bag and took out some notepads and coloured pencils.

'Thank you, Mrs. P,' Jimmy said, smiling at her. 'Look Dan, there's lots of different colours and a big notepad each. Danny smiled and started to draw immediately.

'That's very kind of you, Margaret. Now sit and eat this dinner. You'm ready for it, that's for sure,' Lil said. 'Us haven't seen much of 'ee lately. Us 'ave got a lot to catch up on.'

'It's been a bit rocky at work recently, Lil. They needed more help in the bakehouse and Bert managed to get Maurice back to take Ron's place doing the deliveries for Tuesdays and Fridays.'

'I thought you said 'e 'ad a stall in the market.'

'Yes, but he's got his mother to run it for him for a while. I've been doing some of the cooking with Bert and his team. I've learnt a lot but missed coming out here to see you and Stan.'

'While the school holidays be on, you can come out on the bus, if they ever gives 'ee a day off in that shop.' Lil poured Margaret a cup of tea.

'Will 'ee 'ave some rice puddin', Margaret?' Lil asked, serving out a generous helping before waiting for an answer.

'And what news 'ave 'ee got about Jack? I know 'e was doin' much better.'

'He's home, Lil. A week ago. Suddenly, the door opened and he walked in.'

'Well, but didn't 'ee know 'e was comin'?'

'No, because the post was delayed telling us he was to be discharged. He came home by train and we didn't even meet him at the station, because we had no idea that he had been discharged.'

' "Tis wonderful news, though, Margaret.'

'Yes, but not the sort of welcome we would like to have given him, after he had been away so long. And in the five minutes that he walked from the station, he got soaking wet. We were all over Mum's when he walked in and then, when we got home and got him fed and dried, the air raid siren went off. Diana and I huddled together under the table and Jack grabbed Mary and got into the cupboard under the stairs. He'd forgotten that, apart from keeping the coal scuttle in there, he stored his drum kit there, too. You should have heard the racket as he fell on it holding Mary. His language wasn't any too good either. We heard a plane fly over and then the all clear went. I couldn't stop laughing and then Diana started. Jack took it more seriously and said, "Well, this is a nice welcome home, I must say." Then he saw the funny side of it and laughed.'

'Us never gets any raids round yer, do us?' Lil looked quite offended that a German plane had dared to interrupt the peaceful lifestyle of North Devon.

'They think it may have been a German bomber that had got off course after returning from a raid. Some poor souls suffered from what it had been carrying.'

Jimmy and Danny had been listening to the story.

'Coo, a drum kit!' Jimmy exclaimed. 'Can he play it?'

Margaret pulled a face and said, 'Yes, but badly. What have you been doing?'

'I've written to me Mum and Danny's drew a picture of a peregrine falcon, ain't you, Dan? 'E's very keen on birds of prey and we was invited to a falconer's house to see 'is hawks and falcons. We was "special guests," that's what Mr. Macmillan told us. But 'e's leavin' 'is house to go back to Scotland to help 'is father, and 'e's going to take 'is birds wiv 'im, ain't 'e, Dan?'

Danny shook his head vehemently.

'Mr. Macmillan said 'e'd write to us and tell us all about Scotland and 'ow 'is birds are gettin' on,' Jimmy said.

Danny had put down his pencil and looked crestfallen. Margaret stood up and looked across at the boys' work.

'That's very good to write to your Mum, Jimmy. Danny, you've drawn a lovely picture. Why don't you send a picture of that bird to Mr. Macmillan? He would love that, wouldn't he, Lil?'

'Yes, you can send one picture to your Mum and one to Mr. Macmillan. Uncle will get 'ee the address in Scotland.'

Lil looked at Margaret and shook her head. Danny was still for a moment, then turned a page in his pad and started to draw again.

'I must get on, Lil. Thank you for the meal. I meant to tell you that Jack has found himself a job already, at Hopgoods; part-time at first, which is enough to start with until he is stronger.'

'Good news, Margaret. Maybe you won't have to work so 'ard.'

'You're a good one to talk, Lil. "It takes one to know one." That's what they say, isn't it? Say "Hello," to Stan for me. Bye, Lil. Bye, Jimmy. Bye, Danny. I hope the weather is better tomorrow, boys.'

'So do I, Margaret,' Lil said, with a wry smile.

Chapter 22

The rain had stopped just before Jack left the house to start the first day of his new job. Even so, he had decided to take his mac, had worn his second-best pair of trousers and his best shoes. The trousers still fitted him, although he was beginning to regain the weight he had lost during his illness. He wasn't sure if there was anything he needed to take with him for the work at Hopgoods, but guessed that he would soon find out about that when he started there. In the small, lean-to, glass-roofed building that adjoined the scullery, which they all called 'the greenhouse', even though it wasn't, he'd looked at his pushbike. It had been leaning there itself for nearly two years so perhaps he could smarten it up and cycle to work. The tyres might need replacing but he'd put it on his list of things to catch up on. It was a big list and it would take him some time to work through.

As he passed the Park end of Litchdon Street, his watch showed five minutes to eight. His hours were to be eight till six three days a week. Another man would be working Thursday, Friday and Saturday morning. Jack walked onto the forecourt and went to the office at the back of it, and knocked on the door. There was a woman sitting at a desk. She looked up at him and smiled.

'Good morning. I'm Alice. Are you the new man?'

'Yes, that's right. Hello. I'm Jack.'

Alice got up from behind her desk.

'Wait there, Jack. I'll just pop out to the workshop at the back and fetch the boss.'

They returned almost immediately and Mr. Hopgood stepped forward and shook Jack's hand.

'Your full name is William John Partridge, I believe, but you call yourself "Jack."'

We have a small problem. There is already a fellow working here called Jack, so do you mind if we call you Bill?'

'My family call me Jack but Bill is fine, Mr. Hopgood.'

'Right, Alice, so Jack is Bill while he's working here.'

Alice nodded and sat down at her desk.

'Now, Bill, there are a few things to talk through. I'll go outside with you in a minute and show you how to work the petrol pump. We don't do much trade selling petrol because of the rationing. There are few essential users, apart from the military, but no petrol is sold to the man in the street, as you might say. Even the essential users have to present coupons on purchasing petrol and those coupons are only valid if they are in date. In other words, if they didn't use last month's coupons, it's too late. It's called "use it or lose it." Bill, follow me into the workshop and I'll show you around.' They walked through the back door into a large, covered shed with high windows and overhead lighting. Several men were working on and under various vehicles. It all looked very organised.

'The workshop is busy with repairs and maintenance of cars and vans, but we do sometimes get motor bikes and small farm machinery. I know you said you'd be interested to learn that side of our business.'

'Yes sir, I am very keen to learn as much as I can,' Jack said enthusiastically.

Mr. Hopgood shouted to the men working. 'This is Bill, everyone. He's come to join our merry band.'

The workers looked up and some waved spanners and oily hands in response. Jack followed Mr. Hopgood through the door leading outside from the back of the workshop and round to the front where the petrol pump was located. After a few minutes all had been explained about the use of the pump and how payment and coupons were taken and stored in the office. There was a small shelter next to the pump for the attendant to get under at times of rain but the pump itself was in the open. When there was little demand for petrol, Jack was to be in the workshop, and if a customer wanted fuel, he would ring a bell which sounded in the workshop, so summoning the petrol pump attendant to the forecourt.

'What a lovely rose you have there, Mr. Hopgood,' Jack said indicating the bush, climbing up beside the door leading to the house adjoining the office.

'Yes, Bill. It's been there some years and flowers well in the summer and it doesn't seem to mind the petrol fumes and dust from the tyres of vehicles driving up next to it. Now, I'll leave you to start out here. Get an overall from Alice in the office. You look smart enough to be a bank manager, Bill. Don't wear your best clothes here. You'll put us all to shame.'

He walked away and left Jack to get ready for his first day's work in a long time. The morning passed quickly with no problems and the sun had come out. Jack had decided not to go home at dinner time on his first day and had brought some sandwiches. He was about to cross the road to go over the park and sit on a bench while he ate them, when a man came towards him and greeted him in a friendly way.

'Hello there! Are you the new boy?'

Jack put the packet of sandwiches back in his pocket.

'Yes, I'm Jack, but they've decided to call me Bill.'

'Yes, that's because we've already got a Jack here, as they've no doubt told you. I'm Frank but everyone calls me "Biscuits." '

'Biscuits?' Jack couldn't see how that could be a name for the rather stocky, friendly figure that faced him.

'I thought I'd pop over to meet you. I'll be working the shifts that you don't do, Bill, but it's all interchangeable if needs be. Have they told you what you have to do?'

'Yes, it's all been explained to me but I'll want some time to get the hang of it,' Jack replied.

'The main thing is to keep an eye out for anything that doesn't look right, in the way of forged petrol coupons for instance. Mr. H. is like a hawk over that. I know there are folks about who play the Black Market but anything to do with fuel supplies and coupons and rationing is a big "no" for Mr. H. He plays it straight and expects us all to do the same. Just thought I'd tell you, mate.'

'Fair enough,' Jack answered. 'It's difficult getting fuel to Britain across the oceans, what with the German U-boats sinking the ships bringing it here.'

'Damn right, Bill. Look, if there's anything I can help with, let me know. You can pass a message with the chaps in the workshop and they'll get it to me. I just live nearby, at Silver Street.'

'Thanks. I'll remember that. I haven't worked for nearly two years. I've been away for some time and I feel as if there's a lot to catch up on. I only came out of Hawkmoor a little while ago.'

'Good for you, Bill. My nephew's just gone there, and we're all worried about him.'

'The care there is very good but it's a really strict regime.'

'He'll be able to cope with that, Bill, no doubt about it. We'll catch up again soon, mate. Good to have you join our merry band.' Biscuits smiled.

'That's what Mr. Hopgood called his employees.' Jack looked serious for a moment.

'Just one thing you could answer for me,' Jack paused. 'Why do they call you "Biscuits"?'

'Well, you see, me and my wife used to live in Reading before we moved here in 1935, and I worked at Huntley and Palmers biscuit factory. As soon as the blokes here knew that, there was no other name they could call me, to their minds.' Biscuits turned and walked away, whistling happily.

Chapter 23

'**Oh, Margaret. There** you are. How did the picnic go?' Florrie started to move from her armchair to pour a cup of tea for her daughter.

'Don't get up, Mum. I've just had a cup of tea, thanks. Mary was so tired that she dropped off to sleep as soon as I put her down. Jack is seeing Diana off to bed so I thought I'd just pop over and see you and Dad.'

'Well if you won't have a cup of tea, at least sit down for a while and tell us about Mary's birthday picnic. I hope you didn't carry too much with you and didn't walk far.'

'We thought we'd take a short walk up to the field on the way to Lake and have our picnic there. We were lucky with the weather; not too hot. I took some sandwiches and little cakes that I'd made yesterday. We even lit a birthday candle and sang "Happy Birthday." We had some lemonade, too, and were able to put all the picnic things in the bag strapped to the push chair.'

'Three years old, Margaret. What did she make of it? After all, her birthday was on Thursday, wasn't it, and today is Sunday.'

'Oh, Mary loved it and now she thinks she'll have

a birthday every day. The thing is, I was working on Thursday and it wouldn't have been so easy to fit everything in. In any case, Mum, you gave her a birthday tea so she's done very well out of us.' Margaret went and sat in the empty chair opposite her mother.

'It's nice and peaceful over here. Where's Dad?'

'"Silence is Golden," Margaret. It's good to have the wireless off now and then. Your Dad's gone for a walk by the river. It's a lovely evening, but I was just too tired to go with him.' Florrie settled back in her armchair and sighed. 'Anyway, what did you do after the picnic?'

'We decided to walk on to Lake, and then on towards Tawstock. Mary wanted to walk a lot and we kept stopping to look at wild flowers in the hedgerows and a little pool with newts in it. The children loved it, but after a while Mary got tired and wanted to sit in the pushchair. We should have turned back really, but Jack was keen to go on. He kept telling me he'd got used to doing plenty of walking towards the end of his time at Hawkmoor.'

'Tawstock is quite a long way though, and with very steep hills for walking up and down. Glad I didn't go with you.' Florrie took off her glasses and wiped the lens with the bottom of her pinafore.

'We didn't get as far as Tawstock. Do you remember that steep stretch of road well before the village? It dips down really suddenly. Well, Diana was holding the handle of the push chair and Jack was just about to take over from her because you need to be strong to hold it back on the slope, when neither of them was holding on to the handle, and suddenly, the push chair with Mary sitting up and strapped into it, shot off down the hill. I screamed and we started running but there was no way we could have caught up with it. There were several people out walking and not one of them attempted to get in the way of the runaway push chair and stop it. They just leapt to either side and watched as it gathered speed.'

'Oh my God, Margaret. What did you do?'

'What could we do, Mum? We couldn't catch her and no-one else was going to stop her. We were so lucky that no vehicle was coming the other way. Finally, to our horror, at the bend in the road at the bottom, Mary and the push chair ended up in the hedge with a sudden stop. We rushed down, expecting the worst and a few people gathered round but when we saw Mary, she looked up and laughed and said, "Can we do that again, Mummy?"'

'Wasn't she hurt?'

'There wasn't a scratch on her, Mum, and she thought we'd done it as a sort of game.'

Florrie started laughing. 'That child keeps us all entertained. She's good wartime medicine.'

'It's funny afterwards, but it nearly frightened us to death at the time. Poor Diana ran all the way to the bottom without falling over. It was so strange that none of the Sunday afternoon strollers made any effort to jump in the way of the push chair and stop it. Jack was as white as a sheet but when we heard Mary ask if she could do it all again, we had to laugh.'

'Did you come back home after that, Margaret?'

'We certainly did. I was shaking for a minute or two, but we walked back up the hill with Mary in the push chair and us trying not to make too much of it.'

'It will be a birthday to remember though, won't it, dear?'

'Yes, it will be funny when we look back on it but it could have been far from that, Mum.'

'Margaret, how is Jack getting on with his new job?'

'He hasn't been there long but I think he likes it. As well as getting to know the staff, customers call in for petrol, or for work to be done on their vehicles, and they chat about things happening in their area. Jack says that there is a lot going on around Woolacombe and Saunton and around the coast.'

'I thought they'd laid mines on those beaches. It would have been lovely to take the children there to paddle and build sand castles.' Florrie frowned and looked cross.

'Bloody Hitler and his lot spoiling our summer.'

'Yes, but Jack said that someone told him that the mines have been taken up and a lot of the barbed wire removed. It looks as if the beaches are going to be used in some way.'

'Not by us, though, dear.'

Suddenly the back door opened and Jim and Bill walked in.

'Hello, Dad. Have you been for a walk together?'

'No,' Jim said. 'I met Bill as I was on my way back.'

'I've been over Rock Park, Gran. I've got to know a few other evacuees like me, and some of the local boys. Hello, Mrs. Partridge. I mean, Margaret. I think you told me to call you that.'

'That's right, Bill; or Maggie, if you prefer. It's good you're getting out to meet young people and make friends.'

Margaret moved out of her Dad's chair and he sat down in it. She sat at the kitchen table and Bill sat down opposite her.

'Have you worked out what you're going to do, Bill? At fifteen you can leave school, can't you?'

'Yes. I want to try to get an apprenticeship if I can. I may as well work towards learning a trade while I'm here.'

'That's good, isn't it, Dad?' Margaret thought she would try to get a few words out of her father before he started twiddling the knobs on his wireless.

'Good idea. He could try Shapland and Petter.'

'Yes, Dad. They are really high-class cabinet makers and a much-respected firm. I don't know whether they're making the same sort of things during the wartime though. Still, it's worth finding out about it, Bill. Have you written to your Mum or your Dad yet?'

'Yes. I wrote to Mum soon after I got here to put her mind at rest. I told her it was like home from home here and that Gran is spoiling me.'

Florrie looked pleased. 'He's a good boy and lovely company,' she said with a glance towards Jim, who was busy turning the pages of the Radio Times.

'Well, I must be getting back.' Margaret walked towards the door. 'Bye, everyone.'

'Bye, Margaret,' replied Florrie and Bill, while Jim waved his hand without looking up from tuning in his wireless.

Chapter 24

'Stan, will 'ee just sit there a minute. There's somethin' I need to say to 'ee.' Lil poured her husband a second cup of tea.

'Don't tell me there be another family weddin' an' you'm gwain in Banburys to buy a new 'at?'

'No. Don't be silly! But one of the nieces 'as just got engaged and 'er will get married before too long, I reckon.'

'See? I knew it! You've got more 'ats than Banburys 'ave got in their shop. They should buy 'em back off 'ee, Maid.'

'No. Listen, Stan. 'Tis nothin' to do with weddin's. 'Tis to do with poor old Major Philips down at Stone Cottage.'

'Why? What's up with 'e?'

'Well, Stan, I saw Mrs. Greenslade at Chapel on Sunday and 'er 's worried about the poor ol' boy. She goes there to clean for 'im and to take 'is washin', and she takes 'im 'is shoppin'. 'E used to do a bit of cookin' but 'tis too much for 'im now, 'er thinks. 'E looks after himself in other ways and 'e's always clean and smart.'

'Of course, 'e's clean and smart, Lil. All they years in the army, an' 'is time servin' in the last war was 'is life, and 'e served it well, didn't 'n?'

'Bit of a hero from what us 'ave been told,' Lil said, nodding in admiration.

'And Mrs. Greenslade says 'e still takes an interest in what's goin' on with the war and 'e follows the news all the time, tunin' in to 'is wireless.' She stirred the pot and poured herself another cup of tea. ''E likes to walk along the road from 'is house but 'e don't go far,' she added.

Stan lit his pipe and drew on it thoughtfully.

'I seed 'n in Swimbridge a while back, but I don't blame 'n if 'e likes to keep 'is own company an' don't go far. After all, why would anybody want to go to Barnstaple? Wild' orses wouldn't drag me there. 'Tis too busy and too noisy!'

''Tis a good job us all isn't like you, Stan! But I be worried about 'im. I think us can 'elp 'im out.'

Stan raised his eyebrows but stayed silent.

'I can give 'im 'is dinner every day and you can take it to 'im on the bike before you 'as your dinner.' Lil looked pleased with herself at finding a solution. 'Us can make a small weekly charge for doin' it but it won't cost us much extra and us'll know 'e's had one good meal a day.'

'On the bike, Maid?' Stan looked doubtful.

'You've got a strong basket on the front for carryin' the post, so as long as I puts 'is meal in a deep dish and covers it up, --' She paused and said, chuckling, 'an' you don't fall off yer bike, it'll work.'

'Stone Cottage is less than five minutes from the bottom of the lane on me bike.' Stan smiled. 'You'm right, Maid. Us should do it for the old Major.'

'Good, Stan, I knew you'd want to 'elp 'im. I'll tell Mrs. Greenslade what us is goin' to do when I sees 'er next at Chapel and us can start on the Monday.'

Lil drank the last of her tea and started to gather the dishes together on the table.

'Just a minute, Lil. While the boys be out playin' I can tell 'ee about what's 'appened to Mr. Macmillan's 'ouse.'

'Oh, Stan. Young Danny won't believe that 'e's gone up to Scotland.'

'I know. That's why I want to tell 'ee about it now. I saw Arthur last Friday and 'e told me that there's a new tenant already moved in.'

'Well that be good then, Stan. The Estate wants to keep the place rented surely?'

'Yes, but Arthur bain't sure about the new tenant. Very unfriendly and a bit stuck up, 'e said 'e was. S'pposed to be a distant relation to Lord Fortescue. Anyway, Arthur saw 'n. 'E was drivin' a van with a removal lorry followin' after.'

'Well what's wrong with that, Stan? 'Tis good to 'ave the cottage used.'

' 'Twas somethin' about the new man that Arthur didn't like, posh or not.'

'Arthur spoke to 'im then?'

'Yes. Arthur was just ridin' 'is bike near the entrance to the long lane leadin' to the cottage, when this van pulls up followed by the lorry. The driver of the van puts 'is 'aid out the window and says to Arthur, "So you're the local postman, are you?" "That's right, sir," Arthur says. "Well you needn't deliver anything to me as I've made other arrangements." With that, Arthur says, 'e drives off. The removal lorry 'ad a job getting' through the gate. The driver wasn't used to our roads and Arthur said 'e nearly choked tryin' not to burst out laughin' at the mess the bloke was makin' of turnin' into the lane. There's great 'oles all the way to the cottage. Arthur said 'twas a pity 'e couldn't watch the convoy makin' a real---'

'Yes, Stan. I understand what you'm sayin'.'

'Arthur says, 'e thinks 'tis a bit strange, that's all.'

'Well, they'm city folk, bain't 'em? They just do things different, that's all.'

Stan got up from the table and put his pipe back on the mantlepiece.

'Well, us shall see, that's all I be sayin'.'

And with that, he went out to do some work on the vegetable garden. Lil shouted after him.

'Stan. Check that they boys be all right when you

go up to the shippon. I think they'm gone up the woods.'

At least the weather was dry and they could get out, she thought. She carried on with clearing the table but found herself thinking about the new tenant that Stan was talking about. Wasn't the house furnished? Why would he want a removal van to take a load of furniture there? Perhaps the new chap had a lot of books or something. She wondered why he had a van. With petrol rationed, he'd have to be a doctor or a farmer or someone special like that. She shook herself out of her thoughts at the sound of approaching voices from outside.

'Auntie, there's a lady wants to speak to you. I think she's a lady but she's wearin' trousers.' Jimmy burst into the kitchen, followed by Danny, somewhat breathless, from keeping up with his brother. Lil went out to the front step as a young woman came towards her.

'Hello. I've been told you're Mrs. Webber. I'm working up the woods with a couple of other girls. We're taking down some trees and have run out of something to drink. It's hot work and young Jimmy here said you wouldn't mind me asking for some water.'

'Water? Course you can 'ave some water. Would 'ee like a cup of tea? Jimmy, go an' put the kettle on, please. Danny, fetch the tin with they little cakes in it.'

The boys ran inside and Lil looked at the young woman, dressed in shirt and corduroy trousers and with thick socks and heavy boots on her feet. She still looked attractive in spite of being dishevelled and rather muddy.

'I'm Angela,' she said. 'We three girls are what people call "Lumberjills". We're part of the Women's Timber Corps. I wanted to come and talk to you about the boys. I know they are interested in what we're doing but it is quite dangerous up there. We mostly know which way a tree is going to fall but we wouldn't like there to be an accident.'

'You'm quite right, dear, and good of 'ee to come and speak to me about 'em. They mustn't be up there while you'm cuttin' and 'sawin'. You want your mind on what you'm doin' without Jimmy and Danny in the way.'

'Are they evacuees, Mrs. Webber?'

'That's right, dear. The little one don't talk at all. They 'ad a terrible time with the bombin' in London. 'Tis shock, you see.'

Angela stood on the top step, and looked behind her out over the valley, down the path to the stream and the road, and over the far fence to the bottom field and the woods beyond that. Suddenly, the muffled sound of a train was heard and smoke could be seen curling through the tree tops of those far woods. The white trail of it worked its way along from the Swimbridge direction and on towards Filleigh, eventually disappearing as the train headed on to Taunton, over forty miles away. The gentle chuff-chuffing was the only sound to break the stillness of the place, apart from the contented mooing of the cattle and the odd cackle of the geese.

'What a heavenly place,' Angela said dreamily. She turned back to Lil and shook herself out of her reverie. 'But I expect it's very hard work, isn't it?'

'You'm right there, Angela. But us is lucky to be somewhere safe. Now come in a minute. I can give 'ee a flask of tea and a few cakes to take up the woods. You can let me 'ave the flask when you'm up 'ere next, and you can come yer every time you'm workin' in the woods for the same thing.'

Lil looked at the young woman more closely. Her hair was tied back and had leaves and bits of twigs in it and there was a red scratch across her right cheek.

''Tis a man's work you'm doin' surely, dear?' Angela followed Lil into the scullery and watched her prepare the flask of tea and put some cakes into a bag.

'Yes, it is very tough work but we know where

the men are don't we, and now women have to do jobs we'd never have been asked to do before the war. Perhaps it will change everyone's outlook when this is all over.'

Lil handed over the little picnic to the lovely young woman.

'Well, we love livin' here but I must say, I'd like someone to unchain me from the sink one day.'

'Thank you, Mrs. Webber,' Angela said. She raised her eyebrows as she looked at Jimmy and Danny, who were sitting at the table and tucking into a cake each.

'Don't worry, Angela,' Lil said with a nod of her head towards the boys. 'They won't be up in they woods while you girls be workin' there. Us'll see to that.'

Chapter 25

Diana closed her Enid Blyton book and went out to the scullery.

'Mummy, can you teach me how to knit?'

Margaret was cutting up the cabbage and put down the knife.

'What now, Diana? I'm busy getting the dinner ready.'

'Ugh, not cabbage,' Diana said, screwing up her nose.

'Not just cabbage, but you must eat some. It's good for you and we have to make up our meals with vegetables. Meat is rationed and even then, we can only buy what we can get.' She washed the cabbage and put it in a saucepan.

'Now, what's this about learning to knit? Go in the kitchen and sit at the table. I've ten minutes to spare before I have to carry on with preparing the dinner. Mary is still having her morning sleep so let's see what we can do.'

Diana sat at the table while Margaret went to the cupboard next to the fireplace. She pulled out a large box containing various balls and skeins of wools and a bundle of knitting needles.

'Here's a pair of number nine needles. The

higher the number, the finer the needle, and the thinner wool thread you will have to use. This is about the thickest needle we use these days. Let's see.' She rifled about in the box and picked out a ball of red wool. I keep these small balls of left-over wool to use to knit up multi-colour jumpers. We can't waste wool, but this is fine for you to learn with, Diana.' Margaret placed one needle in each of her daughter's hands.

'That's how you hold them, between your thumbs and first fingers but give them back to me because I'm going to cast on for you.'

'What's "cast on" mean, Mummy?'

'It means "starting off" and getting some stitches on one of the needles. That's something I can teach you later. Now, you've twelve stitches on this needle so put it in your left hand like I just showed you. Good! The empty needle is in your right hand. What you have to do is knit each of the stitches on the full needle to make new stitches to go on to the empty needle.'

Diana frowned. 'It feels funny. I haven't got enough hands to keep hold of everything.'

'Well you can't grow another one, can you? Give it back to me and I'll show you what to do.'

Diana carefully handed the needles back to her mother.

'Are you watching, Diana? Right. Put the point

of the right-hand needle into the front of the first stitch, but still keep the stitch on the left-hand needle. Then you wind the wool under and round the right-hand needle and pull the thread through, and finally slip that old stitch off the needle. There. That's one stitch knitted. I'll knit another one, then you can have a go. See? In goes the needle, round goes the wool, through comes the new stitch and off goes the old stitch.'

Diana was fidgeting in her chair with impatience, and ready to have a try. Margaret placed the knitting in her daughter's hands and put the strand of wool over her right forefinger. 'It's best to have the ball on your right-hand side. We can keep it on the table, here. Remember: in, round, through, off. Take your time.'

After a little while, and with some help, Diana had knitted four stitches. The next stitch seemed to be a problem.

'You forgot to pull the new stitch through, but you're doing well. I really must prepare the dinner but I'll write something down to help you remember it all. Ah! I can use the back of that cardboard clock we gave you when you were learning to tell the time. Here it is, on the top of the bureau.'

Margaret picked up the clock and turned it round the wrong way. On the back of it she wrote, 'IN

ROUND THROUGH OFF' and propped it up in front of Diana.

'I'll leave you to get going. Call me if you need help,' Margaret said, on her way to the scullery. Diana didn't answer. She was already saying 'IN ROUND THROUGH OFF' to herself, as she slowly worked the stitches on the left-hand needle.

'I've finished. I've run out of stitches. What do I do now, Mummy?'

'Just a minute and I'll come and start you on the next row.'

Margaret went to and fro between the kitchen and the scullery until there was a sudden cry of 'help' from Diana.

'What's happened?' shouted her mother while straining the potatoes.

'A stitch has fallen down and I can't catch it. What do I have to do?' Diana wailed.

'Gently lay the whole piece of knitting on the armchair and I'll come and pick it up, but it's nearly dinner time so we'll have to sort it out later. Lay the table, please Diana, and then go and fetch Daddy from the back yard. He's been out there for ages, sorting out his push-bike. I'm going to get Mary from upstairs and we'll all have dinner.'

'OK,' Diana replied, laying the knitting down on the chair.

'And don't say," OK," Diana.'

'OK. Ooh, I mean all right, Mummy.'

During the meal, there was quite a battle trying to get Diana to eat a little of the cabbage. The atmosphere improved when they had their afters, which was stewed apple and custard.

'I think I can get that bike back in working order, Marj,' Jack said. 'It will need two new tyres but it's cleaned up well and I can use it for work.'

'Play with Mary for a while, Diana, and we'll look at your knitting later. Pass it to me and I'll put it somewhere safe or you'll lose all your stitches. Someone small is very interested in it.'

'I'm glad you've reduced your working hours at the bakery, Marj.' Jack stacked the empty pudding dishes together.

'Yes, it's a lot easier to fit things in now we're both working. You didn't see the post this morning, did you, Jack? I've opened it and read it. It's quite a surprise.' She stood up and took the letter from the top of the bureau.

Jack read it and looked up. 'An evacuee? We're being asked to take an evacuee?'

'Yes. It's another worrying story about a London family. Mother is busy helping her parents who never fully recovered after part of their home was damaged in the Blitz. Father is away fighting, so the daughter, Maureen, is left too often to her own devices. When she gets back from school, it's always to an empty house. It all sounds very stressful. The girl is about the same age as Diana.'

'Yes, I saw that. But just as we think things are going to get easier, this comes along.'

'I know, but it isn't as if we wouldn't get money towards her keep, and she would be company for Diana.'

Margaret reached down to give Mary a pat on the shoulder. They were playing nicely and Diana was helping her sister with a jigsaw puzzle.

'Well, if you think it's OK, Marj, go ahead.'

Diana looked up.

'Daddy, you mustn't say, "OK." It's not good English. Mummy told me that.'

'Right, Diana. What your Mummy says goes, as far as I'm concerned. I find it always leads to a more peaceful life.'

Jack looked at his wife. 'Marj, if you think you can manage, go ahead and take the girl.'

'We'll manage. I'll write to the Billeting Officer and get it in the post straight away. There are so many problems in the cities with this war. It's a different life here in North Devon, even with all the food shortages.'

'Yes, but there's more going on than most of us know about, Marj.'

'What do you mean, Jack?'

'Oh, just that with people coming into the garage

from around the area, we get to hear things that we wouldn't otherwise hear.'

'What sort of things?'

'There's a lot of huts being built outside Braunton – Nissen huts – and various vehicles delivering all sorts of stuff there: food, furniture, bedding.'

'Bert in the bakery says that some American troops have been seen around for a while now, especially in the Woolacombe area.'

'But from what I've heard at the garage, the amount of building taking place is for lots of barracks. That's not for a few hundred troops is it? I hear all sorts of stories at work. When you piece them all together, it makes you wonder.'

'Well,' Margaret looked at him teasingly. 'And they say that women gossip.'

Jack looked thoughtful. 'There's something big going on. That's what I think. We just have to wait and see what it is.'

Chapter 26

'Hello, Granma.' Diana and Mary opened their grandparents' front door and ran into the house, followed by their mother.

'We're ready to go, Granma,' Diana shouted.

'We're ready, Ganma,' Mary shouted at the top of her voice.

Margaret held on to the girls' arms as they attempted to push their way into the kitchen.

'Now you two are not going anywhere if you don't calm down. You are lucky that Granma and Grampy are going to take you to Ilfracombe on the train but you have to behave yourselves. There will be other people on the train, other passengers, and they don't want to be near two rowdy, badly-behaved children. Now sit down at the table and wait quietly until Granma and Grampy are ready.'

Florrie was standing in front of the mirror adjusting her hat and securing it with a long hatpin.

'I won't be a minute, Margaret. You've done well to have Mary ready so early.'

'Yes, Mum, but why are you wearing that felt hat? It's going to be quite hot today.'

'Oh, I know but I don't feel dressed without my hat. And I like to have my hat pin at the ready.'

'Don't tell me, Mum. It's your lethal weapon in case anyone should attack you.'

'That's right dear. You never know.'

'Well, anyone trying to attack you would certainly know.' Margaret looked at the pointed end of the hatpin sticking out from the back of her mother's hat.

'We were up early because Jack wanted to make a start on decorating the middle bedroom. It looks really shabby and I want to put the evacuee in that room, sharing the double bed with Diana. Mary's still in our room in her cot. We may take in a lodger in the back bedroom.'

'Oh Margaret, don't overdo it. You'll wear yourself out.'

'Pot calling the kettle black, isn't it, Mum? I want to save up to put some money down to buy the house instead of renting it. Then when we do some work on the place, at least it would be to benefit us instead of the landlord. Anyway, where's Dad?'

'He walked over to the station to check the train timetable. He should be back any minute. I don't know why he didn't check it out before.'

'It was an excuse to get out of the house, Mum. He knows the train timetable like the back of his hand.' Margaret looked worried.

'By the way, don't forget I brought the push chair over last night. Where is it?'

'It's in the scullery, ready to take out the back way when we go,' Florrie replied.

'Mum, are you sure about taking them to Ilfracombe? It's a lot for you and Dad.'

The sound of someone coming downstairs at speed interrupted the conversation. The door was flung open and Bill hurried into the kitchen.

'Ready, Gran. What can I carry? Hello Maggie, hello girls. Aren't we lucky? We're going to see the sea.'

'We're going to see the sea,' Diana and Mary shouted back in unison.

'Oh, are you going with Mum and Dad, Bill?'

'Yes, I am. Gran said she and Gramps would treat me to the train ride. I'll be glad to help carry things. And,' he paused, 'I've never seen the sea.'

'That's wonderful to know you'll be helping out, Bill. I don't know how close to the sea you'll be able to get. Ilfracombe has a shingle beach. I know all the sandy beaches around the coast were mined, and recently, the mines and barbed wire have been removed. Honestly, with this war, it's difficult to know what's going on round here.'

'Well, it's a lot more peaceful than what has been happening in London,' Bill answered.

'And if we can't get to the beach, we can all enjoy the train ride. It is so pretty looking out of the window,' Florrie said.

The back door opened and Jim walked into the kitchen.

'Right. Is everybody ready?' he called out.

'Mum, I know you have some things to eat, but here's a little picnic, I've packed for you.'

'Thank you, dear. That's lovely. Now have we all got our raincoats, in case the weather changes?'

Jim groaned and looked at his wife knowingly.

'How many bloody bundles does that make then, Mother, for us to carry?' he asked, rolling his eyes heavenwards.

'We have to take everything, Jim, so stop worrying. Anyway, Bill's going to help, aren't you, love?'

'Glad to, Gran,' Bill answered, picking up two baskets packed with eats and drinks.

Jim didn't look convinced and went to check that he had turned off his wireless.

'Just make sure that we bring back the same number of bloody bundles that we take,' he went on, adjusting his cap and leading the way out of the back door.

'Oh, Dad, you'll enjoy it when you get on the train, I know you,' Margaret said, kissing Diana and Mary goodbye.

'Be good and help Granma, girls.' Margaret turned to go out to the front door.

'I'd better get back and pick up a paint brush,'

she said. The front and back doors closed simultaneously and the house was left empty and unlocked.

The walk to Barnstaple Junction Station took them about eight minutes. The train was standing on Platform One but they still had a few minutes before it left the station. They all got on, and with the pushchair folded up and baskets and bundles on the floor beside them, they prepared to look out of the windows, with Jim and the girls facing forward. There had been a good number of people on the platform when they arrived but all but a few latecomers had boarded the train when it let its whistle blast and gave out a great cloud of steam. Suddenly, two soldiers in uniform ran to the last open door, jumped on and slammed it shut. To the great excitement of Diana and Mary the train rolled out of the station and followed the tracks in the direction of the back of their own home at Signal Terrace. Jim pointed out of the right-hand window.

'Quick, girls, look! We're going to pass your back yard.'

'You can wave to your Mummy and Daddy,' Florrie said.

'There they are outside the back door,' pointed Diana.

'Hello, hello!' Mary shouted, banging on the

window as the train gathered speed and ran past Shapland and Petter and on to the iron, curved bridge that passed over the River Taw.

'There's the bridge I walk over to go to school,' Diana said. 'I have to hold on to the railings when it's windy so that I don't get blown into the road.'

'The wind blows from the estuary and there's nothing to stop it hitting you,' Jim explained.

'That's why I have my hatpin. I'd have lost many a hat without it. But we're slowing down now, girls.' Florrie adjusted her hatpin more securely.

'Are we there, Ganma?' Mary asked. Florrie laughed.

'No, dear. We've only just got on the train.'

Jim lifted Mary onto his lap and showed her the sign on the platform as the train stopped.

'This is Barnstaple Town Station, Mary. We're stopping here for more people to get on.'

'There's another station in Barnstaple, isn't there, Gramps,' asked Bill.

'Yes, Bill. There's Barnstaple Victoria Road, but that's a different line. You could have arrived in Barnstaple that way if you'd come from Paddington Station instead of Waterloo.'

'Ooh! We're off again,' Diana shouted.

The train gathered speed and they all looked out at the river, with grassy banks on its either side.

'The tide's coming up,' Jim observed.

'That's good. I don't like it when it's a long way out.' Florrie wiped her brow with her hanky and checked her hat.

'The river is broader now.' Bill had his nose pressed against the window.

'We'll stop at Wrafton and later at Braunton.' Jim shifted Mary onto the seat.

Florrie leaned across and lifted her granddaughter up and placed a large hanky under her feet.

'If she's standing on the seat, she'll make it dirty for anyone coming and sitting there later,' Florrie said. 'Keep a hold on her, Jim, in case she falls.'

The train stopped at Wrafton and a few more people boarded it. Were they all going to Ilfracombe, Bill wondered? And would he really get to see the sea?

There was a longer stop at Braunton.

'An extra engine will be put on the back to get us up the steep gradient later,' Jim explained.

On leaving the station at Braunton, the train crossed the road. Diana pointed to the crossing gates which had closed to stop the traffic.

'Those cars and vans have to wait for us,' she said.

Some soldiers had boarded the train at Braunton and one opened the door and came into the compartment.

'Do you mind if I join you folks?' he asked,

removing his cap.

'No. Please sit down.' Jim indicated the seat near him.

'We don't see your sort of uniform around here much,' Jim added. 'Are you American?'

'That's right. I'm stationed just outside Braunton but I've only been in your country a short while and I thought I'd like to see the sea while I have some time off.' He smiled and nodded at Florrie and Bill and winked at the girls. They smiled back.

'It must be hard being away from home,' Florrie said.

'It is but people here are very kind. My name's Andy.' He put his hand into his pocket and took out a small package.

'Would the children like a chocolate bar?' he asked. 'I hope it's not melted.' Florrie gasped. 'Chocolate? Diana, Mary, look! This kind gentleman is giving you some chocolate.' Florrie took it, unwrapped it and broke it in two. The girls looked at the chocolate in wonder.

'Thank you very much, sir,' Florrie said, as she handed the chocolate to the girls

'What do you say?'

'Thank you,' Diana said.

'Sank you very much, sir,' Mary said, biting into the chocolate.

The noise of the engines blocked out any

further conversation as they pulled and pushed the carriages up the steep gradient, the track curving and winding ever upwards towards their destination. There were thickly wooded slopes and green fields, and occasional places where the track had been cut into the rock face. On and up, the train laboured, with clouds of smoke emitting from its engines, front and back.

'I like the chuff-chuff noise it makes,' Diana shouted.

'Are we there yet, Gampy?' Mary asked, as Florrie leaned forward to wipe the chocolate off her face.

'Nearly there, Mary,' Jim answered. 'We can start getting our – bundles together.' He looked at what seemed to be enough luggage for a week instead of a day out. The adults gathered their belongings and stood up as the train pulled into Ilfracombe station.

'Allow me to carry out your stroller for you,' the American soldier offered, moving forward to pick up the push chair.

'Oh! Oh, yes,' Florrie stuttered, realising what he meant. 'The push chair. Thank you. That is kind of you.'

They all got off the train and stood on the platform.

'Right,' said Bill. 'Where's the beach?'

A railway porter overheard him and pointed to the exit sign.

'’Tis a fair walk down to the beach from Station Road, sir.'

'And it'll sure be a longer one back,' said Andy.

They laughed and all set off together.

Chapter 27

'Well, what do you think, Jack?' Margaret stood back and looked at the walls of the middle bedroom, putting the wet sponge down on a sheet of newspaper on the floor.

'Different,' Jack replied.

Margaret frowned. He could be a man of few words, just when some enthusiasm was needed.

'Jack,' she said brusquely, 'it's a matter of doing what we can with what we can get in wartime. And with decorating, we can't get much.'

'No, dear. You've been very artistic.' He was good at thinking quickly on his feet and thought he'd better make an effort to see the positive side of things.

'Light green painted walls with a stippled pink effect overlaid onto them.' Margaret wiped her hands with a damp cloth. 'The pink will pick out the colour of the eiderdown the girls will have on their bed. It's clean and fresh anyway.'

'You mean Diana and the evacuee will sleep in here, don't you, Marj, not Diana and Mary?'

'Oh Jack, I did tell you. I didn't think you were listening to me when I was explaining that Mary can stay in our room with us a bit longer and the back bedroom will be free for a lodger; when we've painted it, that is.'

'Oh God. When are we doing that?'

'Not for a week or two. The evacuee girl will be coming soon. She's called Maureen and we'll settle her in first, although come to think of it, – ' Margaret paused, 'it might be easier to decorate the back room before she comes. It's only a small room and wouldn't take as long to do as this one.'

Jack let out a sigh. 'If you say so, dear. Why don't you go and make a cup of tea and I'll clear up here?'

'Good idea. Then we can move the bed and put the furniture back. I'll have to make up the bed for Diana. They should be home in about an hour so we will just be finished by then.' Margaret ran down the stairs and Jack could hear her singing as she prepared the tea. He wondered where she found her energy. She was a worker, there was no doubt about it. She didn't let the grass grow under her feet and was always thinking of the next step, which could be very exhausting at times. Still, where would he be without her? Florrie was the same. Always on the go. He finished clearing up the mess they'd made and gathered up the paints and cloths and the bucket of water and went downstairs.

'After we've had something to eat, I'll wash over the lino floor, and when it's dry we can move the bed and make it up. Good job we tied the curtains back. You did well not to get any paint on them, Jack,' Margaret smiled.

Praise indeed, Jack thought.

After an hour, they had eaten a light tea and finished work on the bedroom.

They had just fallen into their armchairs by the fireplace when the back door opened and in came Florrie and the girls.

'Hello. How was your day?' Margaret stood up, took the picnic baskets from her mother. and looked at the sunburnt faces of Diana and Mary.

'It was lovely, Mummy. Grampy bought us a bucket and spade each.'

Diana took them out of the shopping bag and handed one set to her sister.

'We digged lots of holes and the water filled the holes and we couldn't stop it and then we found some shells and then we did paddling, and it was fun.' Mary sat down on the floor.

'She must be tired out,' Florrie said. 'I know I am, but we've had a lovely day. The train ride was fun, wasn't it, girls?'

'Guess what?' Diana looked at her parents. 'There was a soldier on the train and he gave us some chocolate. He was very kind but he talked a bit funny.'

'An American soldier,' Florrie explained, 'and ever so nice and polite. He helped us with the push chair but he called it a "stroller". I didn't know what he was talking about at first. Do you know, we saw quite a number of soldiers in Ilfracombe in the same sort of uniform?'

'That's what I've been hearing from some of our customers at work,' Jack said thoughtfully.

'It was good that you could get on the beach, Ma. Shingle, isn't it?'

'Yes, with a lovely little pool when the tide goes out,' his mother-in-law replied.

'Were there many holidaymakers there, Mum?' Margaret asked.

'I think most of the people were locals, just out for the day. The train was quite busy. It's a tiring walk back up to the station but we were so glad to have Bill helping us.'

'He's a lovely boy, Mum, and so mature for his age. He'll have a lot to tell his mother when he writes.'

'It's a pleasure to have him stay with us, dear. Now, I must leave you.'

'Mum, thank you so much, and thank Dad and Bill for us. You must be tired out. We couldn't have painted the bedroom if you hadn't taken the children out for the day.'

'Oh! I forgot about that, Margaret. Can I have a look at what you've done?' Florrie didn't wait for an answer but opened the kitchen door and started to go up the stairs, followed by Diana and Mary.

'I want to see! Let me see!' Mary shouted.

'We can all see,' Margaret said. She and Jack followed the others upstairs and stood behind them as they looked at the newly decorated room.

'Oh, It's lovely, Margaret. I do like the colours. You've both done a lot of work in a short time.' Florrie looked at her son-in-law. 'Are you pleased with that?'

'It'll do,' Jack answered. She looked at her daughter and sighed.

'I think that means he's happy with it, Margaret.'

'I love it, Mummy.' Diana went and touched the pink stipples on the wall. 'And I like these little pink blobs, too.'

'Can I do some painting, Mummy?' Mary asked.

'Only in a painting book, Mary, and perhaps another day. What do you both say to Granma?'

The girls said their thank yous and they all went downstairs.

'Time to get ready for bed, girls. You can have a quick slice of bread and jam, a drink and a wash and then it's – '

'Up the apples and pears,' the sisters chanted together.

'They can't be very hungry, Margaret. They've been eating all day. I'm off now and I'll soon be going "up the apples and pears" myself. Goodnight everyone.'

'Goodnight, Mum,' Margaret shouted.

'Thank you, Ma,' Jack said, as he saw Florrie out the back door.

Margaret prepared some bread and jam for the girls and Jack gave them a drink.

'We've all had a very busy day,' she said to the girls, 'so we want you to behave nicely and get to bed as soon as you have finished your supper. It's too late for a story tonight but if you're very good, I'll tell you about a surprise. Diana, you'll sleep in the middle bedroom as usual but Daddy's opened the window because the fresh paint still smells. Mary, you'll be in your cot in our room.'

Ready for bed and in their nightclothes, Diana couldn't wait any longer for the surprise.

'What's the surprise, Mummy?' Diana asked.

'Is it chocolate?' Mary shouted.

'No. It's better than chocolate.' Margaret looked at Diana. 'You remember me telling you about the friends I've made who live in the country? Diana, you met Mrs. Webber when she was visiting her sister in Landkey.'

'Yes, that's when her sister kept giving me all those coconut cakes. Ugh! But Mrs. Webber lives on a farm doesn't she, Mummy?'

'Yes, that's right. Mr. and Mrs. Webber have a small farm near Swimbridge. We had a letter from them this morning. They've invited us to visit them next Saturday afternoon for tea and you will be able to see the animals.'

'Is that tomorrow, Mummy?' Mary asked.

'No, but it's quite soon and you may only go if you're very good because animals don't like noisy children around them.'

'I'm ready for bed now.' Diana looked sharply at her sister.

'Me too,' Mary nodded.

Chapter 28

'Morning, **Mrs. Webber.**' Graham, the postman for Sunnybank stood on the front step and handed over the post to Lil, who met him with a smile.

'Thank you, Graham. What a lot of post for us.'

'It's not all for you. Some of it's addressed to those evacuee boys living with you. There are two large envelopes, one for each boy, by the looks of it. I see there's a sort of crest on the envelopes. Looks quite posh to me.'

He started to walk back down the steps but paused on the bottom one and turned back in case there was any information forthcoming from Mrs. Webber about the contents. Lil studied the envelopes. The writing was florid and stylish but beautifully neat.

'Well, Graham, these be a mystery to me but they'm addressed to the boys, so I mustn't open 'em. Jimmy and Danny be up the shippon but they'll be back soon.'

Graham was disappointed not to discover more about the post he'd delivered. He liked to keep tabs on what went on in Swimbridge and beyond, and the details of his deliveries helped him to do that.

Until he knew something of the contents of the mysterious envelopes, he would count this delivery as a failure.

''Tis terrible 'ot,' said Lil wiping her forehead with the bottom of her pinny. 'Do 'ee think us'll get any rain? Us needs it, that's for sure. But us 'ave got some friends visitin' this afternoon.'

'It's not going to rain yet, Mrs Webber, but I think we may have thunder later,' Graham replied. He was also good at forecasting the weather, but to his great disappointment had not yet developed the art of seeing through envelopes. Sensing that she was not able to satisfy his curiosity, Lil said, 'I'm sure that Jimmy and Danny will want to tell 'ee what's in they envelopes when they sees 'ee.'

Graham waved cheerily and started back down the lane. Lil went into the kitchen and put the two envelopes on the table. She looked out of the window at the clear blue sky and thought that Margaret and her family would see Sunnybank at its best, even if they sweltered doing it. The start of the school holidays had been wet and the boys had spent a lot of time indoors. It wasn't easy to keep them occupied, and her own working days were often broken by sitting with them to play board games or do jigsaws. The good thing was that they loved being outside with Stan, helping and learning about the animals and the never-ending care that went with looking after them. She knew that Stan secretly enjoyed passing on his knowledge and found the young ones good listeners and good company. A farming life can be a lonely one.

The stomping of boots on the steps heralded their return.

'You two can smell food from far away. Where's Uncle?'

'He's just coming, Aunt,' Jimmy replied. The boys went to the scullery and washed their hands. 'We've been carrying fresh hay from the small shed to the shippon,' Jimmy said.

Stan came into the kitchen with a big smile on his face. He followed the boys into the scullery and washed his hands.

'What be you lookin' so pleased about then, Stan?' Lil strained the potatoes and replaced the lid on the saucepan.

'Jimmy and Danny be my little labourers. I don't know what I'd do without 'em. They be very special to me.' Stan sat down at the table.

'Well,' said Lil, picking up the envelopes and handing them to Jimmy and Danny, 'they be very special to somebody else.'

'Ooh look, Dan!' shouted Jimmy fingering the crest on his envelope. 'Have you got a fancy mark on your one?'

Stan leaned forward. 'I don't see that sort of

thing on my round, boys. Lil, get us a sharp knife to 'elp 'em open they envelopes. That's it. Give it yer. They'm sealed tight and they'm big.' He slit open each one and handed them back to the boys. Jimmy pulled out the contents of his. There was a letter and a picture. He looked at the picture first. It was of a huge stag, standing in the heather on a high hill.

'My, that be what I calls a stag,' said Stan in admiration. 'A red deer, like us sometimes sees round these parts. 'E's got all 'is points too,' Stan remarked indicating the animal's antlers.

'I've got a letter too!' shouted Jimmy.

'Who be it from, Jim, as if I couldn't guess,' Stan said with a smile and a wink at Lil. Danny looked at the picture of the stag as Jimmy started to read his letter, haltingly.

Dear Jimmy,

I have been thinking of you and your brother and hoping you are en – en – ' Jimmy paused and Lil looked over his shoulder.

'*En-joy-ing living on the farm.* Yes, go on then, Jimmy,' she said.

'*My sister painted this stag in water col – col – .'* He stopped and looked up at Lil.

'*Water colours.* They be special sort of paints. My, what a lovely picture. You can put it on your dressing table, Jimmy.' She took the letter and went on reading.

I am busy helping to manage the estate. There is a lot to do and my father is glad I am here to help. Thank you for your pictures and your letters. It was very kind of you to write to me. I will write to you again soon.
Keep safe and be good.

Your friend,
Hamish Macmillan.'

'Well, young Jimmy,' said Stan, you've got friends in 'igh places. Do 'ee 'ear that, Lil? An estate. They owns an estate.'

'My, Jimmy, you'm a lucky boy to get a letter like that. Wait till Mrs. Partridge and 'er 'usband sees that. They'm comin' 's afternoon.'

Danny took his letter and a picture out of the envelope and handed the letter to Lil. He gasped when he saw the picture. It was a painting of Flash, Mr. Macmillan's peregrine falcon.

'Ooh, Danny! What a bootiful painting. Stan, I think us should get two frames for they two paintings. Let's see what your letter says then, Danny. The little boy handed over the letter but moved closer to her to be able to look over her shoulder. Lil started to read.

'Dear Danny,

I hope you like this picture of your friend, Flash. My sister painted it for you. Flash likes to fly high over the mountains. You will see the little bells on his feet. They help me hear him when I can't see him.

When the war is over, I will invite you and Jimmy to come to stay for a holiday. Then you can see how my birds fly here in the Highlands.

Keep safe and be good.

Your friend,
Hamish Macmillan.'

Lil stopped reading and looked at her husband in amazement.

'I can't believe it, Stan. How kind of 'im to write to the boys and to send they lovely pictures.'

'He's a real gent, Lil, that's why. Not like the odd bloke livin' down Shallowford now, accordin' to Arthur. 'E's a book writer, so 'e says, and likes peace and quiet.'

'Well so did Mr. Macmillan like to be left alone.'

'Yes, but 'e was a good sort and 'ad manners. They'm as different as chalk from cheese.'

Lil collected the letters and the paintings and placed them carefully on the dresser. They settled down to have their dinner but Jimmy couldn't stop talking about the invitation that had been given to him and his brother.

'When is the war going to end then, Uncle?' he asked.

'If only us knew, Jim,' Stan replied.

'Only we wants to go to Scotland.'

Lil collected the dinner plates.

'And you wants to see your family,' Lil reminded him. 'You 'ad a lovely letter from your Mum on Tuesday. You can tell 'er all about Mr. Macmillan and your pictures when you writes to 'er, can't you, Jimmy?' She paused and picked up the individual junkets she had made for afters, and deliberately delayed handing them to the children. 'And you too, Danny.'

The boys looked longingly at the junkets and then at Lil and nodded. Stan looked up at his wife.

'Do I get one of they, then, Maid?' he asked jokingly. 'And where's the clotted cream to go on 'em?'

Lil placed the junkets in front of each of them and went to the dairy to fetch the cream. Hopeless, she thought to herself. 'Tis more like three children I be lookin' after.

When dinner was finished, Stan went out to the vegetable garden and the boys helped Lil clear up and prepare for the visitors. When all was tidied, Lil sat down in the armchair and closed her eyes. She always felt tired at this time of the day and could have easily nodded off.

'Boys, go down the bottom of the lane and meet 'em off the bus. They'll be 'ere soon and you can 'elp carry some bags up. The two children will be with 'em so you can all play together.'

Jimmy and Danny ran off down the lane and stood the other side of the gate to wait for the bus. It was very hot and airless. The sun was burning down and Stan stopped working on the vegetables and went back inside the house.

'Too 'ot for diggin' and weedin,' he said, taking off his cap and hanging it on the back of the door. He went to the scullery and pumped himself some water. The sound it made as it came gurgling up from the well was refreshing in itself. As it flowed from the tap, he filled a glass and drank it down in one go. There was nothing as good as their own well water. It was fresh and sweet and cold.

'Do 'ee want a glass of water, Lil?' he shouted.

Lil moved from from her chair and looked out of the window.

'No, us'll 'ave a cup of tea soon. They'm just getting' off the bus, I see.'

The visitors walked up the lane, with the boys and Diana in front, shouting and threatening the geese. Jack carried Mary, who was unsure about the geese but soon joined in the shouting, copying the boys with good effect. The geese beat a hasty retreat, turning and waddling away from the lane to the middle of the field. They had it to themselves as Stan had taken the cows into the shippon to shelter from the full heat of the sun.

'Hello Lil, hello Stan.' Margaret and the family walked into the kitchen.

'Come in and sit down. The children can sit on the floor can't 'em?' Lil asked.

'Course they can, Lil. This is Jack. I've told him so much about you and Stan.'

'And us 'ave heard so much about you, Jack,' Lil answered.

'Wonderful that you'm 'ome again, Jack, and all sorted,' Stan added.

'Thank you. It's good to meet you both,' Jack said, smiling at Lil and Stan.

'We didn't expect to see you indoors at this time of the afternoon, Stan,' Margaret commented.

''Tis too 'ot, Maggie, but I shall 'ave to milk the cows later and you can all come, an' me an' Jim an' Dan'll show 'ee round. Us'll give 'ee the grand tour, won't us, boys?'

He looked proudly at Jimmy and Danny. 'They'm my little 'elpers.'

'I know you can drink a cup of tea and there be some lemonade for the children, and us'll 'ave our "proper tea" later,' Lil promised.

'So, we're going to have our "improper tea" now,' Jack said with a straight face.

The adults laughed.

''Er's always talks about "proper tea,"' Stan explained.

'Well, this don't count. 'Tis just somethin' to keep us goin,' Lil said.

'After you've 'ad a drink and a little cake, children, you can all go out and look round. But first, Jimmy, while I be making a pot of tea, can 'ee show Mr. and Mrs. Partridge what you and Danny got in the post 's mornin?'

The boys were pleased with the 'oohs' and 'aahs' that came from the visitors as they looked at the letters and paintings sent to them from Scotland.

After they'd all had a drink Stan, Jimmy and Danny led Diana outside, followed by Jack, holding Mary's hand as they made their way to the shippon. Margaret stayed in the kitchen to be company for Lil.

'It's lovely and cool in here, Lil. These old cob houses are good for keeping the place cool in summer and warm in winter.'

'They be awful draughty though, Margaret. Us could drive a 'orse an' cart under the kitchen door.'

Stan, the boys and the guests stopped on their way to the shippon to look at the chickens and then the pigs. All the animals had names, which Diana liked. She wanted to know where the horse was. Surely there was a horse. Uncle Stan said that the horse was over the far field, part of which had been fenced off for growing potatoes. Uncle Stan said that horses make a terrible mess of a field, cutting it up with their hooves. He wasn't that keen on horses and preferred tractors but had had Bella for a long time. Diana looked a bit cross and disappointed not to see Bella. Jack told her she could probably see the horse next time she came.

They went into the shippon to meet the cows. Danny went and stood by Madam to comfort her. He knew she didn't like meeting new people and she started to swish her tail and stamp about.

' 'Tis a bit early, but I'm goin' to milk 'em now. 'Tis master 'ot and then us can settle 'em down,' Stan explained. 'Jimmy usually milks the middle one, an' I does the other two. Dan 'ere stands at the top end to keep 'em 'appy.'

Stan showed the visitors how he prepared the cows for milking, by cleaning their udders and lubricating their teats. He took the milking pail, sat on the stool and started milking Buttercup. Jimmy prepared Daisy in the same way and sat on a sawn-off log and started to milk her using a new milking pail that had been assigned especially to him.

'They're very good at it aren't they, Daddy? remarked Diana. 'It looks easy, but I bet it isn't easy to milk a cow,' she added.

'Milk is in a bottle,' Mary shouted. 'That's not real milk.'

Jack and Jimmy giggled and Stan smiled.

'Not at the beginnin', little maid. But 'tis in a bottle by the time you gets it.'

'It's good for them to know where the food comes from,' Jack remarked. 'I expect all this was a surprise to you two, wasn't it, Jimmy?'

Jimmy's head was nestled into Daisy's side as he splish-splashed the milk into the shiny new bucket. He turned his head to the side to be able to see Jack.

'We didn't know nuffink about the country when me and Dan came 'ere, but Uncle knows everyfink and he's passing it on to us, ain't 'e, Dan?'

Dan popped his head out from fussing over Madam to look along her body to the three people from the town. He smiled confidently but said nothing. Mary wanted to go outside so Diana held her hand and they went out into the sunlight.

'I want Mummy,' Mary said. Diana called out to her Father.

'I'm taking her back indoors, Daddy. She's T-I-R-E-D.'

'I'm not tired, Daddy,' Mary shouted. 'I'm hot.'

Jack stepped out of the door of the shippon and called out to the workers inside.

'Thank you, Stan and well-done boys. I'll take Mary back to the house now. Perhaps she'll have a little S-L-E-E-P.'

'I don't want to have a little sleep, Daddy,' Mary frowned.

He picked her up and she laid her head on his shoulder as he carried her towards the house. Her eyes were already starting to close.

Stan milked Madam and when he had finished he sent the boys off to play. He had to sort out the milk, reserving some of it for the house and then clean up, feed the cows with some fresh hay and leave them tied up inside, out of the sun.

'Where be you boys off to?' he asked them as they walked out into the sunlight.

'We're going to play in the quarry, Uncle.' It was one of their favourite places, where they could climb and make up games using some of the parts of old machinery that had been dumped there over the years.

'You mind, then. There be all sorts of things there not good for boys to play with. Us don't want any accidents, do us?'

'We'll be careful, Uncle,' Jimmy shouted, as they ran off.

'What be you doin,' Diana?' Stan started to give the cows some fresh hay.

'I'd like to help you and then go back indoors.' Diana replied.

'Good! Sensible girl, you be,' Stan said, smiling at her.

The quarry was situated up behind the shed which was between it and the shippon. Stan kept a supply of animal feed and some hay in the shed. It wasn't big enough to store much but it saved him a longer trip to the barn which was further away. They had carried some hay from the shed earlier in the day and there was still a trail of it on the ground showing the path they had taken to the shippon.

Jimmy and Danny ran to the quarry and started to climb over its rocky outcrops and look for 'buried treasure.'

'You never know what we'll find here, Dan,' Jimmy shouted. 'It's like after the Blitz when we could climb all over the stones and bricks and find bits of German shells and stuff.'

Danny frowned. Jimmy looked disappointed but thought of something else.

'Well, we won't find that sort of stuff but there's all sorts of other things. Look Dan! Help me lift this big bit of glass. Blimey! It's the front of a car. It's an old windscreen and it ain't broke, neither. If we carry it over by the back of the shed, we can make a den in the dip there.'

They struggled with the glass windscreen to the dip. It almost covered the cave-like hole in the ground but gave them enough room to squeeze in and get under it. Both boys clambered out again and Jimmy looked round.

'Here's an old bit of fencin', Dan. That'll make us a sort of door and we can make it cosy with puttin' down some of the hay what we dropped for a carpet. It'll be our very own hide-out, see?'

After some more fetching and arranging, the two boys had made a den. They squeezed in under the glass roof and kept low. Jimmy said that they were British soldiers ready to ambush a group of German ones.

After about five minutes they climbed out, almost overcome by the heat generated by the glass roof.

'We'll return to barracks, Dan and fight the Germans when it's not so 'ot.'

They turned towards the shed and suddenly both boys stopped. Jimmy sniffed the air and Danny looked behind him.

'I can smell smoke, Dan.' Jimmy shouted. 'There's somefink burning.'

A crackling sound came from the den and the loose hay burst into flames. As they stood in shock, the flames ran across the ground along the line of the hay that had been dropped earlier. It was like a river of orange chasing across the dry ground in the direction of the back of the shed and the shippon below.

'Dan. Quick! Go and get Uncle and I'll untie the cows and drive 'em into the field. Don't just stand there, Dan. Run and get help.'

The cows. Danny could only think about the cows and his precious Madam. He ran down the lane from the shed, past the shippon and the pig sty and on to the house. He rushed into the kitchen and saw everyone sitting around the table. All the faces looked up at his and he gasped for air.

Time stood still and suddenly he shouted, 'Fire! Fire! Help! Help! Cows! Help!'

Everyone came to life and Stan and Jack jumped up and started running out of the door and up towards the shippon. Margaret passed young Mary to Lil.

'Diana, you stay there and you too, Danny. Lil, have you any buckets? There are some up there I expect.'

'Yes, and a big iron water storage tank with a tap that they can draw from. I'll get 'ee another couple of buckets, Margaret, but be careful. The children'll be safe with me. But what's 'appened to Jimmy?' Danny started to go out the door.

'No, Danny,' Margaret shook her head and took the two buckets that Lil had brought from the scullery. 'Don't you worry. I'll fetch Jimmy.'

She hurried from the kitchen and down the steps, running along the path and up towards the smoke.

'Good! Us have got more buckets, Jack.' Stan signalled to Jimmy and they all formed a chain with

Margaret filling each bucket from the tank and passing it along the line from Jack and then to Stan, who threw the water over the wooden wall at the far end of the shippon. Jimmy ran out the back door and round the outside of the building with the empty bucket back to the tank for a refill.

'Where are the cows?' Margaret shouted to Jimmy as she ran the tap into the bucket.

'I untied them and led them out into the field. They was awful scared, especially Madam, cos she 'ad to wait till I got back from takin' out the others.'

'How's it going, Stan?' Jack shouted.

'Well, me feet is wet, Jack, and so is the back wall, so I reckon us 'as done the trick. Tell Maggie 'er can stop now, Jimmy.'

'Uncle, it's my fault. Me and Dan made a den and we 'ad a glass roof for it. The hay and the bits of dry grass caught alight and the fire ran down the hill so fast. I'm sorry, Uncle.'

'You used your 'aid and got the cows out first, Jim. And us was lucky that the shed didn't go up in flames. The door at the back of the shippon was fallin' apart and needed replacin' anyway.'

'But Uncle, how did you and Mr. and Mrs. P. know to come up 'ere?' Jimmy looked puzzled. 'I 'ad to ask Dan to run down to fetch you but after he'd gone, I thought, what's the good of that? 'E couldn't get the words out, could 'e?'

'Oh, but he did, Jimmy,' Jack said picking up a brush and sweeping the water out the back door. Margaret came in from outside.

'Yes, he made it very clear and he even wanted to come with me and help but Auntie Lil and I thought that wasn't a good idea.'

Stan looked around at the mess. 'Us can leave this now and go back to the 'ouse. You go on and I'll follow when I've checked the cows. They'm down the field with the geese, ain't 'em, Jim?'

'Yes, Uncle. Was that right to lead them there?'

'Oh yes, Jim. That was right. And thank you Jack and Maggie for comin' to 'elp. Us made a good team, didn't us?'

Stan walked out and down to the bottom field and the others made their way to the house. It was a good half an hour later before Stan returned to join them there. Jack and Margaret and the girls were wanting to go home but had missed the last bus. Jimmy and Danny were getting ready for bed, having washed off the grime of the day, and in Jimmy's case, the soot from the fire.

'There's no damage done to the boys, and Margaret and Jack be in one piece, Stan,' Lil said. 'What would us 'ave done without 'em?'

'You'm right, Lil. Us be very grateful.' He stood looking thoughtful, and turned to the door to look up at his gun on the hook above it.

'Is everything all right, Stan?' Margaret asked.

'Well, Daisy and Buttercup, they be back in the shippon, but Madam, 'er's still in the field, sittin' down. 'Er wouldn't stand up. 'Tis shock, see.'

'She was the last one Jimmy led out, and the smoke was up her end near the back door, isn't that right, Stan?' Jack remarked. Stan didn't answer but looked at Danny, who turned his big eyes on his brother.

Chapter 29

'I'm just waitin' for the egg to cook, Stan, then your breakfast be on the table.' Lil put the fried bread and a large slice of their own bacon on a plate and lifted the egg from the frying pan.

'I be ready for that, Maid, after the day us 'ad yesterday.' Stan picked up his knife and buttered a large slice of bread, as his fried breakfast was placed in front of him. Lil poured him a mug of tea and sat down to a bowl of porridge. She ladled a spoonful of honey onto it and topped it with a scoop of clotted cream. 'I should have waited up for 'ee last night, Stan. 'Twas good of 'ee to take Margaret and the family 'ome. The car didn't play up, I 'ope?'

'No. I don't know what Wilfred 'as done to it when 'e 'ad it but 'twas runnin' fine. I got 'ome late last night and was late milkin' 's mornin'.'

'That's what I was goin' to ask 'ee about, Stan. 'What's 'appened to Madam? I see your gun bain't there above the door.'

'That's just it, Lil.' He paused to take up another slice of bread to dip into his egg. Suddenly, they heard footsteps hurrying down the stairs. Jimmy came into the kitchen, still in his pyjamas and looking anxious.

'Has Dan 'ad 'is breakfast, Aunt? 'E's not in our room and 'is clothes are gone.'

'Is clothes gone, Jimmy? No, 'e's not been in 'ere. 'Ave you seen 'im, Stan?'

'I've just done the milkin', Jim, and 'e's not been up with me.'

'P'raps 'e's on the toilet. P'raps 'e be ill.'

Lil hurried outside and across the vegetable garden to the Elsan toilet. She came back into the kitchen, shaking her head.

Stan stood up and turned to Jimmy. 'Come on, Jim. Us 'll look up the quarry. I'll go on up there and you get dressed and come up when you'm ready.' He put on his boots and hurried out. Lil went outside the front door and stood on the top step.

'Danny! Danny!' she shouted. Silence. She was suddenly very aware of her own heart beating fast as a feeling of panic took hold of her. Where was he? She would search the house and started running through the rooms downstairs, rooms that were rarely used. Sunnybank was a house of two halves, with each half mirroring the other. Lil and Stan lived in the eastern half and used the western half as a storage facility. It was a large Devon long house and it was difficult enough to heat one half in cold weather, let alone the whole building. Lil made her way through the downstairs rooms on the west side and then went up the stairs to the rooms above. She knew the boys liked to hide around the house, both inside and out, so perhaps Danny was playing some sort of game. That was only a passing thought. She felt, she knew, that he wasn't anywhere in the farmhouse. Jimmy came running down the stairs as Lil returned to the kitchen. At the same time, Stan appeared on the steps outside. 'No sign of 'im,' he said.

They were all still for a moment then Jimmy looked up at Stan. ''E was very upset last night, Uncle. It was the fire, and 'e kept goin' on about Madam. 'E wouldn' go to sleep. 'E said that it was our fault and that 'e'd killed Madam. I tried talkin' to 'im but 'e kept cryin' and then 'e fell asleep.'

'Poor little boy,' Lil said. 'Now, us 'as all got to keep calm and think where 'e's to.'

Jimmy looked at Stan and said, 'Uncle, it sounds funny but I fink I know where 'e might be.'

'Well, Jim, us welcomes any ideas, don't us, Lil?'

''E's gone to Mr. Macmillan's cottage, near Shallowford.'

Lil frowned. 'Why would 'n do that, Jimmy?'

'Dan loved that bird and 'e loved the visit we 'ad at Mr. Macmillan's 'ome. 'E's always on about goin' back there even when I tells him that Mr. Macmillan don't live there anymore. 'E just won't believe it.'

Stan looked at Lil. 'That's because 'e don't want to.'

'But surely, 'e can't 'ave walked there. 'Tis too far.' She looked at Stan.

''E's a clever little lad. I knows 'ow 'e's got there. 'E's gone on the milk lorry. It stops at the bottom of our lane to pick up our churn. Young Danny 'as jumped on the back and 'idden behind they churns. 'Twill be a noisy ride but the lorry goes into East Buckland and on towards Shallowford and Filleigh.'

'That's where 'e'll jump off, Uncle, at Shallowford.' Jimmy looked questioningly at Stan.

'Us'll go in the car, Jim, an' us'll fetch 'im back.'

'Stan, Jimmy 'asn't 'ad no breakfast yet. Let me just go an' make 'im a sandwich to take.' Lil hurried back into the kitchen and started cutting slices of bread off the loaf.

'Come as soon as you can, Jim. I'll start the car.' Stan set off walking down to the garage. Lil handed Jimmy a glass of milk. 'Drink that, Jimmy or you'll 'ave nothing in your stomach; and 'ere's some bread and butter to keep 'e goin'. I don't like the look of the weather. 'Tis still very 'ot but the sky is gettin' dark. Take your coat an' Danny's.'

'Thanks, Aunt. We'll bring 'im back, me an' Uncle. Don't worry.' He ran down the lane as Stan started the car and jumped into the front seat. Once they had left Sunnybank, the car trundled slowly up the hill in the direction of West Buckland. Stan suddenly turned to the right, taking a short cut along a narrow, muddy lane, to save time. After about ten minutes they started to go down over Deer Park Hill, and shortly after arrived at the gated entrance to the lane leading to the cottage beyond Shallowford. Stan stopped the car and got out. He looked at the gate, which was shut but had been unfastened. Perhaps someone had been through recently, as the padlock was on the grassy mound nearby. He made a mental note to ask Arthur more about that, and about the tenant who had replaced Mr. Macmillan. Stan wiped his brow with his sleeve. It was very hot and airless. There wasn't a wisp of a breeze, and suddenly there was a rumble of thunder. He looked up at the sky. It was slate grey. It didn't even take a countryman like himself to know that there would be a downpour very soon. With no compunction, he opened the gate, got into the car and drove through and along the rough unmade road towards Hideaway Cottage in search of Danny. There was another rumble of thunder, longer and louder this time. Jimmy looked out of the window, which was steaming up, as large drops of rain started to hit the front windscreen.

'Not far now, Jim,' Stan said, while silently praying that they would soon find Danny, safe and sound.

The lane was rutted and they felt every bump. The cottage came into view, just as another burst of thunder, followed almost immediately by a flash of lightning shook them both. The rain started with a vengeance, coming down in sheets to make up for the long, hot dry spell that had gone before, as if to say, 'You farmers wanted rain. Now you've got it!'

'Look, it's Dan,' Jimmy shouted pointing ahead of him, as a small boy came running towards them waving his arms. They could hardly see out of the windscreen now as the day almost turned into night. Stan stopped the car, jumped out and grabbed Danny, and pushed him in behind the driver's seat, and got back in himself. The little boy was soaking wet and shivering.

'Pass 'im 'is coat, Jim,' Stan shouted as he tried to work out where he could turn the car. There was nowhere. He would have to drive on to the cottage and turn there. It wasn't far, but he could hardly see out of the window. Jimmy kept trying to wipe the inside of it with a cloth he had found on the floor by his feet.

Just as Stan found a turning place, the front door of the cottage opened and a man appeared with a fierce looking dog, which kept barking at the uninvited guests. The noise of the storm drowned out most of the shouting and barking from the occupants of the cottage, but it was obvious by the gesticulations of the man that unknown visitors would be promptly seen off. He turned to go back inside as Stan drove away up the lane.

It was not an easy journey back to Sunnybank. Danny tried to dry himself with the cloth that Jimmy had used to wipe the windscreen. The boys put on their coats and the rain continued to pour down, hitting the windows of the little car with a noise that almost drowned out the sound of their speech.

'Why did you go there, Dan?' Jimmy shouted to his brother. 'I told you that Mr. Macmillan had gone to Scotland to 'elp 'is Dad on the estate.'

'I wanted 'im to be there, see, Jim?'

'It's not what you want though, Dan, is it? He can still be our friend even if 'e's in Scotland.'

'But it's not the same, Jim.'

'Fings change, Dan. Look at us 'ere with Uncle and Aunt, all 'cos of the war an' that 'orrible 'itler bloke. But we likes it 'ere with Uncle and Aunt, don't we?'

'Yes, I know, but then there's what 'appened last night. There's Madam.' He started crying quietly as Stan turned into the lane and drove up to the garage. The rain had abated somewhat as the boys got out of the car and started to hurry up to the house.

'Stop a minute, boys!' shouted Stan as he walked behind them. 'I want to show 'ee somethin'. Follow me.'

They all walked on up the lane and Stan turned towards the shippon.

'I've got somethin' I want 'ee to see.'

The rain had almost stopped as Stan opened the door of the shippon. All three cows were standing munching quietly on some hay from the rack above them. Jimmy and Danny both gasped as they looked at Madam, relaxed and content, with a scarf belonging to Danny tied loosely around her neck.

Chapter 30

Margaret collected a tray of buns from the bakery and began to lay them out in the window. Now that she wasn't working so much, she was never quite sure where Bert would want her; the bakery, the shop or driving the delivery van. It made the job interesting but unpredictable. Bert came into the shop carrying a tray of loaves and started to stack the bread on the shelves.

'Thanks for coming in half an hour earlier today, Maggie.'

'That's all right, Bert,' she said and carried the two empty trays back into the bakehouse. She returned with a batch of fairy cakes and laid them out on the window shelf. Bert checked the float in the till and looked up at the clock. There was still ten minutes to opening time so they were well ahead, but the early birds were already gathering outside the shop door.

'You're very quiet today, Maggie,' he said, stopping to look hard at her while she put on her apron and adjusted her cap. 'Anything wrong?' He stopped what he was doing and leant against the counter, looking directly at her with the unblinking stare he used when confronted with a problem.

'No, not really,' Margaret said, uncertainly.

He continued to stare at her so she took a deep breath and sighed.

'Well, I'm worried about Jack, you see.'

'Why, he's not ill again is he?' Bert frowned.

'No, it's not that. He's been asked to go onto full-time work.'

'That's good, isn't it, Maggie? That's what you wanted, and now that you've cut your time back here – ' He took a deep breath and stood up straight, as if he were about to make a speech.

'You've been a great help here in this business. You're a clever girl and can turn your hand to anything. You could run this place with both hands tied behind your back, Maggie, I know that.' Bert paused and got his emotions under control.

'I'm grateful for all you've taught me, Bert, and you are over-estimating my ability. I know you've had to make changes to let me work less, and now that Jack will be working more -' Her voice petered out and she sighed. 'The thing is that Jack never told the firm that he couldn't drive. When he went for the interview, he wasn't asked about that. They must have assumed that he could drive, but what with being ill and being away at Hawkmoor for so long, he never learnt. He can ride a motor bike because he had one when he was younger.' She looked at Bert and shrugged her shoulders. 'I don't know what we can do.'

'Well, I do.' Bert put his hand on Maggie's shoulder and looked at her with one of his determined expressions.

'You're going to teach him, Maggie. You're going to teach him to drive. Look how quickly you learnt?'

She stepped back and drew a short breath. 'Me teach Jack to drive? With what, Bert?'

'You can use the van. When you finish on Friday and drive it back here, you can go to a quiet area outside of town and let him have a go there.'

'But what about the petrol we'll be using?'

'You won't use much just petering about, will you, and if you can learn to drive in a quarter of an hour, surely Jack can get it sorted in an hour. You can start this Friday after work.'

'Are you sure, Bert?'

'I wouldn't offer if I wasn't, would I, Maggie? There is one good thing, though.' He looked at Margaret with a straight face. 'He won't need to sit on a cushion.'

They both laughed and Margaret looked up at the clock.

'It's nearly time to open the shop, Bert. Doreen's always here by now. I hope she's all right,' Margaret said.

'I had a message from her Aunt last night to say she'd had a slight accident but would be in later this morning. It's busier now that we're well into August, and with today being Wednesday and early closing there'll be a lot of folks in the town, so I hope she won't be long.'

'An accident?' Margaret wondered what could have happened. Doreen was a sweet young thing but inclined to be flighty. She had a good manner with the customers and they liked her. Many of them were fascinated by the way she followed the fashion trends, not that much of her clothes or her ever-changing hair styles could be seen under the shop's uniform. Bert was a stickler for presenting a professional image to the customer. As he often said, 'The customer is always right, even when she's wrong.'

Bert went back to the bakehouse and Margaret unlocked the shop door. The first hour she was on her own and very busy, but then there was a short lull and she had time to sort out the shelves and replenish what had been sold. It was getting hot in the shop so she decided to leave the door open. At that moment, Doreen appeared, with a scarf over her head and partly covering her face.

'Oh, Doreen,' Margaret said. 'How are you?'

'Stupid, I suppose you could say, Maggie,' Doreen replied removing her headscarf.

Margaret gasped on seeing the black eye, almost hidden by the Veronica Lake hairstyle that Doreen had adopted recently.

'No wonder they call this hairstyle "peek a boo," Maggie. It's supposed to cover one eye and I walked into the bloody door in our kitchen. I should have tied my hair back. I don't suppose film stars have to go to the kitchen cupboard to get out the saucepan for the spuds. Veronica Lake has someone to do that for her, I expect.'

Doreen started to tie her beautiful thick hair back and to put on her cap and apron.

'You poor girl.' Margaret fastened Doreen's apron at the back. 'What a shiner! Have you put anything on your eye?'

'Just a cold flannel, but it really hurts. Course, you're supposed to put a piece of rump steak on it, so that's a laugh. If I had a piece of rump steak I'd put it in my stomach.'

'It'll soon fade, Doreen, and I'm sure hardly anyone will even notice it.' Margaret reassured her colleague as four customers came into the shop. The first was Mrs. Carter, who looked long and hard at Doreen while noisily sucking in her breath.

'Ooh! That must hurt, dear. How did you do it? A tin loaf and four buns, please. Look what this poor girl has done to herself.' Mrs. Carter turned around to alert the rest of the customers to Doreen's injury. Further expressions of sympathy ensued as bread and cakes were exchanged for money across the counter. Shaking their heads and chattering amongst themselves, the customers left the shop.

'What did you say, Maggie? No-one will notice? I may as well be in a bleeding zoo!'

The morning passed quickly and the shop door was locked at one o'clock. After the staff had cleared up and Margaret was ready to go home, Bert reminded her about his offer. He had allowed Doreen to leave early as she had been struggling with a headache.

'Thanks again, Bert,' Margaret said. 'I hope I can manage to teach him to drive.'

'Oh, you can do that, Maggie. Mind you, when I taught my wife to drive, the air was so blue that she didn't speak to me for three days!'

'Well, it could be the other way round with us. Jack is so patient but I've got a very short fuse.'

'Good luck to Jack then, Maggie, that's all I can say.'

Margaret left the shop and hurried home. She had to be ready for when Mrs. Ellington-Smythe called with the evacuee.

Chapter 31

'Oh, my goodness!' Lil said, as Jimmy and Danny came into the kitchen and emptied their baskets of runner beans that they had just picked onto the kitchen table.

'When us 'ave trimmed 'em, there should be over three pounds of beans.'

'We can't eat all of them, Aunt.' Jimmy picked up the longest one from the pile.

'No, but I'll make runner bean chutney with what us don't eat,' Lil said. 'I've been saving up the sugar ration for the recipe. Well done, boys!'

'Do you want us to pick some more, Aunt?' Danny asked, picking up his basket and intending to return to the vegetable garden.

'Only if they'm as good as these. Leave the small ones to grow longer. You can 'elp me get these beans ready to make the chutney. I'll do that after dinner but Danny, 'ere's a knife for you to take off their tops and bottoms. I'll take off the sides 'cos they bits be too tough, and Jimmy, you can chop 'em up into little pieces about 'alf inch long. I'll get 'ee a wooden choppin' board each and a knife for you, Jimmy. Be careful though, boys. My knives be sharp. I sharpens 'em on the front step.'

The little team started to work away in silence until Danny said, 'Ain't it peaceful? You can hear the birds singing outside. It used to be like that at Mr. Macmillan's cottage. That's why I liked it there.'

' 'Tis still like it there though, Danny, surely?' Lil looked up from peeling the sides of the beans.

'No, Aunt. It's not the same.'

'But Dan, there was a thunder storm when you was there and so it wasn't going' to be quiet.' Jimmy placed two beans down on the chopping board and sliced them into half inch pieces. 'Look Aunt,' he said proudly. 'Mass production.'

'You mind that knife, Jimmy. You'm doin' well but us wants you to 'ave all your fingers when you'm finished.' She looked at Danny, who had put down his knife and was looking wistfully out of the window.

'What is it, Danny?' Lil asked him.

'It was creepy there. There was a loud noise all the time when I got near the cottage.'

'I told you, Dan. It was the thunder. And the rain was pourin' down. Look how wet you got.' Jimmy took three beans to see if his knife would cut across all of them to make the job quicker. He wondered how many he could cut across in one go. Danny looked at his brother.

'Yes, but it was another sort of noise, Jimmy. And then that man came to the door and started shouting and then the dog came and started barking and I was scared he would set it loose on me. And all the time that noise went on, and the thunder and the barking went on. I just wanted Mr. Macmillan to be there and I wanted it to be like it was before.' Danny paused and broke the top off an extra-long runner bean with his fingers. 'Why did he have to go away?' Danny sniffed.

'You know why, Danny,' Lil said. 'E 'ad to go back up 'ome to Scotland to 'elp 'is father, but 'e's still your friend. You 'ave to believe that. You do, don't you, Jimmy?'

Jimmy was busy seeing if he could cut through all four runner beans. The knife was really sharp and he didn't want it to slip. He'd lined them up very straight like soldiers at attention. Outside, Bruce had started barking.

'It's Uncle back early,' Lil said, as she started to clear the table. 'We've just finished anyway. What a good job you've done, boys. You two must be gettin' 'ungry. Why don't you go an' play until I've got the dinner ready?'

'What's for dinner, Aunt?' Jimmy asked.

'Some of the ham I cooked yesterday with teddies and runner beans.'

With shouts of joy, the boys ran off outside and down to the stream at the bottom of the lane. Stan came into the kitchen and sat down in his usual seat at the top end of the bench.

'You'm never as early back as this, Stan,' Lil shouted from the scullery while pumping him a cold glass of water. She put the potatoes on to boil and put some of the runner beans in a saucepan, then sat down next to Stan in the kitchen, handing him the water.

'Not much post today. Maybe a holdup somewhere and then us'll 'ave a mountain of it later.'

'Well, we've 'ad some post, Stan,' Lil said, handing over a letter for him to read.

' 'Tis from the boys' mother. 'Er wonders if 'er could come and visit 'er lads next week, bein' that she 'as time off at the factory. 'Er said 'er will find somewhere nearby to stay, but us can't let 'er do that, can us? Poor thing. 'Er can stay 'ere and then 'er can see 'er boys all the time.'

'Lil, why did 'ee give me this yer letter to read if you was goin' to tell me what was in 'un?'

'I didn't tell Jimmy an' Danny that us 'ave 'ad a letter from their mother. I thought us should talk about it first.' She looked at her husband and smiled.

'Us 'ave got cold ham for dinner and those second early teddies what you've grown, Stan. The boys 'as picked so many runner beans and 'ave 'elped me get 'em ready. After us 'ave eaten, I be goin' to make 'ee some runner bean chutney with the rest of 'em.'

'Well,' Stan said slowly, 'if that's supposed to be bribery, it's worked. Course 'er must stay 'ere, Maid. Write back an' tell 'er and then us can talk to the boys later. I'd better go an' change then take the old Major 'is dinner, so keep mine 'ot till I gets back.' He stood up and walked towards the door.

'Stan, before you go, young Danny 'as got something on 'is mind about Hideaway Cottage. While we was doin' the beans' 'e kept goin' on about the noise 'e 'eard there and about the man shoutin' at 'im an' scarin' 'im with 'is dog. 'Tis all a bit strange. Mind you, Danny be very imaginative so maybe us should just take what 'e tells us with a pinch of salt.'

Stan stopped and turned round. 'Or maybe not,' he answered looking at Lil. 'I saw Arthur as I was about to come 'ome and 'e's very interested in what's goin' on at that cottage. 'E's got some idea of goin' there an' 'avin' a mooch round when the tenant be away.'

'You'm not getting' involved with that, be 'ee, Stan?'

'I shall 'ave to think about it,' Stan replied as he went upstairs to change out of his uniform. Lil sighed and went to prepare the dinner.

Twenty minutes later and with Major Philips'

dinner securely packed in the carrier on his bike, Stan walked to the bottom of the lane, taking care not to push the tyres over any large stones in the path. The short cycle ride to the stone-built house was along a narrow road made even narrower by the lush green hedges on either side, as the August vegetation went into overdrive. August was Stan's least favourite month. Although winter made farming life difficult at times, he liked the rest that nature took before spring came with its delicate flowers of yellow and gold peeping through the short grass in the hedgerows. Then came the tiny violets and bluebells, and later the tall stately foxgloves in the woods, standing watchful and waiting for summer to close them down. Early summer was fresh and autumn was a final blaze of orange and bronze goodbyes, but August was over-spent and just too hot.

Stan got off his bike, lifted the dinner carefully out of the carrier and walked towards the back door. The porch walls were needing repairs and some of the stones had fallen to the ground. He carefully stepped round them and called out to his neighbour.

'Dinner's here, Major.' A strong voice called back at him.

'Come in. Come in, Stanley.' The Major got up from his chair by the side of the Aga and greeted

Stan with a broad smile.

'How kind of Mrs. Webber to prepare a meal for me. It has made such a difference. Please convey my appreciation to her.' He took the plate into the kitchen and placed it over a gently boiling pan of water and covered it with a saucepan lid.

'Sit down please, Stanley, if you have a moment.'

Stan sat in a smaller armchair opposite the Major, who had returned to his usual armchair by the Aga. Stan took off his cap and wiped his brow.

'Sorry if it's rather warm in here, Stanley but I never let the Aga out. This room is due north and is fine most of the year but this hot spell makes it rather less comfortable. I never fiddle with the Aga controls. A very good man comes from Landkey and services it once a year and it's more than my life is worth to touch anything other than being allowed to throw logs on it to keep the fire burning and allow it to go out when I know that the engineer is coming.'

'You'm kept warm in winter then, Major, which is a good thing.'

'Indeed, and that is especially helpful for my arthritis. But tell me, Stanley, how are you managing with your evacuee boys? What about the little one who wasn't talking?'

''E's got 'is voice back now. Us 'ad a bit of a fire up by the shippon and 'twas the shock what got 'im 'is voice back. The two boys be a great 'elp to me about the place and they'm 'appy as can be.'

'I hope there wasn't too much damage done. Did the cow shed get burnt?'

'No, only a bit by the back door but us 'ad friends with us at the time an' they 'elped us put the fire out.'

'The grass was very dry before that thunder storm, wasn't it? So, all is well now, then?' The Major looked closely at Stan and raised his eyebrows.

'Well sir, there be one thing I'd like your thoughts on.'

'Oh yes. How can I help?'

'Do 'ee mind the nice chap what lived down at Hideaway Cottage near Shallowford with 'is falcons? 'E's gone back up to Scotland now to 'elp 'is father on the estate.'

'Yes indeed. I met him a few times in Swimbridge when I frequented the pub there. He's a very good fellow and an expert at falconry. He was an advisor to a branch of the Ministry of Defence; something to do with messages carried by pigeons, which could be intercepted by peregrines.'

'You know more about 'im, Major but our evacuees 'ave been befriended by 'im and 'e even writes to 'em and sends 'em paintin's done by 'is sister. The boys be very fond of 'im.' Stan paused and wondered if he should express his concerns to the Major about the new tenant at Hideaway Cottage.

'That is good for the boys to have a friend like Hamish Macmillan. He's a fine man. But that's not what's bothering you is it, Stanley?'

'There's a new tenant in the cottage now and e's a bit – ' Stan paused. 'Well me an' Arthur, 'e's postman over Filleigh way, us thinks there's something funny goin' on, but us can't be sure. Arthur wants to wait till the tenant be out for the day, then go and look over the place.'

'Are you talking about Arthur Morris, Stanley?'

'That's 'e, Major. 'E came to North Devon only a few years ago from away. I don't know much about 'e really.'

'But I do, Stanley. His father was my batman in the last war. Good chap and skilled in unusual ways. We kept in touch for some years, then when I moved here for my retirement, we lost contact. It's a small world.'

'Arthur 'ave never said much about 'is family. 'Is parents be daid, I think. They was livin' in London and got bombed and Arthur met a West Country woman who was up that way 'elpin' 'er aunt. 'Er 'ouse 'ad some damage from the same bomb. Olive, the young woman was called, and she and Arthur started walkin' out together and both came down 'ere and got married. 'Er's a Filleigh maid, see.'

'Yes. Arthur's family is an unusual one, not exactly "run of the mill" as one might say.' Stanley waited for Major Philips to continue.

'They were circus performers, working mainly with animals, but all-rounders, I think. Arthur's father would sometimes entertain us Army chaps doing all sorts of tricks. He probably taught some of them to his son.'

'Workin' with animals, you said, Major?' Stan thought of the dog at Hideaway Cottage. Danny had said that it was about to be set upon him as he ran for safety in the storm.

'There be a fierce dog at the cottage, from what us knows, Major. Arthur's skills could come in 'andy if us goes investigatin'.'

'Tell me, Stanley, is this new tenant seen about much locally?'

'Arthur keeps watch on 'im an' says 'e goes off in 'is van once a week. 'E never 'as any post delivered to the cottage and buys 'is supplies somewhere else. There's one more thing, Major. Danny says when 'e was there lookin' for Mr. Macmillan there was a lot of noise goin' on all the time but us said that was 'cos there was a storm then. Danny won't 'ave it though. 'E keeps on about it. Me an' Arthur will 'ave to go an' 'ave a look round.'

Major Philips sat up straight and looked directly at Stan.

'Danny went to the Cottage after Hamish had moved out but when the new tenant was there?'

'That's right, Major, but that be another story.' Stan got up and started to take his leave.

'I don't like the sound of it, Stanley. Just be careful. I want to be able to see you again, all in one piece.' He smiled but there was a warning expression in his eyes.

Chapter 32

Jack was pleased that he had resurrected his push-bike. It was a quick way to get to and from the garage at Taw Vale, and he had only got wet once during the mostly dry August they had enjoyed. Both he and Margaret had birthdays in August, and Jack always joked that if he didn't get a present on the 15th Marj wouldn't get one on the 20th. Their present giving was modest, not just because of the war-time coupon restrictions but also because they were saving all they could to put towards a deposit to buy the house they were renting. They knew that the landlord was selling some of the houses he owned and that theirs might soon be one of them, so they wanted to be ready to act quickly as sitting tenants when the time came.

Diana had gone back to school to start the new year, accompanied by Maureen, their evacuee, who was in the same class. The two girls got on well together but when Diana was busy with her piano practising, Maureen often went to see Florrie and Jim, and usually spent time playing cards with Bill at weekends, or when he had a day off from his work at Shapland and Petters. Monopoly was their latest craze but that had to be played in the front room because the game went on for so long and they could leave it laid out undisturbed, to continue with on another day.

Life was settling down to a pattern and Jack was pleased with it. Rationing was a problem but thankfully Margaret was a good cook and a clever manager. She was a good driver too, but he wouldn't say that she was a good teacher. His driving lessons had been successful but lively, to say the least. They had two sessions on successive Fridays and Margaret had bought a little gift for Bert as a "thank you" for the loan of the van. Not that Jack had been asked to drive at work but perhaps that would crop up some day. At least he would be ready. Things felt very different around North Devon since the start of September. There were lots of soldiers about. Americans had arrived in vast numbers and were billeted all around the coast. They would come into the town and be seen in the shops and cinemas. There was something glamorous about them; their stylish uniforms, the way they spoke, their friendliness and the fact that they seemed to have an unending supply of chocolate and fruit which they dispatched generously to local children. It was no wonder that they were popular.

Jack got off his bike and wheeled it into the back of the store room at Hopgoods Garage. It was five minutes to eight. He put on his overall and went to the petrol pump. All was quiet but he could hear that a lot was going on in the workshop. Some of the men must have come in early. Mr. Hopgood came out of the office door and shouted to Jack.

'Morning, Bill. It's been rather a rocky start here this morning so you may have to spend your day differently.'

'What's happened, sir?' Jack asked. He often had to remind himself that he was known as Bill at work.

'With so much more traffic on the roads, and with some mad driving on our narrow lanes, there's bound to be more accidents. The Yanks drive their Jeeps about as if they never expect to meet anyone else coming the other way.'

'The lads are in early then, sir,' Jack answered indicating the workshop and raising his voice to talk over the banging noises coming from inside.

'That's just it, Bill. We have our regular customers and we have the results of the collisions I've just mentioned. We've got too much on really, and so I've asked Biscuits to come in and cover the pump sales and I want you to deliver a car to one of our regulars. We mustn't let them down. They're our bread and butter.'

'Deliver a car? You mean drive a car, sir?'

'Yes, Bill. It won't get there by itself and the owner lives in Woolacombe, so I want you to drive it there and then come back on the bus. The keys are in the office. Go steady. It's a nice car and hopefully we've made it look as good as new before it got hit by one of our Allies.'

Mr. Hopgood walked away and Jack took off his overall as Biscuits arrived to serve at the pump.

'Going to the seaside, I hear, Bill.' Biscuits shouted as he put on his overall.

'Yes, Biscuits, but there's no time for a paddle, I'm afraid.'

'We can't get near the sandy beaches these days anyway. The Yanks have taken them over and are having one hell of a time there. They've even made their headquarters at the Woolacombe Bay Hotel. Nice one!' He sounded envious.

'I don't suppose they're on holiday though, do you?' Jack started to walk away but his colleague hadn't finished moaning.

'They were late into this war, just like the last one, and now they've taken over our area and taken our girls. Dances in the town and at Braunton and Ilfracombe and all around. The local lads are pushed out. These Americans have got better uniforms than our blokes, and more glamour. I don't know where it's all going, do you, Bill?'

'Well, no, but we need as much help as we can get to win this war and we mustn't say no to any. I read that Italy has surrendered.'

'Maybe, Bill, but it's all a long way from being finished, isn't it?'

'I suppose you're right. See you soon.' Jack walked towards the office feeling anxious and slightly depressed. His colleague was certainly not in the best of moods and had dampened Jack's spirits somewhat.

'Morning, Alice. Mr. Hopgood wants me to take a car to Woolacombe.'

'Hello, Bill. Yes, that's right. It's Doctor Harding's Morris. It's parked at the back of the workshop. You'll want the details of where to take it. Do you know the Woolacombe area?'

'Only from the top of a bus, Alice. I could do with a map, if you have one.'

Alice reached up to a shelf behind her desk, pulled some maps down and quickly sorted through them.

'This should do it, but it's very easy to get there. You just go straight on from Rolle Street to Braunton and straight on again until you get to a turning to the left for Woolacombe. That's the only time you turn off the road, really.'

'So, I just have to keep on the straight and narrow then, Alice,' Jack smiled.

She laughed. 'You could say that, Bill. Give this envelope to Doctor Harding and here's some money for your bus fare back to Barnstaple. The doctor runs his practice from his home, so here's his address. When you reach the sea front, turn right and drive along the esplanade. His house is at the far end of it, a large rather forbidding stone one, and you can turn into the drive and park in front of the garage.'

'How has he managed without the car?' Jack asked.

'He's had the use of a friend's car, I think, another medical man who'd had to have time off because he fell trying to lob a branch off a tree in his garden.'

'Alice you are a fount of information. How do you know so much about Woolacombe?'

'Oh, I went there with Mr. H. the last time the car had a bit of a prang.'

Shaking his head in disbelief, Jack left the office and went to the back of the workshop to find the car.

It was good that the car was a Morris 8 and not unlike the van on which he'd been learning to drive. There was very little traffic on the road. He motored steadily, but with a few jerky moments at crossroads and a bad stall as he slowed down behind a tractor not far from Braunton. After leaving the village Jack was just beginning to feel comfortable when an American army car suddenly came towards him on his side of the road. There was little time to think, but he pulled on the steering wheel hard to the left and stopped suddenly in a gateway, lurching forward in his seat and hitting his head on the windscreen. The engine cut out and the army car sped past, swerving suddenly to the far side of the road. Jack got out of the car and looked behind him to see the vehicle disappearing at speed around the corner, the driver giving a friendly wave, which Jack took to be a sort of apology. He walked around the doctor's Morris 8 and to his relief, it was still in one piece and looking clean and smart, apart from a few blades of grass under the front left mudguard and a clod of earth stuck to the tyre. He cleaned up the mess, and rubbing his head and relieved to find no harm done to the car or himself, he checked the map and set off again on his journey.

At a crossroads at the top of the same long hill on which he had suddenly stopped, he turned left and motored steadily on through open countryside. After a while, he passed the Mortehoe train station on his left and then the road began a long descent towards Woolacombe. There was more traffic now but it was mostly military vehicles, American ones, so Jack drove slowly, at one point being overtaken on a blind corner by a Jeep. As he continued to drive carefully down the hill towards the village, he drew breath at the beauty of the sea view spread out before him. The sky had cleared, and in the distance the Welsh coast could be seen faintly, with Lundy Island sitting in a sea of blue and, in the foreground, frothy, white waves breaking on golden sand.

Jack forced himself to concentrate on where he was going. He passed some large houses on the right and motored slowly down to the seafront from where the sound of distant gunshots and heavy vehicles grinding their way up the beach could be heard. There were American soldiers everywhere, and as he turned right to drive along the esplanade, two American guards who appeared to be checking the comings and goings of unfamiliar vehicles, nodded and waved him on, seemingly recognising the doctor's Morris. He continued along the road and found the doctor's house exactly as Alice had described it to him. He drove through the wide front entrance, and with a sigh of relief, parked, got out, locked the car and walked up to the front door, which was open, and went into the building. He introduced himself to a grey-haired woman who was sitting at a desk in a room which looked out at the sea and cliffs. She greeted him with a friendly smile and asked him to sit down and wait to speak to Doctor Harding. There were a few patients sitting around the room but when the consulting room door opened and a man popped his head out, the receptionist pointed to Jack and he was immediately ushered in, ahead of everyone else, to see the doctor.

'Hello. I think you're Bill,' Doctor Harding said, indicating a chair to Jack.

'Mr. Hopgood telephoned me to say you'd be coming.' Doctor Harding sat down in his large leather chair facing his desk.

'Yes, Doctor. That's right. Here is an envelope for you and here are the keys.'

'I'm really glad to have my car back, I can tell you. My friend loaned me his car but needs it now that his ankle is better and he can drive again. You've probably encountered some exciting rally driving from our American friends?'

'Yes. I have to say I had a near miss when one of them came towards me on my side of the road,' Jack replied. 'No damage done, though.'

'Well done you, Bill. You must have quicker reactions than me.'

'Hopgoods Garage is some way from Woolacombe, Doctor Harding,' Jack commented.

'Yes, but it's so reliable, and as I have to be at the Infirmary in Barnstaple, once a week, it makes sense to have the car cared for there. Hopgoods is only a matter of two minutes' walk away from the infirmary. Now, Bill, please ask my secretary to make you a drink before you leave. I take it that you are returning on the bus?'

'That's right, Doctor, but I'm not sure where the bus stop is,' Jack answered.

'Just a few yards from here at the corner of the road, and fortunately there should be one in about twenty minutes.' Doctor Harding stood up and opened the door for Jack.

'Thank you, Doctor.' Jack smiled and left the room. His drink was already waiting for him at the reception desk. He sat down looking out at the glorious coastal view and enjoyed the cup of tea. To say that he was relieved to have delivered the car safely was an understatement but he did wonder how long it would be before it was back in the garage for more bodywork repairs.

After a pleasant journey back to Barnstaple on the bus, Jack spent the rest of the day helping out in the workshop before cycling home at six o'clock.

He wheeled his bike into the greenhouse and leaned it up against the cupboard by the wall before removing his bicycle clips and walking into the kitchen.

'Guess what, Daddy?' Diana shouted.

'No, I can't guess. I'm too tired. You'll have to tell me.' Jack sat down in his chair and looked up at Diana and Maureen.

'We're going to go the Saturday Morning Picture

Club, aren't we, Maureen?'

'Yes. Auntie Margaret said we could.'

'When's that then, girls?' Jack asked with a glint in his eyes.

Diana tutted and sighed dramatically.

'It's on Saturday morning, silly.'

'I should never have guessed,' Jack said jokingly

Chapter 33

Stan hid his bike behind a tree at the side of the lane where he had arranged to meet Arthur. The lane was rarely used but was only about half a mile from Arthur's home on the road between West Buckland and Filleigh. The autumn weather had been wet but much of the ground had dried up, the sun had come out, and some of the leaves were starting to turn colour. The air was still. They had chosen a perfect day to investigate. Stan looked up as he heard the crack of a twig. Arthur stood in front of him, with a bag on his back and a stout stick in one hand.

'Today's the day then, Arthur,' Stan stated, greeting his colleague.

'Yes, Stan. Our mystery man has been driving off in the van every Saturday for the last six weeks. He goes at about nine in the morning, and is never back until six or seven, so we should have plenty of time. I've been watching him from various vantage points. He's a canny so-and-so but he hasn't reckoned with me.'

Stan looked at Arthur and wondered what he had in his bag.

'You know I told 'ee about dear old Major Philips

livin' over by us, Arthur? Well, 'e said your father was 'is batman in the last war.'

They began walking towards the gate leading to the lane to Hideaway Cottage. It was padlocked but the two of them quickly climbed over it.

'Walk on the grass, Stan. We don't want to leave any trace of our footprints. Some of the track is still muddy.'

Arthur was silent for a minute then looked across at Stan as they walked on together side by side. 'Yes, I met the Major once or twice back when he used to go to Swimbridge and sit in the corner in the pub there. We got talking and realised what a small world it is. I had to tell him that my parents had died in one of the air raids on London in 1941. That night I was staying with my friend and his house wasn't touched, but ours was completely destroyed. My mother and father had no chance. I had no other relatives so my friend's parents took me in. I worked as a postman then, and one night I met Olive at a dance. She'd come up to London to take her widowed aunt back with her to live in North Devon. I moved here too and married Olive. That, as they say, was that. Meeting Major Philips seemed to tie it all together. He said he thought a lot of my father and wondered if I'd been taught any of his "tricks" as he called them.'

'And 'ave 'ee, Arthur? 'Ave 'ee been taught any

of 'is tricks?' Stan looked closely at his friend.

'We'll see, Stan. We'll soon find out.'

They walked on briskly in silence and after about twenty minutes saw the cottage come into view ahead of them. Almost at once there was the sound of frenzied barking.

'I'll soon stop that,' Arthur said, as he took his rucksack off his back and undid it. He took a package from it and then passed the bag to Stan. They approached the front of the cottage. There was no-one to be seen but the curtains were closed and the sound of barking had become more insistent. Arthur walked to the back of the cottage and Stan followed him, some way behind. There was a large compound, and the dog, a huge bull-mastiff, was inside looking very unwelcoming.

'Keep back, Stan and stay very still,' Arthur ordered.

The gate to the compound was not locked but securely fastened, and Arthur went up to it and bent down. Stan stood back and watched, hardly able to breathe. The dog ran over towards Arthur, who didn't look up but just kept staring at the ground and staying very still. It seemed to unnerve the dog and it became confused, no longer barking but looking around and pawing the ground. After a while, it came closer to the fence and Arthur, still crouching on the ground, slowly and calmly looked up at it. The dog stood perfectly still, looking at Arthur as if hypnotised, and Arthur slowly stood up and opened the gate and walked calmly inside. He held out his hand and pointed slowly to the ground, at which the dog sat down and extended its front legs, lying out-stretched and still. Arthur quietly undid the package he had taken out of his rucksack and offered it to the dog. The animal took it out of his hand and ate it and when it had finished, Arthur patted its head and murmured to it. The dog, totally relaxed, promptly laid down its head and went to sleep. Stan could hardly believe his eyes as Arthur came out of the compound and fastened the gate.

'Right, Stan,' he said. 'Now we can get on in peace.'

'Did your Father teach 'ee that, Arthur?' Stan asked, amazed.

'Yes, among other things,' Arthur replied.

They walked all around the cottage, hoping to see in through the windows but all the curtains were drawn.

'Let's look round the garden, Stan,' Arthur said.

'There be a good-sized shed down the end there, Arthur. That was where Mr. Macmillan kept 'is birds. Us saw it when 'e invited me and the boys 'ere.'

Stan stood still and thought for a moment.

'When this man moved in, didn't un 'ave a van an' a gurt big lorry to bring all 'is stuff? Why would that be if this yer cottage be furnished?'

Arthur looked at Stan and nodded, and they walked up to the shed. There was a window near the door but it had been blacked out.

'When us was yer it wadn't like that,' Stan said. 'There be another window, Arthur,' Stan pointed above them, 'but it be much 'igher up.'

The door was locked with a strong padlock. Arthur looked across at the woods just beyond the shed. There were some broken tree trunks with thick branches attached lying on the ground by one of the trees, and he walked over and started dragging a very large one towards the side of the building where the higher window was.

'You'm not gwain to climb up, be 'ee, Arthur?' Stan looked at his friend.

'Just to get a look, Stan, that's all. That window's not blacked out and will be letting some light in.'

The two men manoeuvred the tree trunk into place and Arthur started to clamber up it.

'Hold it steady, Stan, in case it rocks.' In no time, Arthur was balanced on one of the branches and was high enough to look in at the window.

'Coming down,' he shouted and jumped the last few feet to the ground, landing as light as a feather.

'What did 'ee do in the circus then, Arthur?' Stan

was beginning to enjoy himself. It had been a very entertaining outing so far.

'A bit of everything, Stan, and I had no fear in those days.'

'So, what did 'ee see in there?' Stan could hardly wait to know.

'I think it's some sort of printing machine, but I'll have to get inside to be sure,' Arthur said, taking his rucksack from Stan and searching in it. 'Ah, here we are.' He smiled as he took out a bunch of small metal gadgets.

'What be 'ee doin' of, Arthur?' Stan was starting to get worried. 'Be us gwain' to break the law an' bust in yer?'

'And what do you think this so-called 'distant relative' of Lord Fortescue is doing while he's living here? I'll bet the Estate Manager hasn't a clue what he's up to,' Arthur answered as he started to carefully pick at the lock on the door. Stan looked around. All was quiet except for the sound of the generator. There was no electricity supplied to much of the Estate, and Sunnybank was lit by Tilly Lamps at night, but Hideaway Cottage at least had power from a generator.

'That dog will be out for some time, Stan, so don't worry,' Arthur said, as he patiently worked on the lock. Suddenly, there was a faint 'click' and the padlock sprung open. Arthur pushed at the door and they walked inside. There was a large machine taking up most of the room, and shelves with paper stacked on them. There were cutting implements and bottles of dye and various boxes in tidy order on a table at the far end of the building.

'We have to leave everything in exactly the same place as we find it, Stan. He mustn't know we've been here,' Arthur ordered his friend while carefully examining some prints and rubber stamps.

'What be this for?' Stan asked, about to flick a switch near him.

'Don't touch it,' shouted Arthur. 'I think it starts the machine. It's a printing machine and I reckon he's printing coupons to sell on the black market.'

'So that be where 'e goes to every Saturday,' Stan said.

'Yes, he goes to pass them on. There's probably a big group of crooks involved elsewhere but the noise of a printing machine wouldn't disturb anyone hereabouts, would it? Very clever.'

'Only one person 'eard it. Young Danny, when 'e came 'ere lookin' for 'is friend who'd moved to Scotland.'

The two men looked at each other and were silent for a moment.

'Right Stan. We're going to look around and check that we haven't moved anything out of place. This chap is a clever bloke, whatever his name is.

We'll go out and lock up and make sure we don't leave any trace of our visit.'

'Us'll 'ave to move that tree trunk back into the woods and scuff over the ground where our footprints 'ave been. 'Tis very dry outside the buildin',' Stan remarked.

They went out into the sunlight and Arthur made sure that the door was padlocked, and everything was as it had been. After they had dragged the tree trunk back to where Arthur had found it, and checked that they had left no sign outside the building of their having been there, they started to walk back to the front of the cottage.

'I don't think we should leave by the way we came in, Stan,' Arthur warned, looking towards the approach to the cottage.

''E won't be back yet though, will un?' Stan said. 'Not from what you said.'

Arthur started walking towards the field up from the cottage which led to a tree plantation and on up over to West Buckland, avoiding the Filleigh route.

'I know what I said, Stan, but I've just got a feeling this bloke is a bit savvy and unpredictable. I don't trust him and think he could easily change his routine. Let's get going.'

They walked away from the lane from which they had approached the cottage and, after crossing the field, entered the plantation and were immediately hidden from view.

'What about the dog, Arthur?' Stan asked.

'He'll wake up soon. He just won't be very hungry, that's all.' Arthur grinned.

Suddenly there was the sound of a distant motor approaching from the lane below them. They were well hidden but both of them stopped and stood still, under cover of the trees. It was the tenant returning to the cottage.

They looked at each other and hurried on up through the woods.

'See what I mean, Stan?' Arthur found himself whispering. 'He's changed his routine today.'

''E be a crafty one, all right,' Stan answered.

'Yes,' Arthur said thoughtfully. 'We've got some information but we'll have to think this out carefully before we act on it, won't we?'

Reaching the top of the plantation, they climbed over a fence and on to the road at the top of the hill.

Chapter 34

'**Coo-ee!' Florrie sang** out as she entered the scullery from the green house.

'Hello, Mum. I'm in the kitchen, tidying up and setting the table for tea.'

'Where is everyone, Margaret?'

'They've gone with Jack over the park, thank goodness. I've got time for a cup of tea. Do you want one?'

'I never say no, do I?' replied Florrie, flopping down into one of the armchairs.

'Dad's out for a walk and Bill is meeting one of his mates from work, so it's peace, perfect peace,' Florrie said, stifling a yawn.

'Mum, you look tired out. Is that cleaning job at the vet's too much for you?'

'No, it's not hard work but I don't see how I can dust the huge mahogany table in the dining room.'

Margaret passed her mother a cup of tea and sat down in the armchair opposite her. 'Why's that, Mum?'

'Well, Mr. Cameron is mad on fishing and makes these funny flies with feathers and things and puts hooks on them. Then he leaves them spread out all over the table. There's not an inch between any of them and I don't see how I can dust there without sweeping them all into a cardboard box or something.'

'Oh, I shouldn't do that, Mum, and I shouldn't worry about it, either. I bet Mr. Cameron doesn't notice the dust but he would notice if you moved one of his precious flies, don't you think?'

'Yes, I suppose so, but you know I like to do a good job and it annoys me to have to leave that table untouched.' Florrie took a sip from her tea cup.

'Thanks for the tea, dear. I really came over to ask if you enjoyed the pictures on Friday evening. You know Maureen was over with us playing Monopoly with Bill in the front room. They'd have been there all night if I hadn't sent her home. I don't know why she didn't want to go with you, really.'

'Maureen's mad on playing cards and Monopoly. They even got Dad playing cards last week, you said.'

'Yes. That's was unusual but he quite enjoyed it. Course, he really likes going to the pub, Mugford's, and playing cribbage. He prefers that to cards.'

'Alan's the one for Monopoly, isn't he? I don't suppose you've heard any more from him, Mum?'

'Nothing since we showed you his last letter from Italy. I don't understand it. If the Italians have surrendered, why is the Eighth Army still there?'

'I suppose that's because the Germans are there.'

'That bloody Hitler wants to be in everyone else's country. I'd give him a piece of my mind if he tried to come here, I would!'

'Anyway, Mum,' her daughter said, quickly changing the subject, 'Jack got off early from work on Friday and we went to the first evening performance at the Gaumont to see a film about Lassie, you know that lovely dog, and now Diana wants a dog. That's not going to happen though, is it?'

'I should think not. She'll soon forget about that, won't she? I thought Jack didn't like going to the pictures.'

'He doesn't, but he got persuaded by Diana. He was all right for about half an hour and then he got the fidgets. It's never worth going with him, really. He doesn't like being "cooped up" as he calls it. Anyway, Mum, the thing I didn't have time to tell you about when we came back on Friday night was that as we came out of the cinema an American soldier came up and spoke to us. "Would your little girl like this banana?" he asked, right out of the blue. Course, Diana didn't know what it was. She'd never seen a banana. Anyway, we got talking and he was so friendly. I felt sorry for him, miles from home and in another country. I invited him to tea. He's coming today in about two hours' time. That's why we had an easy dinner today. It helped that Diana and Maureen walked up to St. Paul's Church to Sunday School this morning and Jack had Mary helping him do something with his bike in the green house. You can imagine the mess she got into but at least she enjoyed it and it gave me a chance to cook something for tea.'

'Oh crikey, Margaret, what are you going to give him to eat?'

'I asked him that and he said he would love to have one of our English breakfasts. That seems funny at tea-time but if that's what he wants, then that's what he'll get, rations permitting.'

'Where are you getting the food from, Margaret? I mean, bacon and eggs and things.' Florrie looked puzzled.

'Well I've still got some eggs that Lil gave me a while ago and I've saved our little bacon rations for him. Then I can do some fried bread and yesterday, I bought some laver in Butchers Row.'

'That's quite a feast then, Margaret. And so kind to welcome a young man who's away from his home.' Florrie took out her handkerchief and wiped her eyes.

'Oh Mum, don't cry.'

Florrie pulled herself together and blew her nose.

'It's just that I'd like to think that someone would

do that for my son, for your brother, that's all.' She dried her eyes. 'I'm just being soft. Take no notice, but tell me about the banana. Did you let Diana eat it when you got home?'

'Well, Mary was asleep as you know, and anyway a banana goes brown if it's not eaten right away so we couldn't keep any of it for her. We peeled it, which amazed Diana, and mashed it up and put it in two little bowls with a tiny sprinkling of sugar. I had saved some top of the milk the day before and had made a small amount of clotted cream. We put some on each dish and then we sat down to watch Diana and Maureen eat it. I wish I could have taken a photo. Their faces were a picture.'

'How lovely, Margaret. It's nice to hear good things happening, isn't it? But I must go and let you get on.' She stood up and took her cup and saucer into the scullery.

'I'll come over later and bring you a few scones Mum, if they've left any, that is.'

'Don't you worry. I hope it all goes well,' Florrie answered as she went out of the back door.

The rest of the afternoon sped by and Jack and the children returned from the park. There was a general cleaning up of the children's hands and faces in readiness for greeting their guest and Margaret gave them a small lecture on behaviour. At half past four there was a loud knock at the door.

Within five minutes the young American soldier was seated at the dining room table, answering the family's questions. He gave his name as Oliver D. Johnson, a Corporal in the Army. He was stationed just outside Braunton and it was the first time he had been out of his home country.

'Please call us Margaret and Jack, and may we call you Oliver?' Margaret asked the visitor.

'Pleased to know you, Ma'am, and thank you for inviting me into your home,' Oliver replied. 'And who are these young children?' he asked.

'These are Diana and Mary, our daughters and this is our lovely evacuee, Maureen. Say "Hello" to Corporal Johnson, girls.'

The three girls dutifully responded and the young visitor nodded and smiled at the children.

'America is a huge country, Oliver,' Jack said. 'Where do you live exactly?'

'I come from Boston, Massachusetts, Jack. That's a city in the North East. I can show it to you on an atlas, if you have one.'

'Jack, can you reach for that old atlas from the bottom of the bureau? Sorry, Oliver, we'll have to ask you to move from your chair. Our house isn't very spacious and it doesn't take many people to fill up a room.'

'No problem, Ma'am.' Oliver stood up while Jack found the atlas and passed it to him. The young man sat down again at the table and found the pages showing the United States.

'Here's the state of Massachusetts and here's the capital, Boston.' Oliver pointed to the city and to some other towns in the state. 'You'll see some familiar place names.'

'Oh yes,' Margaret said. 'There's a place called Plymouth.'

'And look girls,' Jack pointed to another town. 'Can you read what this town's called?' Diana and Maureen crowded over the page and Mary pushed her way in under her father's arm.

'Barnstable.' They both shouted. 'Barnstable' Mary echoed, not to be left out.

'Yes, but it's spelt wrong,' Diana commented.

'Yes,' Maureen said. That should be a 'p' not a 'b,' shouldn't it?'

'I guess so if you live here, but where I come from, we spell it with a 'b' at the end,' Oliver said with an apologetic smile. 'Gee, Margaret, these girls sure are smart, aren't they?'

They all laughed and Margaret asked their visitor to excuse her while she left the room to prepare some food for later.

'You may get down from the table and play in the other room until tea is ready, girls, but please look after Mary and see that she has something to play with too,' Margaret said.

'Do you have any brothers and sisters, Oliver?' Jack asked when he and their guest were alone together and his wife had disappeared into the scullery to cook a breakfast for tea.

'Why yes, I have one sister, two years younger than me. She's twenty and works as a librarian but really wants to study and become a teacher. My Mom and Dad are hoping she'll settle down to doing that after the war. But say, what do you do, Jack?' Oliver asked.

'I work at Hopgoods garage in the town. It's a small petrol station but deals mainly with vehicle maintenance and repairs.'

'I guess you're extra busy now that some of our guys are trying to get used to the narrow lanes and corners around here. There's some crazy driving but driving is not part of my work so I can claim to be innocent.' They both laughed.

'It's a beautiful area and the people are so friendly, and it's great to see the sea,' Oliver added.

'Well, feel free to come and visit us. You can call into the bakery in the High Street, where Marj works, or you can find me at the garage along by Rock Park. I'm known as Bill at work because there was already someone called Jack working there when I started.'

'That's real kind of you, Jack. Thank you.'

The kitchen door opened and Margaret entered

with plates of hot food.

'Jack, call the children in please and get them sitting up at the table. We've put an extra little table on the end for them but it's a bit of a squash, I'm afraid. Now Oliver, you said you'd like a cooked breakfast. I'm sorry it's at tea-time,' she smiled putting a large plate of food in front of their guest and one in front of Jack. Margaret went back and forth to the scullery to fetch more plates of food for the rest of them and finally they all sat down together around the two tables. Jack raised his eyebrows and looked sideways at his wife. Where did she get this lot from, he wondered? She never ceased to surprise him.

'This is really swell, Margaret,' Oliver said. 'It's great not to have to sit down to eat with a lot of noisy soldiers in the Mess.'

'Instead, you can sit down with a lot of noisy children here,' Jack said with a smile.

'Jack, don't start them off, please,' Margaret warned.

'Do begin, Oliver, and don't stand on ceremony here,' she went on, passing him the salt and pepper.

'Thank you so much,' he replied. 'Would you pass me the jam, please?'

Diana and Maureen looked up inquisitively, poised with their knives and forks in the air. Oliver removed some chewing gum from his mouth and parked it under the table. Mary put down her spoon and fork and looked at their guest curiously. All three girls were motionless as Oliver started to spread jam upon his fried bread. Margaret and Jack looked at each other but made no comment. Diana couldn't contain herself at the strange sight of someone spreading jam on fried bread and took a big breath while looking in fascination at their new friend.

'Mummy, can I try –' she tailed off as her mother passed the girls a plate of bread and butter.

'Diana, please get on with eating your tea and not chattering so much. Have some bread and butter.' Margaret locked eyes with the girls across the table with a warning glare. It was enough to result in all three girls reaching for a slice of bread and butter followed by a quiet "Thank you" from each of them.

'Oliver, have you ever had laver before? I've put some on the side of your plate. It's quite popular in our area but it's not to everyone's taste. It's seaweed really.'

'Urrgh,' Mary said but Diana and Maureen knew better than to make any comment.

'We have the same thing at home, but not everyone likes it as you say. But I think it's great.'

The meal continued comfortably and Margaret produced some Devonshire scones to finish it. She had made some more clotted cream, just enough to go round, and with a small dish of home-made strawberry jam it proved a great success. The children were excused from the table and the three adults chatted and enjoyed another pot of tea together.

'I will have to be leaving soon but I want to help you with the dishes,' Oliver said.

'Certainly not,' Margaret answered, 'but thank you for offering.'

They all stood up and Oliver produced a little parcel.

'There are four bars of chocolate, one for each of the children and one for you and Jack to share,' he said.

'How kind of you,' Margaret took the parcel, wrapped in brown paper and tied neatly with cord.

'I'll fetch the girls from the front room to thank you, Oliver.'

She called out to them and they came and stood at the doorway looking expectantly at their new friend.

'Oliver has brought some chocolate for you but we'd better keep it until tomorrow after the tea we've all eaten,' Jack said.

'What do you say?' Margaret got tired of prompting their gratitude but continued to do it anyway.

'Thank you,' they all replied while looking at the parcel.

'You're welcome. I'm sorry you can't get some of it over here. We're just lucky with our supplies,' Oliver said. 'What did you think of the banana?' he asked as he prepared to leave.

'It was lovely,' Diana answered, 'but first I thought we had to eat the yellow part.'

'I knew we had to peel it because I've seen one before in London but I never had one,' Maureen added.

'What's a nanana?' Mary asked, feeling she must have been missing something.

'I'll try to get you one, young lady,' Oliver answered, smiling. 'Now, I must be going. Thank you so much for having me, Margaret and Jack. I'll write tell my family how kind you've been.'

They all followed Oliver out to the front door when suddenly Diana shouted, 'You've forgotten something.' She ran back to the dining room table, removed the chewing gum from under it where Oliver had been sitting, returned to the front door and handed it to him ceremoniously. Oliver took it and shook his head.

'Thank you, Diana. You've found me out. That's a really bad habit of mine.'

He smiled and they all waved as he walked away.

Chapter 35

'Long time, no see,' called out Margaret as she walked into Lil's kitchen and placed her basket on the floor.

'Well you'm a stranger, Margaret. Good to see 'ee. Come an' sit down and I'll soon get 'ee some dinner.'

'May I have a glass of water please, Lil? I haven't done the round recently and I'd forgotten how much getting in and out of the van there is. I just didn't find time to have a drink today.'

'Course 'ee, can dear. Comin' right up.'

The friends hadn't seen each other for over four weeks so there was some catching up to do. Margaret enjoyed a plate of boiled ham, mashed potatoes and home-grown leeks, followed by blackberry and apple tart and custard.

'What a treat that was, Lil. I won't be able to eat anything for days. Have you been feeding all the other van drivers that Bert has sent on this round?'

'Of course, Margaret. Maurice has been a few times and another man. I can't remember 'is name but 'e was very nice and 'elped me get a bird out of the chimney while 'e was 'ere. I'd let the range out or us would have 'ad a cooked bird. Stan was workin' with the animals so I was glad of the help.'

'We've been busier than ever in the bakery since so many American soldiers have come to North Devon. It's good for business I suppose, because they come to buy things in the town when they have time off. We even had one young man come to tea with us. He was very nice and gave the children some chocolate. As far as work is concerned, sometimes Bert wants me serving in the shop, sometimes I'm cooking and then, like today, I'm out on the road delivering. I'm sorry I haven't seen you for so long. What's been happening?'

'Nothing changes much here, do it, Margaret, except the seasons and the sort of work us does because of 'em.'

'Yes, but I've been wanting to know how Danny is after he found his voice again.'

'Oh, 'e's fine. You'd never know 'e couldn't say a word when 'e came 'ere first. And 'is Mum was so pleased when 'er came to see 'er boys.'

'Their mother came to stay with you, Lil? How lovely!'

'Yes, 'er 'wrote to say 'er was 'avin' time off from work and could 'er stay somewhere nearby, so us said no, 'er could come and stay 'ere. The school 'ad 'alf term, or whatever they calls it, so the boys spent a lot of time with their mum. She told us that 'er stay 'ere 'ad put 'er mind at rest and she was glad to see Jimmy and Danny so 'appy.'

'And to hear Danny talking again, I expect. Is her husband doing all right?'

'Yes. She showed the boys a card from 'im so they was 'appy, an' they showed 'er what Mr. Macmillan sent 'em.'

'What did she make of that, Lil?'

''Er was amazed an' very proud to know the boys 'ad a good friend.'

'Lil, what about the new tenant at the cottage where the falconer used to live?'

Lil leaned forward across the table. 'You can ask, but from what I knows 'e's a mystery, livin' like a 'ermit.' Lil almost spat the word out. 'Stan knows more about 'n than 'e lets on, and 'e and Arthur over at Filleigh 'ave been in touch an' doin' what Stan calls "carryin' out investigations".'

'Whatever does that mean, Lil?'

'Don't you ask, Margaret, an' I be not allowed to ask. Stan won't say a word about it all, but there's somethin' funny goin' on, that's all I knows.'

'The cottage is quite isolated, isn't it? The postman must go there every day, and the tenant has to shop somewhere, doesn't he?' Margaret put down her tea cup and looked thoughtful.

'Yes, but where? An' the tenant is never seen locally in the village and – ' Lil paused dramatically,

' 'e never 'as 'is post delivered to 'is door, accordin' to Arthur. 'E should know cos 'e be the postman for Filleigh.'

'It sounds shady to me. Is Stan going to do anything about it?'

'Stan 'as told me to keep out of it, Margaret but 'e an' Arthur 'ave met up recently an' talked it over. That's all I know.'

'I should keep out of it then, Lil, and let it take its course. I'm sure it's nothing to worry about,' Margaret said, without feeling any conviction herself. 'The boys are not back from school yet. How are they liking it at Filleigh? This will be Jimmy's last year there, won't it?'

'No. 'E's got another year yet, then 'e'll go on to the big school in South Molton if the boys be still with us. P'raps the war will be over by then.'

'Maybe, but I doubt it,' Margaret replied. 'Our evacuee has settled in anyway, and she and Diana get on well together. It's Diana's birthday soon. She'll be eight. I don't know where the time has gone.'

' 'Tis terrible, Margaret. Christmas 'll be on us before us knows it.'

'Ooh, don't mention it!'

Margaret stood up and picked up her basket.

'Here's your order then, Lil. Is there anything else that you want? Some of these cakes are left over and they're going cheap at this time of the day.'

'Oh, go on then, Margaret. It'll save me a bit of cookin'. Stan and the boys makes short work of food. I can't keep 'em supplied fast enough.'

Margaret wrote out the bill and Lil handed over the money and took her change just as Stan walked up the steps and into the kitchen.

'Hello, Maggie.'

'Hello, Stan, good to see you.'

''Ave you two put the world right while I've been over at the Major's?' Stan smiled.

'No, Stan. Us was leavin' you and Major Philips to do that.' Lil winked at Margaret and busied herself clearing the table as she asked casually, 'What's 'e got to say about that Shallowford chap then, Stan?'

'Not much. The Major wants to check out a few things 'eself and reckons me and Arthur should keep our 'aids down. "Keep a low profile, Stanley," is what 'e said.'

''Thank goodness somebody's got some sense, round yer,' Lil remarked.

'Well I must be off.' Margaret walked towards the door, deciding to say nothing to anyone about the mystery of the new tenant.

'Oh, I nearly forgot, Margaret. I've got a few eggs for 'ee.' Lil picked up a little box and handed it to her friend.

'Oh Lil, that is so kind. I hope you're not robbing yourselves.'

'No. the chickens 'ave kept layin' and you may as well 'ave use of the surplus,' Lil said.

'Shall us see 'ee next week then, Maggie?' Stan asked, removing his boots and sitting down at the table.

'I don't know until I turn up for work and Bert tells me which job he wants me to do. It varies from day to day.'

'You'm a lady of many talents, Maid,' Stan said, 'but we 'opes to see 'ee soon.'

Margaret waved goodbye and walked down the steps and on down the lane to the van where she had parked it at the garage. The light was fading fast and there was a chill in the air. The smell of smoke coming from the chimney above the thatched roof of Sunnybank mingled with the smell of the damp, dead leaves falling on her head as she reached the van. She shivered, placed her basket in the back and got into the driving seat, settled on her cushion and slammed the door. Winter was on its way.

Chapter 36

Diana was starting to get impatient. Having a birthday on a Thursday when she had to go to school was silly. Why couldn't she have had her eighth birthday on a Saturday, or even a Sunday would have been better than a school day. Actually, Diana thought that all children should have their birthdays at weekends or in school holidays. There wasn't time to open any cards or presents before school and the day seemed to go on for ever. There was sums and then more sums, which she hated because, if she didn't understand something, Miss Cutford would suddenly come up behind her and pull her hair. How did that help anyone to understand something? It just frightened her and made her feel lost and unhappy, especially when some of the other children knew the answers. In any case, Miss Cutford had black witches' hair, plaited and arranged in circles around each ear. It made her look really frightening and she never smiled and never praised her, even on the times when she managed to get the right answer. Now Miss Mac, she says things like, 'Well done' and 'I can see you have worked hard at that' and 'It's still got a long way to go but you've improved that piece so much.' Yes, that's the sort of teacher she would be if ever she became a teacher, Diana thought. In fact, she'd quite like to be a teacher and she'd be one just like Miss Mac, and not pull children's hair and not look all cross all the time. She'd smile and praise people, even if they didn't get everything right. Diana felt sorry for one of the boys in the class. He was called Henry and was always getting told off even when he never even said anything. Course, he didn't do anything much either. Diana sat behind him and Maureen sat behind her. It was just as well that they didn't sit next to him because he had nits and had to have his head shaved. That was a sure sign for everyone to move away as they whispered to one another. 'Careful, he's got nits. Don't get too close.' Diana and Maureen kept quiet about nits at home because there was one thing that made life uncomfortable for about two weeks, and that was the nit comb. It was an ugly metal thing and Diana's mother dragged it through their wet hair after she'd put something horribly smelly on it. Even Mary had to have the nit comb. There were ructions but their mother would not relent.

'I'm not having nits and fleas in this house so you have to put up with it. Just remember that you have to suffer to be beautiful.'

Diana didn't quite see the sense of that but sat still on the chair wincing as the nit comb was scraped through her hair. Not that Diana's hair was long. She would like to have had long hair and sometimes plaits, like Shirley, one of the neighbouring children, but her mother said that there was to be no long hair in the house as the nit comb would have to do double its work. On balance, perhaps it was just as well to have short hair, Diana thought.

The rest of the school day was taken up with lessons in hand writing and poetry and singing before home time. Diana loved all of those and the time went quicker. When she and Maureen reached home, the table was being laid ready for the birthday tea. Granma had arrived and was helping to carry in some sandwiches. A big, red, wobbly jelly stood in the centre of the table and a pink blancmange had been turned out perfectly in the shape of a rabbit.

'Ah, here's the birthday girl,' Florrie said, giving Diana a suffocating squeeze. 'I've got something here for you from Great Aunt Maggie, and there's a card and a present from Grampy and me.'

'Ooh thank you, Granma,' Diana answered. It was the moment she'd been waiting for all day. 'Where's Mary? I don't want to open my presents and cards without her here.'

'She's just coming now with Grampy,' Margaret said. 'I can hear the back gate slamming shut. It's a shame that Jack isn't home yet but he doesn't finish until six and I don't want to keep you waiting for your surprises any longer, Diana. Wash your hands, girls and then sit down at the table.'

'Ah, there you are, Jim.' Florrie greeted her husband and took Mary to the sink in the scullery to wash her hands.

'We can all sit around the table with a bit of a squash and Dad, you can sit in the armchair if it's more comfortable for you,' his daughter said.

'You must start off the birthday tea with some bread and butter so it's no good looking like that at the jelly and blancmange, Mary,' Margaret said, passing the bread and butter plate around the table and waiting at Mary's place until she had taken a piece.

'When am I allowed to open my presents, Mummy?' Diana asked looking at a pile of envelopes and small gifts on the top of the bureau.

'After tea, dear.' Margaret looked at her mother. 'We'll save some food for Jack for when he gets home.' Suddenly the kitchen door opened and Jack entered the room. 'Did someone mention my name?'

'Goody, Daddy, you left work early,' Diana shouted. 'You're just in time.'

Jack seated himself in the armchair opposite Jim and food was passed to each of them. Margaret went into the scullery and picked up a plate from the larder. Eight candles had been arranged on the top of an iced cake which she carried into the kitchen and placed on the table. Florrie helped to move some things out of the way and Jack stood up to light the candles.

'Oh Mummy, it's so pretty! You've iced it in pink and white and written "Happy Birthday" on it,' Diana clapped her hands in excitement.

'Now, we all have to sing,' Florrie nudged her husband, in case he was about to nod off to sleep.

They all sang "Happy Birthday" and when they had finished, Diana blew out the candles in one breath.

'I want to blow out the candles,' Mary shouted.

'Yes, of course you may, Mary. Give Daddy a chance to light them again. Do you want to blow out the candles, Maureen,' Florrie asked?

'Yes please, Gran,' Maureen answered standing up to get into a good position.

'Now, does anyone else want to blow out the candles?' Jack asked after all three girls had extinguished them. Before Mary had a chance to answer, the cake was cut and handed out. Everyone said how delicious it was.

'It's a shame to eat it, really,' Florrie mumbled while biting through an extra-large piece. 'It looked so pretty before it was cut.'

'Yes, I was lucky that Bert let me have some of

the icing he had left over to bring home for Diana's cake. There is so little sugar coming into the shop to decorate cakes, large or small.'

When everyone had drunk tea and lemonade, the dishes were cleared away and the tablecloth gathered up and taken outside and shaken.

'Is it time for presents now?' Diana asked as they all sat round as before.

'This is from me and Daddy,' Margaret said taking a parcel from the top of the bureau. It was wrapped in a brown paper bag and tied with a bow of red wool. Diana undid it and took a large flat book from the bag. She laid it down on the table.

'Oh, it's beautiful, Mummy. Look at all the lovely pictures on the cover.'

Maureen looked at the book. 'It's a Walt Disney book, Diana. You know, from the picture. You saw it, didn't you?'

'Yes, that's right. It's "Snow White and the Seven Dwarfs." I loved that picture.'

'Well, open the book and look inside, Diana,' her mother said.

Diana slowly opened the cover and gasped in surprise.

'It's a music book with lovely pictures all in colour.' She turned the pages taking in the details of the songs and words from the story and seeing the stills from the film.

'I love it. Thank you, Mummy and Daddy. I love it and I'm going to learn how to play each one of the songs. Here's my favourite. Look.' She turned back to one of the earlier pages.

'Before you tell us about that, there's a present from Granma and Grampy,' Margaret said.

Florrie stood up and reached for an almost identically-shaped parcel from the top of the bureau and handed it to Diana.

'Happy birthday, dear,' she smiled and kissed the top of her granddaughter's head.

'It looks like the same shape as the other one,' Diana said as she opened the parcel.

'Pinocchio!' Diana and Maureen shouted together as the beautiful book was revealed.

'That will keep you busy,' Jim commented from his armchair.

'Thank you very much. These two books are the best things I could have for my birthday. How did you think of them?'

'We went in to Nicklins, didn't we, Mum, and Mr. Whiting helped us to pick them out. He thought they would be the sort of standard that you'd be able to cope with, Diana.'

'Oh yes, but I will have to practise a lot. I'm going to start with my favourite piece.'

'Which one is that, dear?' Florrie asked.

'It's called, "Heigh Ho! Heigh Ho! It's off to

work we go." That's when the dwarfs start to do the house work, isn't it, Maureen? I can play it and you can sing it, when I've practised it, I mean.'

'That's a good title,' Jack remarked. 'It sounds like what we do every day.'

Jim stood up and said that it was time for him to be off home as there was a programme he wanted to listen to on the wireless.

'I'll be over later, Jim,' Florrie said. 'Diana has to open sister Maggie's card and present yet.'

'Bye, Grampy. Thank you for the lovely book.' Diana waved.

Jack handed the birthday cards to Diana and she opened them and read the greetings written on them out loud. Other than cards from the family, Maureen had made one and drawn a pretty picture on it and Mary had coloured in the bottom of it. There was a card from Bill, who had written a lovely message and put a big kiss after it. He was out with his friends so couldn't come to the birthday tea. The last card was from Great Aunt Maggie from Reading. She had sent a present and Diana opened it to discover a lovely box of coloured pencils.

'Just what I wanted, Granma. I'm so pleased with my birthday presents.'

'You must write to Aunt Maggie at the week end to thank her, Diana,' Margaret said. 'And Maureen, you owe your mother a letter, so you can do your letter writing together, can't you?'

The girls looked at Margaret, not too enthusiastic at the thought but knowing that there would be no escaping from the task.

'Now, I'll do the washing up Margaret, if you want to get a little person ready for bed,' Florrie said, rising from the table

'You mean me, don't you, Ganma? I'm not tired.' Mary looked around to see if anyone else was tired.

'I'm tired,' Margaret said. 'I wish I could go to bed.'

'You wouldn't fit in my cot, Mummy,' Mary replied.

'Always ready with an answer, isn't she?' Jack left the kitchen and went to do some work on his bike. Margaret looked at Mary.

'You can have a little while longer to stay up, Mary, if you go into the front room and play nicely with Diana and Maureen.'

'Mummy, I want to try out my Snow White piano book.'

'You can do that later, Diana, before you go to bed.'

The girls went off to play in the front room.

'It's quite cold in there, Mum,' Margaret said. 'We've got the fire going in the range in here but it gets really chilly in that room. Diana doesn't seem to mind but it's not winter yet, is it? She has some mittens and wears them sometimes when she practises, I notice.' The two women washed the dishes and when everything was put away, sat down in the armchairs in the kitchen.

'How are those friends of yours, Margaret?' Florrie asked.

'Oh, you mean Lil and Stan? They're well, and as busy as ever. Their evacuee boys are very happy and the little one has settled down and chats away now. Of course, it is a wonderful spot there, Mum. There's not another house in sight. You should come out with me some time. They would give you a lovely welcome. I've told them all about my family.'

Florrie was thoughtful.

'Do they have running water, Margaret?'

'No, they have a pump, and they pump their water up from a well.'

'Oh, that's hard. And what about electricity? They've got electric lights, haven't they?' Florrie was starting to feel uncomfortable.

'No, they have Tilley Lamps and use candles.'

'Oh, crikey, Margaret! I suppose they do have a proper toilet?'

'Yes, of course they have a toilet but it's not exactly a proper toilet; not like you'd expect it to be.'

'It's outdoors then, is it?'

Florrie was beginning to think she had returned to her early years. She could see her poor mother carrying buckets of water and sharing the washing facilities with the neighbours, and she remembered the row of communal toilets in the lane at the back of the little gardens in Southampton. Surely these friends had moved into the twentieth century.

'Our toilet is outdoors, Mum, but when we can afford to buy the house, we'll put in a bathroom and be able to have it indoors.'

'That'll be good. You and Jack will do it, dear, I know you will. But this toilet where your friends live in the country, is it just outside the back door?'

'No, not exactly, Mum. You have to go down the front steps and across the yard, then go through the top of the vegetable garden and it's there.' Margaret looked at her mother, waiting for a reply.

'Does it flush, Margaret? Do you pull the chain?' Florrie seemed to be fixated by the whereabouts and workings of the toilet at Sunnybank.

'No, it doesn't flush. It's just a bucket really. It's an Elsan toilet in a little wooden hut with roses hanging round the door.'

'Oh my God, Margaret. I don't care if there are gold sovereigns hanging round the door. You won't get me there however nice the folks are.'

'It's not their property, Mum. They rent it from the Estate.'

'Well, the Estate should get them a proper toilet. I dread to think what it must be like trekking across the garden to get to a bucket. They have a po under the bed, like all of us, I expect, but a bucket – ' Florrie stopped and shook her head.

'No, I couldn't come with you to see them, Margaret. My bladder might not last the visit.'

With that, she stood up, kissed her daughter and left to join Jim and his wireless, feeling grateful for their upstairs toilet.

Chapter 37

Stan pulled in to the grass verge at the side of Stone Cottage, got out of the car and walked up to the porch door. Just as he was about to knock, the door was opened.

'Ah, good morning, Stanley. I thought I heard a car.'

'Good mornin', Major Phillips.'

'Come in, come in. Your friend isn't with you, then?'

'No, Major. I've just dropped my wife at Swimbridge Chapel and the boys at my sister-in-law's 'ouse. The boys be 'avin' dinner with 'er and 'er family in Landkey, then they'm all comin' back to our 'ouse 's afternoon for tea.'

'Splendid. Splendid. I expect you will have to go back to collect Mrs. Webber after the service?'

'I will, Major, but Lil always stays on after the service for a good tell with all the others there.'

'Ah, yes. Excellent. Now, Stanley, sit down in your usual place. I have moved my dining chair next to your armchair for Arthur, then we can all sit around the Aga to talk things over.'

'You'm glad of that range today, Major. 'Tis a lot colder now us is well into November. Before

I forget, Lil 'as sent over some eggs.' The Major's eyes shone with gratitude as he took the box and placed it carefully on the table.

'How kind. She has made my day and I will have a boiled egg for tea,' he paused, 'with soldiers, of course.' They both laughed but were interrupted by a loud knock at the door.

'That will be Arthur, I suspect. Stanley, would you be so kind as to let him in? Your legs are younger than mine and once I sit down it takes some effort to rise again.'

'Straight away, Major.' Stan went to open the door and returned with his friend. Arthur walked straight up to the Major and handed him a small package.

'Good to see you, sir. No, please don't get up. My wife has baked you a small carrot cake for your tea.'

'Please thank her. I am being thoroughly spoiled today. Place the package on the table there, Arthur, next to the eggs from Mrs. Webber. What a treat I'm going to have at tea-time! Now, before you sit down, Arthur, would you fetch three glasses from the shelf on the dresser there, and you'll see a large bottle of whiskey on the table. I think we have a serious matter to discuss and we will need some decent fuel to help us to do it.'

Arthur poured three glasses of whiskey and

handed one of them to the Major and one to Stan. With each of them seated and holding a glass, Major Phillips raised his and said, 'Cheers.'

The two visitors responded and sipped the excellent malt which they suspected was a favourite of the old gentleman.

'Now, Stanley, now, Arthur,' the Major looked directly at each one of them in turn, 'about this tenant who resides at Hideaway Cottage. I must start off by asking you not to discuss anything that I might tell you now, or anything that you think you know about him with anyone at all. I don't only need your agreement, I need your word.' There was a short silence as Major Phillips leaned forward to look at the two younger men. The light-hearted banter had gone and his face was deadly serious.

'Of course, Major. You can rely on us.' Arthur rested his glass on his knee and looked at the Major.

'And you are not to discuss anything about the matter with your wives or anyone else. Is that agreed?' Major Phillips pressed on.

'Certainly, Major.' Stan looked anxiously at the Major.

'Us won't say a word outside this room.'

'I have been making enquiries through contacts of mine. Suffice it to say that I number among my friends men who shared some of the campaigns from the last skirmish with me. One in particular has a son who has a very senior position at Scotland Yard. You may know, Arthur, that Stanley calls in every day to bring me a meal prepared for me by his dear wife. It was on one of those visits that he told me about your little investigation. While I can't help admiring your adventurous spirit, you both took a big risk, apart from the fact that you were trespassing. I gather it was a near thing as the tenant arrived back at the cottage much earlier than expected. This tells me that he is suspicious and will now change any routine that he may have adopted previously. I think you had a feeling about that didn't you, Arthur? There is much of your father in you. He was a very special and able man.'

'Thank you, Major. I know that and I miss him. He taught me a lot.'

'Indeed, and you had Stanley there to help you with your dubious investigation.'

'Us wouldn't like to do it again, would us, Arthur?'

'I'm glad to hear it, Stanley because my friend's son has said that you are definitely not to do it again. I have had contact with my friend on the telephone and told him what Stanley told me about your little escapade. He in turn discussed the matter with his son at Scotland Yard, who was very grateful for the information. He has said that I am to tell you that there is a huge investigation going on into the illegal production and distribution of petrol and clothing coupons. They think the printing of these coupons is done in more than one place and you have discovered one of those places. What the police want to do is to track the chain of distribution. The forgeries are very good. These criminals are experts and have probably been involved with forging all sorts of documents before the war. Scotland Yard is listing all the cities where they think the forgeries are handed over for distribution. They probably never appear anywhere near where they have actually been printed. They are sent on up the line for inspection and eventual sale to people who have the money to buy these illegal coupons. You will know, Stanley, that you may use your car because you produce food. My doctor may use his because he has to drive to see his patients if they are too ill to go to the surgery. But I don't need to tell you all this. However, in the cities, where it is more difficult to check on who may and who may not have use of a car or motor of some sort, these forgeries are turning up. The police may find them but they haven't been able to track the route taken from start to sale of them and there is big money in it. Of course, forged clothing coupons can also find their way to people who live the high life, and dress to match it. Apart from it all being illegal, this matter is taking up time which is better given to the war effort.'

'So, the tenant at Hideaway Cottage is part of a chain of criminals then, Major?' Arthur looked thoughtful.

'Yes, and you and Stanley have unearthed a very important link in that chain.'

'But us mustn't rock the boat, must us? Us must leave well alone.'

'Yes, Stanley, but I expect that at some time in the future you will both be contacted by the police in order "to help them with their enquiries", I think the term is.' The Major sighed deeply and looked at the two men.

'In the meantime, another glass of whiskey each wouldn't go amiss, after all this excitement.'

'I'll pour it shall I, Major?' Arthur offered, standing up.

'Then I must go an' fetch Lil from the Chapel, Major,' Stan said.

'Of course. Thank you both for your time. We will do nothing and await developments, men,' said Major Phillips, lifting his glass to them and downing its contents in one.

'I'll be back later with your dinner, Major. 'Tis cold lamb and boiled spuds and pickle today. What I calls an "after prayer dinner".'

'Perfect, Stanley! I shall look forward to it.'

Arthur and Stan let themselves out, and Arthur set off on his bike towards Filleigh as Stan turned

the car and drove back to Swimbridge to collect Lil
from chapel. Both men uttered not a word to each
other before they left Stone Cottage travelling in
opposite directions. They had been given plenty of
food for thought.

'How did 'ee get on with the Major 's mornin' then,
Stan?' Lil had washed up the dinner things and laid
the table ready for tea. She sat down in her usual
place, looking out of the window towards the gate
at the bottom of the lane.

'Oh, 'e was so glad of they eggs, Maid. 'E was
plannin' one for 'is tea. And Arthur 'ad brought a
carrot cake 'is wife 'ad cooked, and the old Major
said it made 'is day.'

'That's good, Stan, but I means what did'n say
about the tenant over at Shallowford? You'd told
'im 'twas all a bit fishy, so did 'n say what'n thought?'

'Only that there was nothin' to worry about
and us 'ad best keep out of it in case us gets into
trouble. If the tenant wants to bide on 'is own an'
live peaceful like, then that be 'is business. And us
shouldn't talk about 'n and listen to gossip. 'E just
wants to get on with 'is writin' us thinks, an' us
should leave 'im to it.'

'Oh good. I'm glad the Major 'ave talked sense
into the two of 'ee. "Live and let live." 'Tis a good
proverb, Stan and I'm glad you'm listening to the

Major.' Lil stood up and announced, 'They'm comin' up the lane and Wilfred and George be with 'em.'

'I don't know what us 'ave done to deserve that,' Stan answered.

'Behave proper now, Stan. 'Tis Sunday, after all.'

'Hello, Lil. Hello, Stan.' George and Wilfred stepped into the kitchen, immediately making it feel smaller. Edith and the boys came in behind them and everyone sat round the kitchen table.

'Hello, George, Wilfred, Edith.' Lil and Stan smiled at the visitors and Lil vanished into the scullery to make a pot of tea and fetch some lemonade for Danny and Jimmy.

'We'll have our proper tea later, if that's all right with you,' she shouted as she pumped cold water into the kettle. 'Thank you for having the boys, Edith.'

Lil returned to the kitchen and sat down to join the others while waiting for the kettle to boil.

'Did you say thank you, boys?' Lil looked at Jimmy and Danny. They didn't look very clean. Their hands were filthy and there was some sort of grease on their faces.

'Oh yes, Lil,' her sister answered for the boys. 'They were very polite and other than eating everything that was put in front of them, I haven't seen hair or hide of them.'

'They were out in the workshop with you, Wilfred, weren't they?' his father asked.

'They're my new apprentices,' Wilfred boasted, who was in the same role himself, and still learning from his father.

'So, can I 'ave 'em mend my tractor, Wilfred?' Stan asked with a laugh.

'Not yet, Uncle, but we've brought the part you wanted and we'll fit it while we're here,' Wilfred answered.

'Bits keep falling off that old tractor, Stan,' George said. 'Time to buy a new one.'

'Oh no, George. Not while there be life in the old dog yet.'

Lil poured tea, and lemonade for the boys, and passed some cakes around the table.

'Wash your 'ands, you two, and after you've 'ad a drink an' a cake why not go and play outside. It'll be dark all too soon.' Jimmy and Danny ran out to the scullery and washed off some of the grease under the water pump.

'With cookin' a dinner for everyone, Edith, you couldn't go to church,' Lil said, taking a sip from her tea cup.

'I'll go tonight, Lil. We won't stay too long. George sings in the choir, as you know, so we'll go together.'

'I don't know why you don't come to church in

Landkey, Lil,' George cut in.

Lil made a show of passing more cakes around the table. It was always like this. They were 'church' and she was 'chapel' and George didn't let her forget it.

'Well you lives in the Landkey Parish and us lives in the Swimbridge Parish, George.' Lil replied, topping up his tea cup.

'In that case, why don't you go to the Swimbridge Church instead of the chapel, Lil? They've got a choir there too but not as good as ours at Landkey,' he added proudly.

Stan, who didn't go to church or chapel, had heard enough and decided to change the subject.

'Out you go then Jimmy, and you too, Danny. You can 'elp me with the milkin' soon.' The boys ran off and Stan looked at his brother-in-law.

' 'Ow's business then, George?'

Stan had hit upon one of George's favourite subjects and sat back in anticipation of a long list of motor problems that George and Wilfred were dealing with.

'Can I come out to the scullery and give you a hand, Lil?' Edith asked.

'Thank you, Edith. I know you 'aven't got much time, so we'll get the tea earlier than usual. The ladies left the room and Wilfred stood up and said that he would go down the lane to the garage and fit the part they had brought with them for the tractor. Wilfred's exit to sort out the tractor gave his father full reign to hold forth on the ups and downs of his business.

'Well, Stan, we're quite busy although there's no private motoring on the road, what with the petrol rationing, but there's the agricultural side of things and that's where our business mostly lies. So many farms have had more land set aside to produce food, and the machinery has to work harder as well as the farmers. That's where we come in.'

'That be more business then, George. And 'tis good that young Wilfred be such a 'elp. An' don't 'ee forget to tell me what I owes 'ee for that tractor part.'

'Not much, Stan. It's a second hand one from our spares box. Yes, Wilfred is a natural. He grew up with a spanner in his hand.' George paused. 'There's one thing I wanted to ask you, though. What do you know about that new tenant who lives near Shallowford?' The directness of the question almost threw Stan for a moment and he reached for his pipe and filled it with tobacco while he thought what he would say.

'I don't know much about 'n really. Only that 'e's a writer an' likes to be left to bide by 'eself.'

'What about that chap, Arthur? He's a postman. He must know something about him.'

'No more than us do, George,' Stan said lighting his pipe and puffing hard on it.

'Well, we've had two run-ins with the man, Stan. First, I was driving a tractor and towing a piece of farm machinery on the way to deliver it, when who should come towards me but this bloke from Shallowford. I recognised his van. I only have to see a vehicle once and I can photograph it in my mind. I'd seen him driving through South Molton back along. Course, he never comes to Landkey for anything and I don't suppose he comes to Swimbridge, does he, Stan?'

'I don't go there meself, if I can 'elp it,' Stan replied dryly.

'Well, anyway, we meet face to face, or bumper to bumper, as you might say, on the single carriage road leading to Stags Head from Shallowford and I sit there waiting for him to go back.'

'Did 'n go back?' Stan asked, knowing the answer before it was given him.

'No. He just sat there. And I just sat there on top of the tractor. He could see I was towing and he still just sat there, so I got down off the tractor to explain and then the funniest thing happened. He pulled a cap down over his eyes and started to reverse at speed until he got to a gateway wide enough for me to pass. I got back up on the tractor and when I'd driven alongside him, I leaned over towards his door to thank him and he turned his head away from me. Totally ignored me. What do you think of that?'

'Bit rude, George,' Stan said noncommittedly.

'And then,' George went on, fully wound up by this time and waiting for information from his brother-in-law to shed light on the matter, 'only last Saturday, I had to go up on Exmoor; to Brayford to look at another tractor. Who should I see but this same van with the mystery man driving it. I think he saw it was me and we passed each other at the top by Forty Beeches. Now if he's a sort of hermit, what's he doing up there, Stan?'

'I think e' must like walkin' in the countryside. 'Tis master quiet up there, bain't it? If 'e's a writer, p'raps 'e writes books about nature. There's plenty of it up on Exmoor.' Stan puffed away thoughtfully at his pipe.

'Well, I think there's something strange about him, that's all, Stan. He's not normal. That's what I think.'

Lil and Edith suddenly entered the kitchen as Wilfred and the boys came in for their tea.

'Normal?' Edith repeated. 'Do you think you're normal, George Tucker, 'cos I don't; a man who runs around the garden with a plate of porridge, because he can't cool it fast enough?'

'And us can't say Stan's normal, can us?' smiled Lil

as she set down two plates laden with sandwiches and scones.

Chapter 38

'No, I don't want to go off to work. I'm tired. It's not time to get up. I'm sleepy.'

'No, you are not Sleepy. You are Lazy,' was the reply. It was a funny, croaky, old voice. 'Yes. That's who you are. You are Lazy.'

'I'm sleepy, I tell you. I should know.'

'Listen,' the croaky, old voice said,' I'm in charge of the Eight Dwarfs and I know every one of you. There's Grumpy, Dopey, Happy, Bashful, Sneezy, Sleepy, Doc – that's me, – and Lazy, and that's you. And I am telling you that it is time to get up and start Heigh Ho-ing because it's off to work we go time.'

'No, it isn't. I'm not getting out of this bed yet. It's not time to get up, not until the bell rings.'

'I don't know what you are talking about. Mr. Disney wants us to sing 'Heigh Ho' and you have to get up to join us to sing it. We're all waiting for you. You are Lazy.'

'I am not lazy and I won't get up until the bell rings. In any case, you and your friends have very strange names. You say you're called Doc and you are in charge?'

'Yes. Mr. Disney put me in charge, but I don't

think he should have had eight dwarfs. "Snow White and the Eight Dwarfs" doesn't sound right. We could do with one less dwarf and then we could all start singing and marching off to work together. We're going to be late as it is. Can't you hear the music has started?'

'Not that bloody music again, surely?'

'Ooh! Mr. Disney won't allow swearing. I think he will give you the sack and then you won't be allowed to go off to work. You'll have no job. What about that, Lazy?'

'I am not lazy, I tell you. I am not lazy and the bell hasn't sounded yet so you can go off to work without me. I am not called Lazy. I am called Jack. I am not Lazy. I am not Lazy. I am not Lazy.'

A gentle voice sounded close to his ear.

'Of course, you're not lazy. Jack, you've been dreaming. Jack, Jack, wake up.'

Someone was shaking his arm and a loud bell was ringing.

'Wake up, Jack. Whatever have you been dreaming about? You've been mumbling all sorts of nonsense. That's the alarm so we'd better get up.'

Margaret noticed that Mary had managed to climb out of her cot and had gone downstairs from where the sound of the piano was emanating. It was seven o'clock and the piano practice had started early. Diana and Maureen were to be performing 'Heigh Ho' at the Saturday Morning Picture Club later. Jack groaned and sat on the edge of the bed.

'If I hear that – music one more time,' he muttered.

'We must encourage her, Jack. She and Maureen have worked hard to be ready for today, so think of some nice things to say.' Jack grunted and sighed.

'What's the attraction, anyway?' he asked, putting on his socks and slippers.

Margaret sat at the dressing table and brushed her dark hair.

'Well, if a child or a group perform a little entertainment before the films start showing, they are allowed in free the following week.'

'Ah, now I can see the attraction,' Jack nodded.

'Yes dear. A chip off the old block.'

They went downstairs and the family gathered at the table for breakfast.

'That piece is harder than I thought it would be,' Diana said as she started on a plate of porridge.

'The right hand keeps moving up and back on the keyboard and at the same time the left hand puts in some little chords.' She put down her porridge spoon and drilled the rhythm on the table cloth. 'So the right hand goes "Heigh Ho" – that's the song bit, and in between the song bits the left hand goes "plonk, plonk," – that's the little chords, you see.

I'm a bit nervous about doing it really.' She picked up her spoon and sat looking at her porridge. She didn't feel like eating it now.

'And what about you, Maureen?' Margaret asked. 'Have you learnt it by heart?'

'Yes, Auntie Margaret, and we can do it quite well, usually,' Maureen answered. 'But I don't think we will be next to each other when we perform the song. The piano is below the stage and I will have to be on the stage to sing into the microphone.' Diana frowned. She had not thought of that.

'I'm sure it will be fine, girls, and you will be helped by whoever is in charge, won't you?'

'Yes,' Maureen answered. 'There is a really jolly man who comes on and smiles and laughs and shouts a lot. He'll help us.'

'Well, good luck to you both,' Jack said, getting up from the table.

'I want to go and see it,' Mary said. 'Why can't I go and see it?'

Margaret cleared away the dishes. 'Well, we'll all walk over there together and wait outside during the performance.'

'You won't be allowed in, Mummy,' Diana said.

'That's because you're too old,' Mary said.

'Thank you, Mary. If you've finished, you may leave the table now.'

'Too old, Marj. That's nice.'

'Everyone who is over the age of ten is too old as far as they're concerned Jack,' Margaret replied.

'Now, we'll let Daddy get off to work, then you girls can get washed and dressed in your best clothes. You won't have much time, so go and make sure you have your music packed in the case, Diana.'

'It's not very often that I have to work on a Saturday,' Jack said, 'but you can tell me all about it when I come home.'

'Are we all ready?' Margaret asked, 'and have you girls been to the toilet?'

The answer came in the affirmative and even Mary chipped in with a 'yes.'

'Where's your music case, Diana?' Her daughter held up the brown leather case that her mother had bought second hand.

'Oh good, you've got it. Don't forget to bring it back with you.'

Suddenly, the back door opened and Florrie came in, dressed for town.

'Do you mind if I come with you? I know we're not allowed into the cinema to see you perform but I have to do some shopping anyway.'

'That's fine, Mum. We'll walk to town together.'

'You two look very smart in your best clothes. Turn round the back,' Florrie said, twirling her hand. Diana never could understand why her grandmother always told people to turn round the back in order to inspect their clothes. Perhaps they should walk backwards in the first place.

'Very smart, and If you sound as good as you look, you will be fine.'

There couldn't be a kinder person than her grandmother but sometimes the things that she said came out wrong.

'Right. Now put your coats on, everyone. It's cold outside.' Margaret was looking at the clock.

'Do you like my dress, Ganma?' Mary asked, turning round the back to show every angle.

'Yes dear, you look lovely. Is that the one you made out of that remnant from Banbury's, Margaret? It looks really good on her.'

'Yes, that's right, but I only just had enough material, Mum,' Margaret replied as they all walked out of the front door.

'Do you sing and play after the pictures or before, girls?' Florrie asked, adjusting her hat pin.

'We are on first, Granma,' Diana answered, her voice a little shaky.

'Mary, you can go in the push chair and walk later. We want to reach the cinema in good time for Diana and Maureen,' Margaret said, pushing Mary at a brisk pace with everyone else hurrying to keep up. Margaret's family were used to the speed of her walking. It was more like a trot. She couldn't bear to waste time and dawdling was never acceptable to her. They soon arrived at the Gaumont along with what seemed like hundreds of noisy children who were queuing on the pavement back up through Boutport Street.

'I think we have to go in before them,' Diana said, opening the heavy door with the brass handles. They all went into the foyer and were stopped by an usherette.

'It's children only for the Picture Club, and you girls will have to queue outside until it's time to come in,' she insisted.

'But we're playing and singing today,' Maureen said indicating herself and Diana with her hand.

'Oh, that's different,' the young woman smiled. 'Follow me.'

'Good luck,' Margaret and Florrie called out after them as they disappeared into an office nearby.

'I'd better get on,' Florrie said.

'I wish we could hear them, Mum.'

At that moment, the commissionaire came towards them wearing an immaculate maroon uniform and a smart braided cap.

'Are you the mother of those girls?' he asked, looking at Margaret?

'Well, one of them is my daughter and the other is our evacuee,' Margaret answered.

'You know I can't let you into the cinema, but if you want to hear them, come back in about quarter of an hour when the wild mob queuing outside is seated and you can stand at the back of the foyer over there and listen with the door slightly ajar. How's that?' he asked with a grin.

'That's very kind, and my young daughter won't make a sound, will you, Mary?'

Mary answered by putting her finger to her lips and squeezing them together tightly.

'Is it all right for me to stay, too? I'm the grandmother,' Florrie said.

'As long as there aren't any more of you, and you blend into the surroundings, that's fine,' the commissionaire replied drawing himself up to his full height and looking more serious.

'We'll meet back here in ten minutes, Mum. We don't want to be in the way when they let in that lot outside.'

A few minutes later the doors to the foyer were opened and the young Saturday Morning Picture Club Members flooded in, shouting and cheering, and were directed to their seats by the long-suffering usherettes. After about ten minutes the children were seated, late-comers sorted and Master of Ceremonies came onstage, smiling and waving to rapturous applause and cheers from the young audience. Standing in front of the red velvet curtains, dressed in a smart black suit, white shirt and black bow tie, he waved and shouted into the microphone.

'Good morning, young picture-goers!'

Screams and foot-stamping was the response.

'Are you ready for our Saturday Morning Entertainment?' He opened his arms wide, as if he were the entertainment.

'Yes!' the children screamed back at him.

In the wings Maureen waited with baited breath, and below stage, Diana stood gripping her music in the orchestra pit, almost hidden from sight.

'And now, boys and girls, your Saturday morning start to our programme this week will be a song from one of your favourite Walt Disney films. It is none other than "Heigh Ho, Heigh Ho" from "Snow White and the Seven Dwarfs."'

More cheering from the audience.

'And to perform it, we have two friends: Maureen, who will sing it for us and Diana on the piano who will accompany her. Please give them a warm welcome.'

Further cheering and foot stamping. There was a creak from a door somewhere at the back of the auditorium while Maureen walked to the microphone and Diana sat at the piano and opened her music book. Diana looked up to see if Maureen was ready but the level of the floor of the stage was that of her own eye level. She could see Maureen's short white socks and black shoes, the same sort of socks that her mother had knitted for each of them. Silence fell on the audience. Maureen cleared her throat. It sounded like a lion roaring into the microphone. Diana decided to start and began playing the introduction. Maureen came in with a confident 'Heigh Ho' and the song went along without a hitch. In no time at all they had reached the end and cheering and clapping had broken out. The Master of Ceremonies reached down and offered his hand to Diana who, taking it, was hoisted up onto the stage to take a bow alongside Maureen.

'What about that, then, children?' he said. More cheering.

'Next week, Diana and Maureen will come in free as their prize for entertaining us, and don't forget, you too can come in free if you have a short entertainment to offer us. Thank you, girls.' He pointed to the side of the stage and the young performers left amidst more applause. Diana wondered why there was so much clapping and cheering. They'd only played a short piece and yet the children listened well and seemed to enjoy it. As they waited offstage, the Master of Ceremonies raised his hands and spoke quietly into the microphone.

'And now, what you've all been waiting for – '

Even louder cheering.

'the continuation of our weekly serial – '

A crescendo of cheering and foot stamping ensued.

'Starring none other than – Roy Rogers.'

Rapturous shouts and yells as the Master of Ceremonies left the stage and the red curtains parted to show Roy Rogers and Trigger at the start of the highlight of the week. Diana and Maureen were shown to their seats for the show, and in the foyer, Florrie shook her head in disbelief.

'What a noise! I thought that a fire had broken out when I heard that racket.'

'The children love the pictures, especially Roy Rogers, Mum. Didn't the girls do well, though?'

'Yes, they did, dear. What did you think, Mary?'

'I liked that big lollipop thing, Ganma.'

'What does she mean, Margaret?' Florrie was confused.

'She means the microphone, Mum. Yes, it does look like a lollipop, Mary but it makes the singing sound louder.' They thanked the commissionaire who'd heard Mary's comment and found it most amusing. Outside in the street, Florrie turned to Margaret and took something wrapped in brown paper out of her shopping basket.

'I popped into the bakery for a loaf of bread and

saw Doreen. You'll never guess what she gave me.' She passed the object to her daughter and Margaret unwrapped it.

'A banana!' Margaret showed it to Mary.

'Doreen said that a really "dishy" – I think she called him – young American soldier called in to see Margaret and asked that the banana should be passed on to Mary.'

'It must have been Oliver. You know, Mum, the one I invited to tea. He said he'd try to get a banana for Mary because she missed out when the others tried one last time.'

'What a lovely chap, Margaret. Doreen thought so too.'

'Yes, Mum. I'll bet she did!'

Chapter 39

It was a cold, bright December morning and the temperature was just above freezing. He was glad that he had decided to leave early and he thought it was a good idea of his to change his route. The front lights on the van were insufficient to allow him to travel at any speed. Wartime restrictions resulted in only being able to see a very short way ahead, but there was no traffic on the road, apart from the odd milk churn lorry. As he headed up through East Buckland and on towards Brayford, the sun started to show itself, gradually making driving easer.

He began to relax. All his contacts with the gang were by using public phone boxes. Each member of the team only knew the arrangements of who to meet with and where that meeting was to be. He was the start of the chain, of course, and vital to the success of the whole operation. The gang was known as The Chain Gang and each member was part of the chain but no-one knew how many links there were in it, but they did know that it was headed by two men, only known to the members as 'The Clasp'.

Now it was time to close the whole thing down.

Every illegal venture was never taken too far, which was why the gang was so successful. He'd made a lot of money over the last few years with various jobs, using his expertise. 'Quit while you're ahead' was one of their mottos. Yes, they were all really smart and that was why he was relieved to hear that the job was being shut down. He had an uneasy feeling about the place he'd been renting; a feeling that he was being watched. There was no proof but he had learned to trust his feelings. They had kept him out of prison and made him quite well-off. His wife wanted for nothing, even in wartime, but he felt he needed to move on, buy something in the south of France when this war thing was over. It had put a real damper on everything, but the Clasps seemed able to take advantage of every situation, and after a spell of lying low would soon think up the next ruse. The two men who had come down with the removal lorry were to collect his personal belongings from the cottage and send them on to him later, to load the printing machine and the rest of the equipment, and remove any trace of what had been in the shed, leaving no sign of the work that he had had to do. Now it was almost over. Apart from this, his last delivery, the forged clothing coupons had been passed along the chain and had ended up in various cities, never the same one twice. There were plenty of well-off people who were ready to part with large amounts of money for coupons on the black market. The plan was that he was to deal with the forging of clothing coupons while somewhere else there was a member of the gang with similar expertise to his own who was dealing with the forging of petrol coupons. This was the final chapter. He'd got the last lot of coupons in the back of the van, beneath other legitimate items of stationery which would present no reason for suspicion if he were to be stopped and anyone looked in the vehicle. Not that anyone would be very welcome should they try to do so, as his dog was comfortably settled down there and wouldn't be happy to receive visitors. He was almost becoming fond of the dog but still hadn't got around to giving it a name. His wife wanted a dog and like everything she wanted, it had to be big and different from anything anyone else had. It was certainly that all right. It nearly took his hand off once but they had got to know each other and it turned out that the animal had become a deterrent for any unwelcome visitors. After all, he had put it about the village that he was a recluse.

He was beginning to feel cold. It was certainly colder up here on the moors than down at Hideaway Cottage. There was nothing to look at here. He hated the country. God, it was boring. Nothing ever happened. Just look outside the car windscreen.

Hills rolling up and down. Where were the towns and the pubs, and what did people do? Farming. You don't have to be smart to do that. He liked the life and noise in the cities, the clubs and pubs. Even in wartime, there was plenty going on. Of course, the blackout had put a real damper on his social life, but at least there wasn't the bombing like at the start of the war. His knee played him up now and then, but it had kept him out of the forces. It was a lucky accident really, falling off that wall when he was a nipper. He'd thought he could reach the open window and climb in and pinch something. The owners of the house were well-off and had gone out and left the window open. That was their fault. He'd lost his balance and fallen badly. After a while some passers-by had found him on the ground, crying and taken him to the hospital. He'd told them he'd tripped in the blackout on a raised paving slab.

He found himself thinking about the people around Swimbridge and Filliegh. What did they know? Where had they been? They'd never make as much money as any of the Gang and would miss out on all the fun and travelling that would come his way when this little lot paid off. He'd had a big advance and it was in the bank, safe and sound. As for today, he had his journey mapped out. After Exford, he'd drive on to Wheddon Cross and head for the coast road that would take him in the direction of Bridgwater and on towards the outskirts of Bristol. There was a quiet little pull-in, screened by trees near a village where he was to meet his colleague. He shook himself out of his musings. He'd left Simonsbath well behind and thought that he must be only a few miles from Exford. The road started to drop away steeply and he soon became aware that the tyres were failing to grip the icy surface. For the first time since he'd been driving the van, he felt out of control. He tried to slow down and touched the brakes when he should have gone down a gear. Too late. The van began to slide and there was nothing he could do about it. Suddenly, an enormous animal jumped out of the beech hedge on his right and stopped in the road ahead of him. He wrenched the steering wheel to the left with all his might to avoid it and the van careered into the nearside hedge and stopped with a jolt. The engine cut out and there was only silence.

The creature started to come towards him. What was it? A deer of some sort; a reddish-brown colour with huge antlers. The beast came slowly on and stopped at the front of the van, towering above it and lowering its massive head to stare at him. He sat stock still. The dog started to growl quietly from the back of the van without being able to see out of it. The deer looked in at him, its antlers seemingly out of all proportion to the size of its head and he sat, frozen with his mouth open, looking out at it. He felt that the animal could see into his soul. He had never experienced anything like this before. After what seemed ages, the deer turned away and leapt, from a standing position, back up into the hedge from where it had come. He was shocked and amazed that it could do that. Nothing much had ever surprised or impressed him in his life but this was different. For a while he sat still, staring out at the empty road. He was sideways into the hedge. Pulling himself together, he tried to restart the van. After several futile attempts, the vehicle coughed and spluttered into life. He reversed, and pulling hard to the right on the steering wheel, managed to get back on what people like to call a road in these parts. He proceeded forward slowly for a while in bottom gear, watchful of the ice and mindful of anything that might jump out at him from the hedge.

The rest of his journey was uneventful. He hardly saw a soul, apart from a few tractors and then some vans delivering produce to outlying farms. There was more traffic around the Bridgwater area but he felt he had done the right thing to avoid his usual route via Taunton. Once he'd handed over the documents, his colleague would deliver them to a lock-up in Bristol and the stuff would be collected from there. Then, he would drop off the van at an appointed garage and make his way home, by train of course, to London. Yes, it had all gone to plan. There would be a time of lying low until he was contacted to take part in whatever was being planned for the next job. He was flexible and had developed a number of different skills, the main one being to keep his mouth shut. Clubs and Pubs were fine but he shunned close friendships. He was a good listener, not a talker. You learned a lot that way.

He stopped the van at the meeting place, turning off the road onto a muddy grass track that went towards some woods. His colleague was already there, having parked his car to allow space for him to park the van. He gave his name as Mark, which it wasn't, of course, and in return, the other man gave his as Matthew. Very biblical, he thought. It didn't take long for them to empty the van and load the vital contents into the boot of Matthew's car, a rather smart Hillman. He looked in at the back seat. There were all sorts of bottles and pots and tubes piled up on it, the sort of stuff a vet might use for treating sick animals. Perhaps his colleague really was a vet. His use of a car in wartime would be legitimate. It would be a good cover story if he were ever stopped, and there would be more money illegally earned in a short time than even a vet could make in a year. Thinking of animals reminded him to let the dog out for a few minutes. He didn't want it running off so he tied a long rope to its collar and wound the rope around a small tree. The dog wagged its tail and shook itself. It looked at this new man and continued to wag its tail. It was a clever dog and obviously knew they were all on the same side. He gave it a bowl of water and a few biscuits.

The two men didn't hang about. They shook hands and went back to their own vehicles. Perhaps they'd meet again in the future if something else came up. He opened the door of the van on the front passenger side and the dog jumped up and settled itself on the seat. There was just enough room for his colleague to reverse past him and set off first. He got in behind the wheel and feeling that the end of this little escapade was in sight, he attempted to start up the engine. It took several tries before it was successful and with a sigh of relief he reversed out onto the grass verge and then drove onto the road. The motor was not running as well as it had done since before he'd ended up in the hedge on Exmoor. There was a rattling sound and the brakes were sluggish, too. He was quite good with cars and had some idea of vehicle maintenance, or at least, he thought he did. The bosses, the Clasps, didn't stint. They always provided vehicles that were kept up to scratch, although driving on West Country roads and lanes with all their potholes and terrible surfaces wouldn't be something that the big boys would be expected to recognise. He couldn't wait to get back to civilisation where he knew what to expect.

He was approaching the edge of Bristol and there was a big crossroad some way ahead at the bottom of a steep hill. It wouldn't be long before he could dump the van at the garage and he and the dog could get a train to London. A few cars ahead of him was his colleague. He must have stopped somewhere for petrol. He put the van into second gear and applied the brakes as he approached the cross roads. There was hardly any response and he started to pick up speed as the gradient of the hill increased. He stamped again on the brakes. Nothing. He fought to get into a lower gear and, in desperation, tried applying the hand brake. The van careered into the car in front which in turn shot into the back of his colleague's car. The traffic lights were at red but the Matthew's car was hurtled forward heading straight for the side of an ambulance coming from his right. Luckily, the Hillman only scraped against the front side of the ambulance as its driver was quick to take evading action, pulling hard to the right of the steering wheel and finally stopping with a shudder. A small lorry coming up behind the ambulance couldn't stop in time and crashed into the back of it. Although the traffic had not been fast moving, a concertina of vehicles started to pile up from different directions and an increasingly tangled mess had developed. The lorry driver could see that Matthew's car was starting to move away slowly from the centre of destruction. There was no response from the engine of the van. It was time for quick thinking; time to ditch the van and leg it. He didn't intend to get caught up in this mess. He grabbed his bag and jumped out. The dog followed and they ran around the tangled huddle of dented vehicles and shouting drivers and raced towards Matthew's car. He saw them, slowed and shouted to them to get in. Jumping in the back of the car amongst the assortment of veterinary equipment, the Hillman shot off at speed away from it all, leaving the broken-down van halfway across the road junction.

Now it was time to put on some speed. They would both have to get to the lock-up garage, leave the car with its valuable contents, take their own belongings and get away. It was a good car but Matthew didn't own it. He had his own but the veterinary stuff in the back of the Gang's car did belong to him. He would need to take that as well. It was more than just 'props'. It had been good cover but now it could be the undoing of him. There was silence from the two men as the car raced ahead. The dog was shaking but sat in the back amongst all the tubes and bottles, panting, with its head down.

Once he had driven about half a mile from the accident, Matthew slowed down. They decided not to draw any attention to themselves. He looked in the driving mirror. No cars were chasing him. They discussed the likelihood of being apprehended and hoped that no-one had had the time to take the car's number plate. There was more traffic now but no sign of a police car. Matthew turned the car into a narrow road by the docks and stopped outside a lockup garage with a grey painted door. He got out and took a key out of his pocket and unlocked the door. Once he had driven the car inside, they quickly took out their belongings and, leaving the forged coupons in the boot, went outside and locked up.

'Thanks, Matthew, for coming to our rescue,' Mark said, patting the dog's head.

'You'd do the same for me,' Matthew replied as he turned and walked away.

Mark wondered if he would, and suddenly he thought of the deer. It had been quite a day. He took a lead out of his pocket and attached it to the dog's collar.

'Come on, dog,' he said. 'Let's go home.'

Chapter 40

Margaret took off her coat and scarf and hung them on a hook in the passageway outside the bakehouse.

'Is that you, Maggie?' Bert's voice bellowed from inside the bakehouse. He came out carrying a tray of plain buns on his way to the shop. 'I want you working in with me and Frank for an hour or so. Make a couple of pounds of pastry and finish some of the small cakes. When it gets busy in the shop, you can go in there and work with Doreen,' he said, balancing the tray on his head and opening the door to the shop. He didn't wait for a reply and Margaret didn't stop to give one. She hurried into the bakehouse, put on a large pinafore, found the ingredients she needed and got to work.

Wednesday morning. Early closing, thank goodness, especially as it would be Christmas Day on Saturday. She'd left Diana and Maureen finishing their breakfast, with orders to wash up and make their bed. Then they could go and play out in the street as long as they wore their coats and mittens and didn't cross the railway line to go and play over the Marsh. That was more than they dare do, as the fear of being hit by a train was outweighed by the wallop they'd get from Margaret if they disobeyed her. She'd dropped Mary with her mother and the girls would join her there at dinner time. Margaret planned to dash off when the shop closed at one and catch the bus to Swimbridge. She'd brought the Christmas presents for Lil and Stan with her and a little something for each of the boys. But that wasn't the only reason she was going out to Sunnybank. Lil wanted Margaret to wash and set her hair in readiness for some sort of social event. Then there was something she had to do to their Christmas cake. She wasn't sure what that could be as the ingredients for almond pasting and icing Christmas cakes were nigh near impossible to get. Even the bakery was struggling and had to make do with all sorts of rather bizarre alternatives. Apart from the odd moan and shaking of heads, people accepted the fact that everything, whether food or clothes, was a case of make do. In fact, the wartime slogan was 'Make do and Mend'.

Margaret was pleased with the gift she had knitted for Lil, which had been made with wool she had unpicked from a sleeveless pullover she'd knitted some years ago that used to be Jack's. He'd hardly worn it and now that he had recovered from his illness and put on weight, he could no longer get into it. It was a fine three-ply wool in a sort of lovat colour and had knitted up well after she had unpicked it and washed the wool. Yes, she was pleased with it and as Lil was quite slim, there had been enough wool to make a short-sleeved jumper. Once it had been pressed, it looked like new.

'Make do and Mend!' her mother had exclaimed. 'That jumper would win a prize, Margaret.' Florrie didn't knit. Her eyesight wasn't up to it and neither was her patience, although she was so patient and tolerant in other ways. 'It wouldn't pay for us to be all the same, would it?' her mother often said. Margaret reluctantly agreed. She wasn't a very patient person in many ways. She knew that. She was a quick thinker and felt that she had not fulfilled her talents at school, and now she had responsibilities and just had to get on with life as it was. She had ambitions, though, and was ready for hard work to realise her dreams. She had a surprise for the family which she couldn't wait to tell them about. She'd keep that for a day or so. It would be like a Christmas present for her and Jack. Better than a Christmas present.

The bakehouse door swung open and Bert came in from the shop, going at his usual speed of top gear.

'Is that pastry ready yet, Maggie? Good. I was longer in the shop than I wanted to be, and then I had to go off to the bank to get some small change.' He turned to his apprentice.

'Those loaves look good, Frank, but you know we're not allowed to sell them until tomorrow. We'll keep them on the shelves at the back of this room.'

'Criminal, Bert, that's what it is!' moaned Frank. 'Criminal!'

'I know, Frank, but it's the law. You see the government knows that you make such wonderful bread that if the customers were allowed to buy it and eat it on the day you take it out of the oven, they'd want more of it and there wouldn't be enough to go round.' Frank smiled proudly. That was praise rarely given from Bert so he decided to say no more.

'Is this pastry for mince pies, Bert?' Margaret asked.

'Yes, Maggie, but not as we used to know them. There is so little dried fruit coming through from the wholesalers that we have to compromise. It's been the same with the Christmas cakes. As for the almond paste and icing, I never thought I'd see myself mixing some of the ingredients that have had to replace what we used before the war.'

'I was lucky you gave me those two little bowls of icing that I used for Diana's birthday cake back in November.'

'That was only some of our left-over icing back when we actually made some icing, Maggie,' Bert answered, as he started to mix the ingredients for the filling of the mince pies.

Suddenly the sound of voices could be heard coming from the shop.

'I think it's getting busy in there. You'd better go in and help Doreen, Maggie. She's in a bit of a dream today,' Bert said. 'I had to tell her twice to clean the top of the counter. She was just standing and staring out of the window.'

'Right, Bert. See you later, Frank.' Margaret hung up her overall and left the bakehouse. In the shop she donned her white apron and cap and started to serve the queue of customers that had built up. Doreen was very quiet, not as chatty with the regulars as she usually was. After a while the early morning rush quietened down and Margaret looked at Doreen, who had gone to the door and was staring up and down the street. She came back into the shop and smiled at Margaret.

'Looking for someone, Doreen?'

'No, no-one in particular,' Doreen replied.

'Your hair looks lovely, Doreen, now that you've tied it to one side.'

'Do you think so, Maggie? I'm glad you like it.' She went to the back of the shop and started fiddling with the baskets on the shelves, moving them a little to the right and then shifting them back again. She turned to Margaret and said casually. 'Oh, by the way, a friend of yours came in here yesterday. He's called Oliver and said that you had invited him to tea at your house,' Doreen turned away again and continued rearranging the baskets of buns behind the counter without looking at her colleague.

'Ah, yes. We do know him, Doreen. He's one of the Americans posted to North Devon. He's such a nice chap.'

'He's been in here a few times asking after you and Jack.'

'Has he, Doreen?' Margaret raised her eyebrows. 'How many times has he been in the shop?' She could see Doreen's face in the mirror on the back wall starting to colour.

'Say "Hello" to him from us when you see him next, then.'

Doreen turned round and looked up at Margaret, her eyes shining.

'Well, as a matter of fact, Maggie, he's asked me out.'

'Really?' Margaret smiled, trying to sound surprised. 'How lovely!'

Doreen looked as if she was going to burst with excitement but managed to get a grip on herself to smile at the first of another group of customers who had entered the shop.

'May I help you, Madam?' she asked.

'Yes dear,' was the reply. One of your day-old loaves and some of what poses as mince pies nowadays, please.'

'Just in time, Madam, for the first batch of them,' said Bert coming in with a hot trayful. 'These mince pies are unique. You won't find anything like them anywhere.'

'I'll believe you there. Just two, please, and I'll be back for more if I survive them,' answered the customer.

Chapter 41

There wasn't a bus to West Buckland when Margaret finished work so she had to take one to South Molton and get off at Swimbridge. Even then, she'd had to run to catch it and jumped on just as it was pulling away. It stopped near the Church at Swimbridge and Margaret stepped down onto the pavement just as Stan arrived to pick her up in the Austin Seven.

'Perfect timing, Stan, but I was happy to walk to Sunnybank. It's a cold day but at least it's a dry one.' Stan held the passenger door open for her and she climbed in. He started up the car and turned off the road to drive up Station Hill.

'No trouble, Maid, as long as you don't mind walkin' the last bit from the old Major's 'ouse. I took 'im 'is dinner but 'n wants to see me an' Arthur 's afternoon, so I can drop you off at 'is place. Arthur be comin' on 'is bike an' meetin' me there.'

Margaret wondered why the Major wanted to talk to the two men, but she knew better than to ask.

'I expect he's glad to have some company, Stan, living on his own like he does,' she commented. 'Of course, I can walk the last few hundred yards from his house. It won't take long. Thank you for coming to meet me.'

'I know that Lil be lookin' forward to you comin'. 'Er said somethin' about 'avin' 'er 'air done.'

'Yes, I think she is going to some kind of social function at the Chapel tomorrow afternoon. It'll be a chance for her to dress up and relax for a while. Wouldn't you like to go, Stan?' Margaret asked, knowing what the answer would be.

'I bain't Church nor Chapel, an' I don't like big get-togethers; so much noise with folks all talkin' at once. Gives me 'aid ache.' He slowed down and stopped outside Major Philips' house.

'You get out, Maid, then I'll pull in tighter.'

'Thank you, Stan.' Margaret shut the car door and waved as she walked away.

'See you later.' After walking along the narrow road towards Sunnybank and passing two cottages but without seeing a soul, she arrived at the bottom of the lane to the house and opened the gate. Usually there was a cackling sound of geese and she'd have to wave and shout at them but they were nowhere to be seen. Margaret walked up the lane and then over the stony path and up the steps to the front door. She knocked and shouted, 'Hello, Lil,'

'Come in. Don't' stand there knockin,' Lil's voice shouted back at her.

Margaret opened the front door and walked into the kitchen. She hardly recognised it as the room she had been in so often.

'Hello, Margaret. I'll make 'ee a 'ot drink. Sorry 'tis all a bit of a shambles 'ere. 'Ave 'ee 'ad somethin' to eat? I 'aven't 'ad time to make dinner but I can give 'ee some bread and a slice of braun.'

'No, Lil, thank you. I had something from the bakery and ate it on the way. I only just caught the bus. It was good of Stan to meet me at Swimbridge.'

Margaret moved some bags and towels along the window seat and sat down. Lil filled the tea pot, poured milk into two cups and flopped down in her usual seat at the table. She looked as if she had been in a fight. Her pinafore was messy and her hair was sticking out in all directions and there were some little white feathers caught in it and one stuck to the back of her left ear.

'Whatever have you been doing, Lil?' Margaret asked.

'Oh 'tis the time of year. Stan 'ad one of the pigs killed last week and us killed some chickens on Monday and three of the geese Tuesday. I 'ates it but it 'as to be done, so yesterday I was pluckin' chickens and today I plucked the geese.' She took her handkerchief from her pinafore pocket, sneezed into it and blew her nose.

'You must be tired out, Lil. Where are the boys?'

'Yesterday they was up at their friend's 'ouse at West Buckland and today they'm over at Filleigh for another boy's birthday party.' Lil poured the tea and passed a cup to Margaret.

'That's good, Lil. I don't expect they're comfortable with all the killing of animals that has to go on.'

'Well they understand things more now, Margaret. They know that us can't keep the animals as pets, even if Stan thinks more of 'em than 'e do of most people.'

'Have they heard any more from Mr. Macmillan?'

'A parcel 'ave come for the boys this mornin' from Scotland. They 'aven't seen it yet and us won't let 'em open it till Christmas Day. There's something from their mother, too. I made 'em make Christmas cards for 'er and for Mr. Macmillan. They did 'em lovely and wrote inside 'em too.'

'You and Stan have done a wonderful job with those boys.' Margaret put down her tea cup and looked at her friend. 'Now, what can I do for you, Lil?'

'Well, just look at me. You said you could set me 'air to smarten me up a bit for tomorrow afternoon. As you can see, the place is a mess and I be a mess. Tomorrow mornin' I'll set about sortin' this room out but if I go an' wash me 'air now, can you see if you can sort me out please, Margaret?'

'I'm not a hairdresser but I'll have a go, Lil. I've brought some Kirby grips and a hairnet, and after I've set your hair I want you to keep it all pinned up until just before you're ready to go out tomorrow. Then you can take out the grips and pins and brush it all out.'

Lil finished her cup of tea and went into the scullery. She took off her pinny and blouse and started to pump the water up from the well. Reaching for a bar of soap, she rubbed at her hair, rinsing it as she continued to pump the cold water over it. When she had finished, she came back into the kitchen with a towel over her head and a comb in her hand.

'I'll just put me blouse back on, Margaret.'

'That's fine, Lil. You sit in your usual place and I'll stand behind you and get started. We don't want to dry your hair too much. You've got a slight wave in it so that's a big help. Now, while I do what I can, tell me all about this "do" you're going to tomorrow.'

'It's a Christmas Bring and Buy in the afternoon, endin' up with some carol singin'. I'll 'ave to take something to sell, p'raps some holly and a few cakes.'

'Sounds really nice,' Margaret said combing through her friend's hair and parting it on the side. 'What are you going to wear?'

'That's the problem. I've got clothes I've worn to weddin's but they be too fussy and not warm enough for December.' Lil adjusted the towel around her neck.

'We'll talk about that later, Lil. Perhaps we can come up with an answer.'

After about a quarter of an hour, Lil stood up and looked in the mirror and adjusted her hairnet. 'Very professional, Margaret. You can turn your 'and to anything. Should I put a turban over it?'

'Yes, but we'll allow it to dry for a while and then I'll wrap the turban tightly around your head to keep all the curls in place. Of course, you'll have to sit up in bed all night!' Margaret smiled at her friend teasingly and looked around the kitchen. 'Now, Lil, there is something else you wanted help with; the Christmas cake, wasn't it?'

'Oh yes, please. I've put the almond paste on it, as best as I could. At least I 'ad real eggs to mix with the soya flour instead of they dried things but 'tis bright yellow and very sticky. What's s'posed to be almond paste kept fallin' off an' I kept stickin' it back on.'

'That's the same as mine, Lil. No ground almonds available, that's the trouble. We just have to do what we can. Did you manage to get some almond essence?'

'Yes, but I thinks that I've used too much of it.

Us'll just 'ave to slap on some icin' over the top of it and if they'm 'ungry they'll eat it, won't 'em?'

'You're right. What ingredients have you got for the icing, Lil?'

'Ah, there's another thing; no icing sugar but us 'ave saved up the ordinary sugar from our rations.'

'That's what I had to do. And I've brought some dried milk powder for you to mix with the sugar. I thought that as you have your own fresh milk, you wouldn't have milk powder in house. Now if you go and fetch the ingredients you do have, and the cake, we'll see what we can do.' Margaret started to clear a space on the table.

'Oh Margaret, you think of everything,' Lil said going off to the scullery. She returned with the cake, which was covered in a tacky substance in a rather startling yellow colour.

'Well, here goes, Lil. Pass that bowl and we'll mix together what we've got and hope for the best.' Margaret added two dessertspoons of water to four dessertspoons of sugar and six tablespoons of dried milk powder, together with some lemon flavouring and stirred it up. It was too runny so she added some more milk powder. 'That's all we can do, Lil. Now to put it on the cake.'

After some delicate manoeuvring with a palette knife, the cake was covered in the icing mixture. It was a sort of off-white. The sides looked as if the icing might just about stay there and the two women decided that the top should be roughed slightly to indicate snow. Lil had found a porcelain Father Christmas that had seen many Christmases and put him carefully on the top.

'Do' ee think it needs somethin' on the sides, Margaret?' Lil asked, standing back and looking at their work.

'I wouldn't chance your luck, Lil. Don't touch the sides until you cut into it.'

'You'm right. Us'll leave well alone now. Thank you for what you've done. I'll go and put it in the dairy. 'Tis cold in there. Then us'll 'ave some tea. Stan's still not back from the Major's. I don't know what's goin' on there, Margaret.'

'The Major wanted to see him and Arthur, Stan told me when he picked me up in the car.'

'But the trouble is, 'e'll be late with the milkin' and 'e 'as to pick up the boys from Filleigh afore that. 'Tis gone three now.'

'I mustn't stay too long, Lil. Mum's got the children.' Margaret picked up her basket and took out four packages from it.

'Now, I have brought something for you for Christmas, but I think that you should open it today. You'll see why when you unwrap it.' She handed the largest parcel to her friend.

Lil looked surprised and unwrapped it slowly.

The delicate woollen jumper fell out and she caught it just as it was about to hit the floor.

'Ooh, 'ow bootiful, Margaret. Did you knit it yourself? I've never 'ad anyone give me anything so bootiful. Can I try it on?'

'Yes, but mind your hair. There are little buttons at the back which are undone at the moment so you can get it over your head.'

After taking off her pinny and blouse, Lil had put the jumper carefully over her head and looked in the mirror. It was a perfect fit and suited the delicate colouring of her rosy cheeks.

'Lovely, Margaret. I can wear it tomorrow. I've got a plain skirt that'll go with it. Thank you so much.'

'That's why I wanted to give it to you today, Lil. Now here is some tobacco for Stan and some little gifts for the boys.'

'That be so kind. Now, us 'ave got something for you. 'Tis for all of you really. I'll just go in the dairy and fetch it.' She hurried out through the scullery and soon returned with a large, and what appeared to be a heavy parcel.

'You better not open it right up,' Lil said, putting it down with a bang on the table. There was lots of brown paper and string and Lil cut the string and pulled the paper at the top apart to reveal a very large dressed chicken. Margaret's mouth opened and no sound came out. She looked at the bird and at her friend in amazement, finally emitting a little 'ooh' sound. Then she suddenly burst into tears.

'Thank you. Thank you both so much,' she croaked, wiping her eyes and shaking her head in wonder. 'It is so generous of you.'

'Us thought you could all tuck into that. 'Tis a big bird. Us 'aves a goose and us gives one to Edith and family and one to another sister that us don't see so much. But you gets more meat on a good size chicken than on a goose. There be some enterlean bacon in there too, Margaret. It makes the bird go a bit further.'

Margaret had recovered herself and blew her nose.

'I can't tell you how much this will be appreciated by all of us, Lil. It is very kind of you and Stan.'

'We all 'elps each other, Margaret. Give and take. That's what Christmas be all about.'

After Margaret had started the short walk towards Sunnybank, Stan decided to wait outside the Major's house for Arthur to arrive, and to use the time to clean the car windscreen. He found a piece of cloth almost as dirty as the windscreen, spat on it and started rubbing away at dirt accrued over many months. Fortunately, his efforts were soon interrupted as Arthur drew up on his bike.

They both greeted each other and went to the door of Stone Cottage together, stepping aside from a newly fallen piece of cement that had been holding part of the porch wall together.

'Come in, gentleman,' a voice called out from inside.

Arthur and Stan opened the door and were immediately handed a glass of sherry by Major Philips.

'Sit down now and warm yourselves by the Aga.'

Both of the visitors expressed their thanks and sat in a semi-circle alongside the Major, who raised his glass and smiled warmly at them.

'Congratulations are in order. I wonder if you have read in the newspapers about the arrests made in various parts of the country?'

There was no reply from Stan and Arthur, who looked puzzled and sat waiting for a further explanation.

'No? Well, I have the advantage of not only having read a report in yesterday's paper, but also of having had a long conversation on the telephone with Chief Inspector Armitage of Scotland Yard. You will remember that I told you that the son of one of my Army colleagues from the last World War holds a high position at Scotland Yard? He telephoned me yesterday evening and gave me details of the arrests that have been made and the further ongoing investigations regarding the forging and distribution of clothing and petrol coupons. He said that it is largely down to the two of you that they have been successful in putting most the pieces of the jigsaw together. What about that then, Stanley? What do you think of that, Arthur?' The Major raised his glass, his eyes shining with pride.

'Cheers!' he said, looking at the men and waiting for a response.

'It's not often that I'm lost for words, Major but – ' Arthur stopped and looked at Stan.

'The tenant at Hideaway Cottage, 'ave 'e been arrested too, Major?'

'That's right, but only yesterday afternoon, so I was told on the telephone by the Chief Inspector. He'd like to meet you two at some time if you'd agree to it.'

They all looked at each other and downed their glasses in one.

'So, he won't be coming back to live in North Devon any time soon,' said Arthur.

'And I bet 'e's no more related to Lord Fortescue than I be,' laughed Stan.

'There was a string of events that led to a good number of arrests,' the Major continued. 'I'm sure you'd like to know about them,' he added, warming to the unwinding of his tale. Stan thought that although the old Major's house was falling down bit by bit, at least he had contact with the outside world with the use of his telephone.

'Arthur, my throat is getting dry. I think we all need another glass of sherry, don't you?'

Arthur nodded and refilled the empty glasses.

'There was a serious accident on the edge of Bristol. A pile-up, I think is the modern expression. A van went into the back of some cars at traffic lights and caused a large number of vehicles to hit one another. The thing was that the van driver tried to restart his vehicle but the engine and the brakes had failed so he made off, leaving it there. He then jumped into another vehicle that had only suffered a few scratches and that car drove away at speed. There was a bus involved in the crash and the driver was able to give lots of information, including the number plate of the car that was driven off. One more thing he said was that a large dog also jumped from the van and leapt into the car, a Hillman, it was, with the van driver.'

'Us knows who that was, don't us, Arthur?' Stan looked at his friend.

The Major resumed his account of the accident.

'The bus driver ran to a police phone box to report the incident. There was a police car in the vicinity and it was contacted and the driver managed to find the Hillman and follow at a discreet distance. Other police had been called to the accident and had inspected the van and its contents. They, in turn, contacted Scotland Yard, who took over the management of the investigation. The culprits were seen leaving a lock-up garage near the docks in Bristol and finger prints were taken from the Hillman left there. The police didn't remove anything from the car but lay in wait for the collection of the forged coupons. Then they followed the two men who came in a van to pick up the coupons. Some of these were left at a drop off point for distribution in Bristol while most were driven on for selling at cities in the Midlands. And so, the links in the chain went on. In fact, Chief Inspector Armitage told me the gang is known as "The Chain Gang".'

'There's a lot of money to be made from these forgeries then, Major Philips?' Arthur commented.

'I'm told the forgeries sell for about ten pounds a sheet in the cities, where some people have money to spare,' the Major answered.

'And what about the tenant of Hideaway Cottage, Major? Where be 'e now?' Stan leaned forward, keen to know that the man had got his just deserts.

'Locked up, and the man he met and escaped with has been traced, too, and is also under arrest. He's a vet, would you believe. A disgrace to his profession and should be ashamed of himself.' Major Philips frowned and pointed to the sherry bottle.

'Another glass, I think please, one of you, if you'd do the honours.'

'What about all the gear in the shed behind the cottage?' Arthur asked.

'Thanks to you two the authorities had been informed about that and kept watch in the Shallowford area. At the end of last week what looked like a removal lorry arrived and two men were arrested while removing personal items from the cottage, and emptying the shed and loading the lorry with the forging machinery. Investigations are still ongoing and the case is far from closed. Chief Inspector Armitage doesn't think they will ever get the criminals at the top of the whole thing. They have found another machine used for forging petrol coupons at some out of the way place up in Cumberland.'

'I wonder what our tenant said when he was arrested,' Arthur said, looking at Stan.

'Oh, we know that,' Major Philips cut in. 'It was rather odd, according to Chief Inspector Armitage. He said, "That bloody stag. It was that bloody stag's fault." He kept swearing about the stag and shouting "Country Bumpkins." They couldn't quite work out what he was shouting about. Do you think it could have been anything to do with you two?' the Major asked. 'And do you want to be interviewed on the radio and have your names in the papers? You could become very newsworthy around here.'

'Please pass on our regards to the Chief Inspector, Major, but I can't think of anything worse than having my name in the paper. I'd like to remain anonymous. What about you, Stan?' Arthur turned to his friend.

Stan raised his glass and smiled.

'Same for me Major. I be 'appy to be a "country bumpkin."'

'Oh, at last. Stan, could 'ee drive Margaret to the bus stop in Swimbridge, an' then go on to collect the boys in Filleigh? Then you'd better get back yer to do the milkin'.'

''Tis all go, Maggie, at Christmas. I see you've been busy tryin' to improve on nature.'

'Hello, Stan. Sorry, but I need to be home soon and would be so grateful for a lift to the bus stop. How did you get on at the Major's house?'

'Us got on very well. There be one bit of news. That tenant us don't like 'ave been arrested for forgin' clothin' coupons. It's all in the papers.'

There was silence in the room.

'That be all to do with what you an' Arthur 'ave been up to,' Lil said.

''Tis all done with now, Maid, and 'e be gone and detained at 'is Majesty's pleasure.'

'So, will you have to give evidence then, Stan?' Margaret asked.

'I shouldn't think so, Maggie. Us don't know much really,' he said, unconvincingly. 'In fact, 'tis slipped out me 'aid already.'

It was gone half past six when Margaret reached her parents' house. Jack was there drinking a cup of tea with Mary on his lap and the older girls were in the front room starting a game of monopoly with Bill.

'I'm so sorry, Mum,' Margaret said, putting down the heavy parcel on the kitchen table. Stan gave me a lift to Swimbridge and I had to wait for the bus then walk with this parcel from the bus station at Barnstaple.'

'That's all right, Margaret,' Florrie said, pouring her daughter a cup of tea. 'They've all had their tea except Jack. He hasn't been here long, have you, dear?'

'No, Ma, I was late leaving work today.'

'Margaret, you know I said I'd try to get something for Christmas dinner?' I've been scouring the town with Mary in the push chair, haven't we, Mary, and there's no meat to be seen anywhere, not even rabbit. I'll go out again tomorrow but everyone's on the hunt for something.' Florrie looked at her husband.

'Jim, you've got some vegetables from the

allotment, haven't you and I've bought potatoes but I don't know what we can do to make a Christmas dinner.'

'I do, Mum,' Margaret said. 'Look at what Lil and Stan have given us.'

She undid the parcel to show the large chicken and the slab of enterlean bacon.

Gasps went up all round and everyone started talking at once. Diana, Maureen and Bill came into the kitchen from the other room and all stood around the beautiful bird in amazement.

'Oh, how wonderful and how kind of them, Margaret,' Florrie said. Then she asked one of her frequent questions when it came to buying poultry before the war.

'Did it run about?'

'It did once, Ma,' Jack replied dryly.

Chapter 42

It was becoming more and more difficult to get Mary to bed as Christmas Day drew nearer. Frequent assurances that Father Christmas wouldn't come and leave presents at the bedside of little children who were still awake were not convincing Mary to settle down and go to sleep. It was already a quarter to eight and she was still calling out from upstairs. Jack wanted to complete the work he had been doing on the wooden cradle he had made for the doll that Margaret had bought for Mary. He had applied an undercoat of paint the evening before and intended to finish off with a top coat and finally apply some pretty transfers. Margaret had already knitted a set of doll's clothes and had planned to ice the Christmas cake that evening while listening to "The Messiah" on the wireless. It was being broadcast on the Home Service but she had missed the start of the performance and was hoping to be ready with all the ingredients for the cake laid out on the kitchen table, together with a battered copy of the score, in time for one of her favourite choruses. She went to the foot of the stairs and listened in the hope that Mary had stopped talking to herself and had settled down to sleep. All was quiet apart from Diana practising some Christmas carols in the front room. Maureen was in the kitchen making a bobble to go on the top of a hat that Margaret had knitted for Diana. Maureen was working in silent concentration so Margaret switched on the wireless just in time to hear the start of "Every Valley Shall Be Exalted." She began to measure out the ingredients to make the icing, the same miserable recipe that she had had to use for her friend's cake the day before. She wouldn't attempt anything too fancy in the way of decoration, just a snow scene. If the mixture stuck to the cake, it would be a success of a sort. She had almond pasted the cake a few days earlier, although it was done without using any ground almonds. Everyone was doing what they could, Margaret thought, and any hardship was nothing compared to what the men fighting suffered and what many people had endured in the cities. Margaret added some water to the mixture and stirred steadily, keeping time and joining in as the choir sang "And All Flesh Shall See It Together." She turned the page and accidentally dropped a blob of icing on the part where the sopranos go up to a top 'A.' She hurriedly wiped it off with a cloth and started to cover the cake with the icing, Margaret dipped the palette knife in a jug of boiling water and wiped it dry so not to make the mixture even wetter as she ran the knife over the top and sides of the cake. That was the easy part for her with all the tricks she had learned in the bakehouse. She had searched out a few treasured decorations saved from previous years for the top of the cake and would put them on when the icing was almost dry.

Margaret carried the cake into the scullery and placed it on a shelf on the wall, hoping that the icing would dry out overnight. She cleared away all the dishes and bowls she had used and washed them up while "The Messiah" continued towards the end of Part One. Returning to the kitchen, she sat down by the fire and turned the pages of the score to catch up with the performance and sing along with the chorus of "Glory to God."

'Finished!' cried Maureen triumphantly, holding up the bobble she had been making. 'But I don't know how to tie it off so as it doesn't come undone.'

'Come over here, Maureen,' Margaret said, putting a marker in the score and closing the book. 'I'll show you how to finish it if you pass me the scissors.' After a few minutes, a fluffy, bright red bobble was held up for Maureen to admire.

'There, Maureen. Well done! Now all we have to do is sew it to the hat I knitted; or would you rather wrap it up and give it to Diana and then sew it on afterwards?'

'I'd rather wrap it up so she knows I made it for her.'

'Yes, I think that would be a good idea.' Suddenly the door to the greenhouse where Jack was working opened and Bill came in.

'What a strong smell of paint, Jack. That looks very professional. I can guess who it's for.' Bill looked at the cradle with interest.

'The smell of the paint is overpowering, Bill, but it's cold with the door open.'

'Sorry, Jack. I've come to ask for something. Have you got any old newspapers?'

'We don't buy a regular newspaper other than the Journal, and when we do we save them and cut them up to use for hanging in the lavatory.'

'Oh, yes. Of course.' Bill looked disappointed.

'But go and ask Marj. She's in the kitchen with Mr. Handel.' Not understanding what he meant, Bill squeezed past Jack and went through to the kitchen.

'Sorry to bother you, Maggie, but do you have any old newspapers I can have to make paper chains? I've painted and cut up all that Gran has, and am ready to stick them together but I wanted to make some for you.'

'Oh, that would be lovely Bill. Yes, I've managed to save some but haven't had the time to make paper chains with them. I'll fetch what I've put by if you wait a moment.'

'Can I go and help Bill make paper chains, Auntie Margaret?' Maureen asked, putting the red bobble in a paper bag and hiding it at the back of the kitchen cupboard.

'Well, it's getting late but I don't see why not. Do you want Diana to come as well, Bill?' Margaret asked, hoping that she could have some time to listen to Part Two of "The Messiah" without any interruption.

'Yes. That would get the job done tonight if there are three of us,' Bill smiled, holding out his hands and taking a small pile of newspapers from Margaret, who went from the kitchen and into the passage to call out to Diana.

'Diana, Good King Wenceslas has been looking out quite long enough. Stop practising that carol now and come and help Bill make some Christmas decorations.' The piano playing stopped and Diana joined everyone in the kitchen.

'Gran has let us use the front room to make the paper chains because Gramps is listening to "The Messiah" on his wireless in the kitchen,' Bill said.

'And woe betide anyone who interferes with that,' Margaret added with some envy.

'Now put your coats on, girls, and you'd better take some scissors and a bottle of glue. Try not to get it on yourselves.'

'We won't,' they shouted as they inched past Jack and followed Bill out of the greenhouse door, shutting it with a bang.

'I think it would be easier trying to do this at Waterloo Station,' Jack said, putting down his paint brush.

'Oh, Jack! That looks lovely. Mary will be so thrilled. Where are you going to keep it so she doesn't see it before Christmas?'

'I'll hide it behind something up on that top shelf until it's dry, then I'll put the transfers on tomorrow night.'

'Good idea, Jack.' Margaret fell silent for a moment. 'I wanted to tell you something before I tell Mum and Dad. You know that we've been saving for a deposit to put down to buy this house?' Jack waited for his wife to continue.

'Well, I've looked at our savings in the Post Office and we have enough. We will have first chance as sitting tenants and I've contacted the landlord and he said he is happy to sell.'

'He's probably glad to get it off his hands, Marj. There's plenty that needs doing to it.'

'But we can do it, can't we, Jack?' Jack looked thoughtfully at his wife.

'We can do it,' he answered smiling and wiping his hands on an old paint cloth.

'There's something else that I want to do here,'

Jack added. 'Why don't you make the most of the peace and quiet and go and listen to the wireless, Marj?'

'That's just what I was thinking,' Margaret answered, going into the kitchen and sitting by the fire. She turned up the wireless, picked up the score and found the page she was looking for at the start of Part Two. The music was beautiful and she relished the time to listen to it in peace for a while.

'Jack,' Margaret said, opening the scullery door and looking into the greenhouse. 'I didn't realise how late it's getting. I've listened up to the end of Part Two of "Messiah", but I'd better go and fetch those girls from Mum's. They'd stay there all night if they could.'

'They must have finished making paper chains by now, Marj. You didn't have that much newspaper, did you?'

'No, but why have you been out here so long? You must be frozen.'

'Oh, I finished painting the cradle some time ago,' he replied. He picked up a pair of high heeled shoes and looked at the heels.

'Oh good, Jack. You've put new heels on them. Thanks, dear.' He handed them to his wife and picked up his own shoes.

'And I've heeled and soled my work shoes,' he

said coming into the scullery. 'I'm going to make a hot drink, Marj. Do you want one?'

'Not until I come back and have seen those girls into bed. I'll tell Mum and Dad about our plans to buy the house,' she said, smiling and picking up the torch as she went out the back door.

Margaret opened the front door to her parents' house and walked into the dark passage. She could hear talking coming from the front room but walked on and opened the kitchen door. A single candle and faint light from the fire burning in the grate dimly lit the room and cast a shadow on her mother sitting with her eyes closed in the armchair opposite her father's empty one.

'Whatever's happened, Mum? Why are all the lights off?' Margaret went and sat in her father's chair.

'And where's Dad? Part Three of "Messiah" is on the wireless now.'

'I know, and he's missing it. He and Bill are outside in the shed. Oh, I put the chicken out there in a box, all closed up but with some holes in the box to let some air in.'

'Never mind about that, Mum. Whatever's happened? What are they doing out there?'

'They've got two torches but they're looking for some fuses. It's my fault really, or for certain I'll get the blame for it. I found a lovely old Christmas decoration, one you could plug in that lights up. It was Mother's and I thought it would look perfect fastened to the holly decoration that Bill made. He plugged it in and he fused all the lights right in the middle of "The Hallelujah Chorus."' Florrie wrung her hands and looked distraught. 'You know how your Dad loves to listen to it on his wireless. Everything went black.'

'And silent,' Margaret added, 'but I bet Dad had something to say about it that was a bit stronger than "Hallelujah!"'

'He jumped up out of his chair and I thought to meself, I know people like to stand up for "The Hallelujah Chorus", but they don't swear while they're doing it. Anyway, Bill apologised, thinking it was his fault and now he's out there in the shed with Jim.'

'So, are the girls still making paper chains in the front room? It's getting late, which is why I thought I'd come over and see what's happened. And before I forget, I wanted to tell you and Dad that Jack and I have saved enough for a deposit to put down on the house so that we can buy it.'

'Oh, Margaret, that's such good news. With the start you and Jack had to your marriage, you should be proud of what you've managed to do. I'll tell Jim later when he's calmed down.' Florrie leant forward and poked the fire, then threw another shovelful of coal on it. 'Oh, yes,' you've come over for the girls. They finished making paper chains with Bill and then he brought out the Monopoly and started them off playing. Then I called him in here to plug in Mother's Christmas light. The lead on it was a bit frayed but, well I told you what happened. I took a candle in for Diana and Maureen, and they've got the oil stove to give them some warmth, but as I said, Bill is out in the shed with Dad. I don't know what we'd do without that boy. He's not very old but he has a wise head on his shoulders.'

Margaret stood up. 'But I really must go and take the girls home to bed.'

Florrie nodded and the two women looked at each other as the sound of a loud crash came from the shed outside.

Margaret sighed and sat down again. 'Perhaps I'd better stay on for a while, Mum. Do they know where the fuse box is?'

'Yes, Your Dad isn't very practical, as you know, but I think he knows where it is,' Florrie answered without much confidence.

'You're getting good at this game, Diana,' Maureen said as she picked up the little glass jar that was used as a shaker. 'I heard the front door open. I think your Mum has come over to fetch us,' she added as she threw a three and moved her red counter along the board and landed on The Old Kent Road.

'Do you want to buy it, Maureen?' You've just passed Go and collected £200.'

'I know, but I had to pay £100 tax at the last place I landed on. In any case, it's not posh enough.'

'Isn't it very posh in the Old Kent Road?' Diana asked, not knowing anything about London other than a lot of it had been bombed.

'The thing is, I keep landing on boring places like Income Tax and Chance and Community Chest. I really want to land on somewhere posh that I could buy and build houses and hotels on, then when anyone lands on my properties they have to pay me a load of cash.'

Diana was new to the game and picked up the shaker and sat looking at the board thoughtfully.

'I like the green colour ones. Are they posh, Maureen?'

'Quite posh, but the purple colour ones are the best. That's where all the very rich, posh people live in London.'

'But weren't they bombed, too?' Diana asked.

'Not very much, cos if old Hitler wins the war, he'll want to come and live in the poshest part of London, won't he?' Maureen explained.

Diana frowned and shook the glass jar furiously.

'Four,' they both said in unison. Diana moved her green counter from Pall Mall.

'I should have bought that really,' she said but I don't like the colour. 'But I'll buy Mary – Mary – le –' Diana stopped trying to work out how to say the word and said instead, 'I'll buy that one because it's like the name of my sister and I like the little green train.' She handed £200 across to Maureen who was acting as the Banker in Bill's absence.

'Marylebone,' Maureen said, taking the money and putting it neatly in a pile in the corner of the table. She dropped one of the notes on the floor. The light from the candle was so dim that they were struggling to see well, but Monopoly was the latest craze for them and they couldn't get enough of it.

'I may put a house on Marylebone later,' Diana announced, looking serious.

'You can't, Diana. It's a railway station. You can't put a house or a hotel on a station, but if someone lands on your station, they will have to pay you rent. And if you buy more stations, they'll have to pay you even more rent.' Maureen took the jar and held it, listening for noise from the next room.

'I thought I heard a door open, Diana. I wonder when they'll get the lights back working again.'

'I don't think we should play much longer anyway,' Diana replied. 'I feel cold in here now. Has someone left the front door open?'

'Is it all right to finish after my turn? I was the third one to play when we started the game with Bill,' Maureen asked.

Diana shivered. 'Yes, because we can go on with it tomorrow, can't we?'

Maureen shook and threw a six and landed on Chance. She groaned and picked up a card which said, 'Get Out Of Jail Free.' 'That will be useful if I go to jail,' she announced.

'You won't go to jail, and nor will you, Diana. I know you are good girls,' a voice said. Both girls sat up and peered through the dim light towards the door.

'That's not Bill's voice,' Maureen said.

'No. It's somebody else.' Diana stood up, picked up the candle holder and directed the dim light towards the door. 'I know who it is. It's – '

'Shhhhhh!' The man smiled and put his finger to his lips. He beckoned the girls to follow him out of the room and stand in the passage, outside the door to the kitchen.

'You go in first,' he whispered.

Diana threw open the door. Suddenly all the lights came on and the final, triumphant chords of the Amen Chorus came bursting out of the wireless.

'Look who's here!' she shouted. 'It's Uncle Alan!'

'Alan?' his mother cried.

'Yes, Mum, it's me, Alan.' He put down his bag and took off his cap.

'Home on leave. Happy Christmas, everyone.'

About the Author

After attending Barnstaple Girls' Grammar School the author studied at The Guildhall School of Music and Drama and had a long career in music teaching, primarily in North Devon. She has written plays and pantomimes, songs and a religious cantata. *Just Making Do* is Dia Webb's first novel. She is married to Leslie and they have two children and seven grandchildren.

Acknowledgements

It took the terrible Covid 19 pandemic and having to shield at home for me to sit down and write the book I'd wanted to write for years. Looking at what everyone was struggling with, the sense of community and the heroic efforts of NHS workers, it took me back to my childhood and the 1940s. I thought about the efforts of family and friends during wartime, not appreciated by me as a child at the time. They were part of a generation that had lived through so much hardship and knew all about 'Just Making Do.' My memories of them will attune with others of my age and older, and may raise a smile or a tear along the way.

There are many to thank who have helped me in the writing of this book.

Firstly, my husband, Leslie for his patience and interest, my daughter Debbie, and my son, David for their help and ideas, my granddaughter, Emily who often rescues me from my frequent computer tech problems, and then kindly tells me that I am doing well. Vielen Dank to my sister Mary in Germany who shared so many of those bygone times with me.

Thanks especially to Yvonne Reed, my wonderful proof-reader, whose kindly but eagle eye helped me to tidy up my literary efforts.

Thanks too to Cheryl Thornburgh who spent hours researching and painting the cover illustrations, bringing those far away years to life again, and to her husband, Edward, also an artist, for his support and enthusiasm.

Jenny Savill and Louise Henderson have been a great help in giving their professional advice to me, and my friend and fellow author, Berwick Coates has fired me with his own enthusiasm and directed me to put my book into the capable hands of Mark and Anne Webb and their staff at Paragon Publishing, who have been patient and encouraging.

Nearer to home, I am so grateful to Mike Matthews of Lineal Software Solutions and his staff for arranging the scanning of the paintings and for putting up with me when I get lost on my computer.

Finally, for their knowledge of how things were, and how they were done back in the early 1940s, my thanks go to Dorothy Baker, John and Tania Hussell, André Muxworthy and Brian Watts.